Praise for
Falling Under

"*Falling Under* is a lush, romantic, and captivating novel. It took my breath away."   —Sarah Beth Durst, author of *Ice*

"*Falling Under* is absolutely irresistible. A lush, dark fairy tale full of magic, intrigue, and love. Genuinely scary and swooningly romantic in all the best ways, once I fell into this book, I couldn't stop reading. Theia and Haden's story utterly enthralled me, and I can't wait to read more about Serendipity Falls."

—Rosemary Clement-Moore, author of *The Splendor Falls*

"Hayes's first YA novel seasons its Romeo and Juliet theme of separated lovers with horror and languid eroticism . . . a satisfying story that hints at more promising dreams to come."

—*Publishers Weekly*

"In an eerie, intriguing YA debut that is sure to have some crossover appeal for *Twilight* fans of all ages, Hayes has spun a magical, sometimes terrifying tale of teens caught at the intersection of the human and demon worlds and their struggle to save their souls and escape the evil threat that could destroy them both."   —*Library Journal*

"*Twilight* fans will be tripping over themselves to read Hayes's new series. This powerful love story will take your breath away as you are transported to the world of Serendipity Falls."

—*RT Book Reviews*

"A plot that leaves you guessing until the final page, a mysterious boy who could give Edward Cullen a run for his money, and writing that brings the characters to life in front of you as you read."
—Chapter Chicks

"Loved it . . . I totally got wrapped up in this one."
—Forever Young (Adult)

"A new, sexy take on demons and the battling of lust versus love."
—Scarrlet Reader

"Fascinating."
—Genre Go Round Reviews

"Beautiful, lyrical writing."
—Fiction State of Mind

"*Falling Under* has some similarities to books like *Twilight*, but it whomps all over them . . . lush, evocative, and incredibly creative."
—Errant Dreams Reviews

"A gripping tale of demons and the Underworld . . . *Falling Under* just about ticked all the right boxes."
—Nice Girls Read Books

BOOKS BY GWEN HAYES

Falling Under
Dreaming Awake

DREAMING AWAKE

GWEN HAYES

NEW AMERICAN LIBRARY

New American Library
Published by New American Library, a division of
Penguin Group (USA) Inc., 375 Hudson Street,
New York, New York 10014, USA
Penguin Group (Canada), 90 Eglinton Avenue East, Suite 700, Toronto,
Ontario M4P 2Y3, Canada (a division of Pearson Penguin Canada Inc.)
Penguin Books Ltd., 80 Strand, London WC2R 0RL, England
Penguin Ireland, 25 St. Stephen's Green, Dublin 2,
Ireland (a division of Penguin Books Ltd.)
Penguin Group (Australia), 250 Camberwell Road, Camberwell, Victoria 3124,
Australia (a division of Pearson Australia Group Pty. Ltd.)
Penguin Books India Pvt. Ltd., 11 Community Centre, Panchsheel Park,
New Delhi - 110 017, India
Penguin Group (NZ), 67 Apollo Drive, Rosedale, Auckland 0632,
New Zealand (a division of Pearson New Zealand Ltd.)
Penguin Books (South Africa) (Pty.) Ltd., 24 Sturdee Avenue,
Rosebank, Johannesburg 2196, South Africa

Penguin Books Ltd., Registered Offices:
80 Strand, London WC2R 0RL, England

First published by New American Library,
a division of Penguin Group (USA) Inc.

First Printing, January 2012
10 9 8 7 6 5 4 3 2

 REGISTERED TRADEMARK—MARCA REGISTRADA

LIBRARY OF CONGRESS CATALOGING-IN-PUBLICATION DATA:
Hayes, Gwen.
    Dreaming awake/Gwen Hayes.
       p. cm.
    ISBN 978-0-451-23554-1
    [1. Demonology—Fiction. 2. Supernatural—Fiction. 3. Love—Fiction. 4. High schools—
Fiction. 5. Schools—Fiction.] I. Title.
    PZ7.H31458Dr 2012
    [Fic]—dc23   2011032112

Set in Adobe Caslon
Designed by Alissa Amell

Printed in the United States of America

PUBLISHER'S NOTE
This is a work of fiction. Names, characters, places, and incidents either are the product of the
author's imagination or are used fictitiously, and any resemblance to actual persons, living or
dead, business establishments, events, or locales is entirely coincidental.
    The publisher does not have any control over and does not assume any responsibility for author
or third-party Web sites or their content.

The scanning, uploading, and distribution of this book via the Internet or via any other means
without the permission of the publisher is illegal and punishable by law. Please purchase only
authorized electronic editions, and do not participate in or encourage electronic piracy of copy-
righted materials. Your support of the author's rights is appreciated.

For Harrison John—already a hero in so many ways

ACKNOWLEDGMENTS

The care and feeding of a writer is a complex endeavor that necessitates a special kind of patience and, most important, a good sense of humor. Without the support of my friends, family, and colleagues, there would be no book—just a strange woman in the corner talking to the voices in her head.

I'd like to thank my editor, Anne Sowards, for never letting me settle until I've written my best, even when I whine and complain about how hard it is. Also for letting me borrow Kat Sherbo from time to time because she is super smart. I'd also like to thank Jan McInroy for wrangling all the commas, and Erin Galloway and Kayleigh Clark for keeping publicity fun. There are a lot of other people at NAL/Penguin who work behind the scenes on my book that I'd like to thank also. I really appreciate all they do even though I don't get to work with them directly.

Thank you, Jessica Sinsheimer, who is the most professional, savvy, witty, classy, and fiercely fun woman I know. She's also my agent and represents everything I love about publishing and being female. She is a positive force in not just my career, but my life.

This book would not be if it weren't for: my readers, my Twitter friends, the YA book bloggers who keep me excited about not just my book but *all* the books, Michael Graham for letting me borrow his duck, Bob and Janet Hayes for my name, and the Zone 91.3 (special shout-out to Jeremy, Pol, and Jon because I told you I would). Thanks to my inner circle of writer friends who send me encouragement, critiques, advice, and sometimes NSFW pictures.

And, as always, my deepest gratitude to my family for always believing in me. And for being understanding when I spend too much time on the computer.

And to my husband, Travis, thank you times one million still doesn't cover it. You are my world.

DREAMING
AWAKE

HOMECOMING

Danger doesn't always greet with bared fangs. Sometimes it seduces with a willowy caress, a sigh of pleasure, and then turns carnivorous with whipcrack intensity.

Falling in love is the same.

Love had seduced my heart and soul, changed me forever, and then, in one promise made under duress, jeopardized my very humanity. And yet I couldn't regret it.

These were my thoughts as I cartwheeled back through the supernatural veil that separated two worlds—the one I was supposed to live in and the one from which I was escaping. The place called Under.

Existing on the other side of dreams, Under wasn't a place a person could journey to and from freely. On this night, my course had been set by a demon-summoning spell.

And it summoned *me*. Because now I had the blood of a demon running in my veins.

Brilliant streaks of light flashed around me. I was neither here nor there. I was everything and nothing at the same time. Like a comet, I brushed past the whole world, painting it with light.

The crash of my body onto a hard wooden floor jolted the part of me that still swam in the alterverse. Then came a sharp tug on the metaphysical line that tethered my spirit to my flesh and bones. I slammed into myself and drew in a harsh breath of oxygen.

And just like that I was home.

CHAPTER ONE

One week later

Sometimes it seemed that nothing had changed since the night I saw the burning man fall from the sky.

I stared out of my window into the cold, dark night. Behind me, my pink and ivory bedroom was reflected in the glass. A picture of a world that felt like a cage and a haven all at once. I tried to remember that everything was different now, that *I* was different now, but it felt like I'd stepped into a time warp. One that brought me once again to peer into the night and long for some unnamed freedom from being Theia Alderson—the perfect daughter, the perfect teen girl, the perfect ingénue from every gothic romance ever written. A doll in a box.

But I wasn't that girl anymore. Even if I was the only one who recognized it.

I didn't dare dwell on those thoughts for too long. There were shadows in my own heart and soul that I didn't want to get to look at too closely. Best to keep them at bay since a small part of me was curious about the new darkness inside me. Too curious.

I pushed away from the window and roamed my bedroom, brushing my fingers against the furnishings of my old life as if they were touchstones for keeping me earthbound. Tomorrow would be my first day back at school since my "return." All of Serendipity Falls thought I had run away, including my father. I could hardly have told him I'd been held prisoner in Under, the realm where nightmares were born. He'd have had me sedated and carted off to the nearest mental ward if I'd explained that demons exist and that not only was I dating one, but his mother had turned me into some kind of a monster as well.

So my father didn't look deeper and accepted the fact that I had run away because of his overbearing rules and because I couldn't handle learning the truth about my mother.

He never recovered from losing her; neither of us had, really.

My father was wrong about my running away, of course. When he was finally truthful with me about the circumstances of my mother's death, a little of the ice around his heart began to thaw and I felt hope that we might be able to build a better relationship. He'd seemed to be realizing that he had tried so hard to keep me safe that the life of structure he had built around me often made me feel like a princess trapped in her castle turret.

But then I was taken to Under, and now our relationship was strained in a completely different way.

I closed my eyes and replayed the memory of returning home a few days ago. I hadn't known what to expect. The counterfeit cheerfulness of the hulking Victorian house where I lived had never seemed so false as when I stood on the street in front of it working up the courage to go inside. It had never been a home to me, not the kind you remember with sentimentality. The way it rose too proudly from the well-manicured lawn and loomed over everything it saw reminded me too much of the way I'd felt about my father most of my life.

I'd knocked cautiously on my own front door. My breath had come in shallow puffs meant to imitate breathing but falling short. The door opened in slow motion, as if it was cracking an entryway into my fears.

"Oh, thank Jesus!" Muriel, our housekeeper, had cried as she pulled me into the house and into her arms. She'd been baking and smelled like apples and brown sugar. "Mr. Alderson, she's home! Theia is home!"

Muriel patted me here and there, inspecting me for damage. She'd kept her red hair short and still wore appalling mom jeans and an embroidered sweatshirt. I loved every unfashionable stitch.

She'd cooed and murmured comments about my being too skinny and too pale, but her eyes were filled with happy tears. I was glad she answered the door first, and not my father. She was a respite for me. She always had been.

I'd felt it in my bones when my father saw me. The chill in the room became arctic.

He'd aged ten years in the time I'd been gone. Deep lines

framed his eyes and mouth and his hair seemed thinner and lighter. If I'd lost weight in Under, he'd lost more here. His normally impeccable clothes hung loosely on his frame, the fabric gathered in pleats where it should have been flat.

His stern face was all the more frightening paired with his sunken eyes.

I took a step towards him but stopped when he flinched.

My lower lip trembled and tears formed and stung, but didn't fall. "Daddy?" I'd whispered. I'd rarely called him that, even as a young girl. "Daddy, I'm sorry," I cried. "I'm so, so sorry."

He didn't hug me that day or since. In fact, we'd barely spoken. He didn't ask where I'd been, if I was all right. He didn't welcome me with open arms. "We'll talk tomorrow" was all he said.

Only *tomorrow* hadn't come yet, despite the passing of many days. The nonreaction cut deeper into my heart than harsh words would have. His coldness covered my heart like freezer burn. I would have preferred a stern lecture or an angry tirade; instead, he'd sealed himself off from me once again.

He hadn't even talked to me himself about going back to school. His assistant called me after she made the necessary arrangements to reenroll me in my classes.

School. I shook my head in disgust. My friends had convinced me that trying to get back into the routine of normal life was the best thing I could do, but I was not looking forward to returning to high school.

Serendipity Falls is a small California town very different from my childhood home in England. Fitting in had been a problem even before I'd been cursed with demon blood. My British accent, overly strict father, and extreme introverted tendencies put a bull's-eye on my back when Father moved us stateside and I enrolled at the small, cliquish school. Luckily, I made two friends that year who cared very little about fitting in and still cared very much about me. Donny and Amelia were my family. And now I had Haden too.

I smiled to myself even as the fire-hot blush stroked my cheeks as it always did when I thought of Haden. He wasn't the sort of boy a girl could easily bring home to meet the parents— even if she had normal parents and not an imposing, authoritarian father like mine. Haden, despite being half-human, had been raised in Under. He was unpredictable and wickedly handsome. He had the manners of a hero from a Jane Austen novel, but was equally at home in the high school cafeteria.

As if he knew I was thinking of him, my phone buzzed and lit up with his name on the caller ID.

"What are you wearing?" he asked as soon as I answered.

I smiled into the phone and looked down at my nightgown. "A clown suit with big red shoes."

Haden chuckled low, his voice tickling something deep inside me. "Liar. You hate clowns. Are you ready for your first day of school?"

"As ready as I'll ever be." I slid into my sheets and turned off the light, my restlessness abated by the sound of Haden's voice.

"I just called to tell you good night. Get some sleep, Theia. Tomorrow is a big day."

"I would sleep much better if you were here." As soon as the

words spilled out of my mouth, I wanted to die of embarrassment. Haden and I were close, but we hadn't gotten *that* close
yet. "I mean . . . it's just that when you're near I'm not as agitated. Not that I want to sleep with you." I needed to stop
talking—I was making it worse.

"You don't?" He was teasing now. "Now you've hurt my
male pride."

"You know what I mean. Stop trying to fluster me." We
weren't really ready for *that* yet—but I did think about what it
would be like. I just didn't want him to know I thought about it.

"My greatest joy comes from flustering you. Your cheeks
pinken so sweetly. I bet they're warm right this very minute."

I brought my fingertips to my face. *Scorching.* "Not at all."

"Good night, Theia. Sweet dreams."

"Good night, Haden."

I never thought I'd fall asleep. As I approached the edge of
it, despite knowing better, I let it welcome me back.

It had been a long time since I'd awoken while dreaming.

One moment, I'd been lying in bed drifting into slumber;
the next, I was standing outside. Stars danced across the navy
blue sky and the moon provided an ambient light. A blanket of
red and black rose petals carpeted the ground beneath my bare
feet, soft and delicate. Not far from where I stood, a small gazebo glowing with white lights that twinkled like stars on a
string drew my gaze. It was breathtaking. In the center a small
table was set for two.

I looked down at my white cotton nightgown, chagrined to once again find myself in Under barely dressed. I should have been used to it. I also should have been afraid, but I wasn't.

A red petal floated past me and then another. Slowly, they began falling from the sky like unhurried snow. The black ones were interspersed lightly throughout, but when I put my hand out to catch one, it was heart shaped.

I twirled in a slow circle, catching petals and wondering where they fell from with no clouds in the sky. They were fragrant whispers of delight, and I couldn't help but kick at the pile under my feet as if I were a child playing in autumn leaves or in a puddle from the summer rain.

I immersed myself in the ambience, letting the cool petals brush my skin as they settled around me. The atmosphere felt as decadent and lush as it did innocent and childlike. It seemed to fit my current state of mind—a crossroads between girl and woman, between human and demon.

I continued to play in the flowers as they settled at my feet. I came across a thicket of silvery bushes that were dipped in glitter. I couldn't resist touching the jeweled leaves. The branches were sturdy transparent tubes filled with a viscous red liquid and barbed with razor thorns. They parted on their own and revealed a center of three beating hearts. I shivered as the hearts squeezed and pumped their blood through the stalks. I stepped back in time to avoid a barbed vine reaching out to lash me. It was good to remember that even the beauty of Under was laced with deadly terror.

I went back to playing with the rose petals, though a little more cautiously, until I felt a cool sensation on the back of my neck and turned. Where there had been nothing, there was Haden.

Theia was beautiful.

The petals settled around her like she was the center of a snow globe and time seemed to slow. A few stray petals caught in her curls like unmelted snowflakes, and she reminded Haden of a forest nymph. Her cheeks were rosy and the way she caught the light dazzled him.

He watched her frolic, charmed by her playfulness and how comfortable she felt here, despite everything she'd been through. He'd hoped she would enjoy the interlude he'd planned. He wanted to give her some relief from the intensity of the last few months. He'd brought so much drama with him, he wondered why she hadn't severed ties with him the moment she found out what he was. It was time he gave her some joy to temper all the sorrow.

She sensed him, the romantic bond they shared so powerful that it was hard to comprehend. A stronger person would let her go now, but he'd already tried that. Easing away from Theia was a challenge Haden was not built for. No, it was going to have to be enough that they grab what little happiness they could. He would savor these moments and put them away to relive in the future, because the future was one thing they would never have.

Just like the night we first met, when he stole into my dreams and introduced me to Under, Haden cut the picture of a dashing rogue. He'd worn his dark suit with tails again, knowing I'd be in a nightdress. I scooped up a handful of petals and flung them at him, laughing as they stuck in his hair and in his cravat and starched collar.

He wore his Victorian ensemble so elegantly, and yet the clothes didn't conceal his real nature. As formal as his wardrobe and manners were, the effect was tempered by his black-painted fingernails and the very modern chain belt. Haden was always a mix of decorously proper and deliberately uncivilized.

"Where are we? I don't remember this place. Is it safe from Mara?" I asked as he shook the flowers off him. Mara, the demon queen, hadn't let me go willingly.

"You're as safe as you ever can be if you're mixed up with me." He bowed deeply, a man from another time, but he seemed a little sad.

As if to underscore his words, a pair of birds began a woeful call unlike any birdsong I'd ever heard. The sound seemed to chisel at my bones with its intensity. Their pitiful lament crescendoed from a moody song to a hysterical, deafening screech, but by the time I'd lifted my hand to my ears, all was silent again.

Haden looked down at his feet. "There are places in Under even my mother can't go, but that doesn't mean they are safe."

"I feel safe with you. And you can make it rain roses," I said, blowing a heart-shaped petal off my hand like a kiss to cheer him up.

He smiled and closed the distance between us, reaching for my hand and pressing it against his lips. "I am full of tricks."

He brushed a stray petal from my hair. "You deserved a little break from real life. I know you're worried about tomorrow."

"I'm dreading it. I'm not sure it's a good idea, Haden. We still don't know how Mara's curse will affect me."

"I wish I could have stopped you from taking a blood oath with her. You shouldn't have risked yourself like that for me."

I touched his lips with my fingertips. "Your soul was at stake, Haden. I would do it again."

"Never say that, Theia. Don't ever put yourself in danger for me again." He paused. "I'm sorry. I invited you here to put you at ease and I'm not doing a very good job of it. You look beautiful." Haden offered me his arm, and I tucked mine into his as we walked to the gazebo.

"I feel very underdressed," I admitted as he sat me at the small table.

"I happen to enjoy your nightgowns more than words can say."

I rolled my eyes. "Yes, nothing is quite as tempting as a long cotton nightgown."

Haden's expression turned warm, so warm I wondered if my skin was melting like butter under his gaze. "Theia, you have no idea how sexy it is or you would wear a suit of armor to bed."

A tremor of pleasure made me shiver slightly, but I held the eye contact and the tremor deepened into something so strong it ached. Haden looked away first, for a change, and a gentle pink dotted his cheeks.

He lifted the silver dome in front of me to reveal an elegant chocolate mousse garnished with chocolate shavings, raspberries, and a mint leaf. The dish was a work of art.

"One of the things I love the most about you is the way you react to chocolate." Haden gestured to the spoon. "Wait until you taste it."

He was right. As soon as the frothy chocolate touched my tongue, I sighed. "This is what heaven tastes like."

Haden leaned across the table and stole a kiss, licking the corner of my mouth. "Yes," he agreed. "Heaven."

He sat back, and my heart squeezed. He'd awoken someone new inside me, and something delicious and edging on wicked blurred the lines of who I used to be and who I wanted to become.

The rich darkness in his eyes caught the glow from the candlelight and threatened to drown me in the surge of wonder that this perfect boy loved me. *Me.*

But he wasn't a boy. Haden Black was a dark mystery, a demon with a human soul. He embodied all that shouldn't be in a glorious presentation of everything that was ideal. His chiseled features would have been too harsh on a mere mortal, but gave him a unique appearance—as if he was sprung from a well of dreams. I suppose he was.

And he knew very well the effect he had on me.

Haden didn't feign ignorance about his sex appeal—he enjoyed the attention, courted the reaction. That's not to say he was egotistical. He'd be the first to admit his failings. His smoldering appeal was just part of what made him Haden. Desire was a natural state of being in his world—using it, feeling it, receiving it was all the same to him.

As if he knew what I was thinking, a slow grin eased

across his face. So much of our courtship had been spent by me trying to cipher whether Haden had really wanted me or not. He had pushed me away every time he had drawn me close, and the seesaw of tumultuous emotions had been exhausting.

I didn't have to wonder now.

When Haden looked at me, I no longer felt perplexed by his feelings. His heart beat strong and true, and there was nothing ambiguous about the desire I read in his eyes. He wove a spell over me, enticing me from the safe world I'd been sheltered in and into a place where I didn't know my way but trusted that I would find it with him.

Heat kindled the air between us. Nerves dashed throughout my body, making me aware with prickles and tingles that I was not just nervous—but also excited.

Haden said, "Your cheeks are pink."

I didn't answer, but my skin felt too hot and tight and my lips were parched. I licked them and Haden inhaled sharply.

Answering my questioning look, he said, "Sorry. I'm a little too focused on your mouth right now. Perhaps we should change the subject."

"I'm not sure we were talking about anything." *Was he blushing?* It was nice to know that he was just as overwhelmed by his feelings. It made me feel like my lack of experience wasn't as monumentally important—that we were both charting new waters.

"Well, we should talk about something, then. Something normal couples talk about," he said.

Unfortunately, that would be easier said than done. "I have no idea what normal couples say to each other. I've never even been on a date before."

A wistful expression softened his features. "Me either. Someday, we should try for a really normal one. Maybe go to a movie or bowling."

"Bowling?" I laughed, imagining Haden in rented bowling shoes. "Okay."

Haden cleared his throat. "I have no idea what is wrong with the male population of Serendipity Falls, but I can't tell you how much it means to me that I will be your first."

I glanced up sharply, but realized he meant first date, not first . . . lover. Still, the words hung between us as if suspended in a cloud. He realized what he'd said and his eyes widened. Suddenly his dessert plate became very interesting and he concentrated on his mousse.

The part of me that wasn't embarrassed loved that he bounced between dark, dangerous demon and slightly awkward boy. It made up for my mostly awkward girl moments.

I pushed the spoon through the mousse, trying to think of small talk that would defuse the tension. I couldn't think of anything to say that would qualify as inane chatter when there were so many things that needed to be discussed. Things we'd avoided since my return.

I didn't know what I was and I didn't know what I was capable of anymore. Under had changed me in more ways than one and he was the only one who could understand. I looked up to find him watching me intently.

"What is it?" he asked. "And don't tell me 'nothing' because you are a horrible liar."

I bit my lip. "I have questions."

Haden leaned back casually, but there was something so ethereal about the way he moved sometimes that it didn't seem as casual as he probably thought it was. "You know I'll answer whatever I can, Theia."

I had to know. "The summoning spell our friends performed . . . the one that brought us both back from Under last week . . . it was a demon summoning, right?"

Haden nodded, knowing where I was headed with my questions but letting me form them.

"So, I'm a demon then . . . since it obviously worked on both of us?"

"You have demon attributes because you made a pact with Mara using blood. You're not a demon, though. Not technically."

I closed my eyes and relived the memory of almost stealing Haden's essence while I was "not technically" a demon in Under. "She taught me things." I couldn't look at him. "Mara showed me how she steals souls from people in their sleep. She taught me how to be a mare demon—like her."

"Did you—?"

I shook my head. "I almost did, that one night . . ." The hunger I had felt that night would haunt me forever. It was like being possessed—like I was watching something else take over my body and mind while I stood in a corner unable to stop it.

"I remember," he said simply. Quietly. Of course he remembered the night I almost took his human soul. "But you stopped, Theia. You overcame it."

But would I be able to stop the next time?

The unnatural desire had racked my body physically, but what it did to my mind was much, much worse. The primal urge to feed overcame everything and became who I was for those few hours. My entire sense of self boiled down to my needs and urges. The person I knew myself to be was an annoying gnat to demon blood trying to take over. I was weak and useless. I was a silent scream.

A mare demon usually preys on human victims in their sleep. I didn't know all the correct demon taxonomy, but as a species, humans tend to lump the mare together with sex demons like incubi and succubi. The myths say the demons visit the sleeping humans and feed them nightmares—sometimes erotic ones—while absorbing the essence, the soul, of their prey. What the myths don't talk about is that mare demons can feed on souls that are awake as well—and the demons use their demon-given charms, called the Lure, to entice their prey into wanting to hand over their essence gladly, just to be near the mare demon. The demons absorb the human spirit through touching and kissing . . . and other, more intimate ways.

"Have you ever fed on a person's soul?" I asked, but wasn't sure I wanted the answer.

"I don't need to feed to survive, because I'm half-human. I've never drained a soul completely—but I have to admit that I've swiped a bit of essence now and then. Does that bother you?"

Well, it didn't make me think of puppies and rainbows.

"You're a demon, Haden. There are things that I have to expect will make me uncomfortable."

"It doesn't hurt them if you just take a bit. I know that isn't an excuse, and I haven't done it in a while. It's not always easy to resist." He didn't look away from me, almost as if he was daring me to turn away from him. As if I had any right to judge.

"I understand that it's difficult." I didn't want to admit how difficult it had become. "I have these cravings that come and go. Fleeting, really," I lied. "That night she showed me how to take your soul . . . it was so hard to stop myself. . . ."

Haden covered my hand with his warm one and I instantly felt calmer. "If we can find a way to rid you of her curse, I swear I will do anything."

"I worry that we've made a horrible mistake bringing me back, Haden. I think everyone was safer when I was trapped in Under."

Sometimes during the last week, I even missed Under a little. It was dangerous, and yet there was an eerie, captivating beauty to it also.

A string quartet began playing in the distance. I couldn't see the musicians, but the haunting song reached into my soul, entwining around my memories and dreams, twisting, turning, and reliving them . . . making the melancholy sweet . . . turning the sweet arcane. My eyelids drifted shut and the sound washed over me. I hadn't picked up my violin since I'd returned from Under. When I opened my eyes, I found my suitor standing in front of me, offering his hand and all of his old-world charm.

"The way you catch the light takes my breath away, Theia."

Haden sent me a smoldering look, the kind that made me

glad I was already sitting down, because my knees would have been useless. He arched one brow, quite aware that he was undoing me with just a look and quite proud of himself for it.

I placed my hand in his, sliding my palm across his until our fingers linked, and he pulled me out of my seat. He pressed an openmouthed kiss against the back of my hand, curling my toes with wicked pleasure.

We began to dance in an elegant pattern of a waltz he'd taught me before we knew that our hearts would shatter a million times in our quest to be together. This time during the dance, Haden touched me, something he'd been unwilling to chance when we first met. The weight of his hand on my back was not as heavy as the gravity of his gaze. The twinkling lights danced in the reflection of his onyx eyes. I wanted to capture this moment like a firefly in a jar.

We moved together as if we'd been dancing partners for centuries, when in fact I'd never danced until Haden taught me. I loved him more in that moment than I thought possible, but I felt a sadness seeping between us. We danced as if we had no worries, and yet we knew full well what torment might come.

We twirled and dipped and the world raced around us to keep up.

He scanned the horizon. "It's almost time."

"So soon? It feels like I just got here."

Haden kissed my temple. "Good morning, Theia."

I blinked, and my bedroom was awash in the light of a brand-new day.

CHAPTER TWO

My best friends were waiting for me at our usual before-school bench in front of the main building. I stood back a moment. I didn't remember ever being nervous about spending time with Donny and Amelia, but there it was, coiling in my stomach like an angry snake.

I'd seen them since they brought me back with the summoning spell, but this was different. This was about walking back into my old life, picking it up where I'd set it down. What if it didn't fit anymore? What if *I* didn't fit anymore?

Amelia was telling a story of some kind. I couldn't hear her words but, as usual, she used her whole body to talk. She'd dyed the ends of her black hair pink and she wore black leggings under a denim miniskirt, a tie-dyed T-shirt, arm warmers, and Dr. Seuss Chuck Taylors. Donny was laughing at whatever Ame was telling her, her dangly earrings catching glints of sunlight. If that didn't attract attention, surely her tight T-shirt would, especially since it just grazed the top of her belly button ring.

Ame caught sight of me over Donny's shoulder. Her smile was brighter than the sun and she raced towards me.

I let go of my fear and met her halfway. We squealed and clung to each other. She smelled like pears and the incense from the metaphysical bookstore she loved to go to.

She pulled back enough to look at my face. "I bought everything we need to do a super-duper protection spell. It's totally going to work this time. Can we meet tonight?"

"I don't know. Maybe. Did you get it from the Internet?" I asked. "And your hair is pink. It wasn't pink the other day, was it?"

She put her arm around my shoulder and walked me towards the bench. "No. I couldn't sleep last night, so I colored it. And no, not the Internet. I found a really old book of magic at the thrift store last week. It's the real deal. It's not even all in English. Varnie and I had to meditate over a few of the pages to get the secret text to show up."

"It sounds amazing. You think it will work on Mara?"

Ame bounced on the balls of her feet. "Totally. You'll see."

Amelia had learned a lot about the metaphysical world lately, especially being tutored by Varnie. "You've been spending a lot of time with Varnie lately."

Varnie and Haden were odd roommates, but it seemed to work for them both. I'd first met Varnie when he was dressed like a woman reading tarot cards. Apparently, his clients took him more seriously in a muumuu and turban than as a nineteen-year-old surfer. His methods were unconventional, but his clairvoyance was real.

"He's so amazing," Amelia enthused. "He's not only a psychic—he's more than just intuitive. He's taught me soooo much. He says I'm a natural. We were both a little freaked out by how strong my powers got so fast. It's like someone just flipped a switch in my head and I'm this metaphysical badass now."

"I'm really happy for you, Amelia. I know you've always been interested in that world, and I'm glad you're learning new things. But please be careful. Mara's dark magic isn't a good place to try your wings. I've seen what she does to people— what she did to me. I don't think she's going to give up and I'm afraid I've put you all in her line of fire."

Ame scoffed. "It's not your fault. If she comes back, we'll deal with her, just like we've done before."

She didn't understand. "Mara torments people. I think some of the creatures that live in Under used to be human. Now, they're just . . . warped. I told you about the handmaids, right? There were three of them that went everywhere together. And they were stitched together from each other's body parts. Someone hacked them apart and put them back together as if they were interchangeable." I shuddered, remembering the black floss stitches that had sewn their wobbly heads to their necks, how their eyes had been mix-and-matched. "I'm serious, Amelia. I don't want you poking around magic when it comes to Mara. You're in over your head."

Amelia's brow furrowed, but not because she was worried

about Mara. Because she was worried about me. "I know she's powerful—but there is a reason that her kind of magic doesn't rule the world. The good stuff—the kind that creates balance and harmony—it always wins in the end. Just remember, a dark shadow needs light to exist—but light doesn't need darkness to be luminous."

I hugged her tightly. She was so precious to me and I appreciated her more now than ever. "Thank you for being just the way you are. I love you."

We rocked a bit. "I love you too, Theia."

Donny sighed heavily. "Oh, my God, are you two about done? I've heard enough psychobabble this spring to last me through at least ten of my supposed reincarnations."

I let go of Amelia and turned to Donny and laughed.

"Hey, English." We made eye contact and she said with her eyes all the mushy things she would never utter out loud. Instead, she grabbed an iced coffee for me from the cardboard carrier on the bench and said, "I asked for an extra shot of chocolate for you."

That was good enough for me. I loved my friends.

Awkward silence ate up the time as the three of us tried to decide where to begin with the conversation now that the welcome-back portion of our morning was done.

"Can we start with normal, everyday things?" I asked after I had my first sip. "I just really want to feel normal for a change."

Ame began, "I totally froze on the SAT last week. I started geeking out about how important it was and couldn't read the questions, let alone come up with the answers."

I patted her back. "Oh, Ame. I'm sorry. You can retake it in the fall, right?"

She nodded. "Yeah—and you'll be able to take it then since you . . . missed it."

The iced coffee tasted wonderful, so I concentrated on that instead of what else I'd missed. Luckily, Haden still had many loyal servants who had made sure I was well cared for during my time in Under. I didn't think he knew how much they still loved their prince there.

Ame shoulder-bumped me and coerced a small smile from my lips. I looked into her almond-shaped eyes and found the comfort I'd missed so much while I was gone. Ame never failed to mother everyone she came into contact with. Her maternal instincts were spot-on. She always knew when I needed a hug or a word of encouragement.

She had a great mom of her own, but she still understood what I was going through when I missed the mother I never knew. Amelia had been adopted from Korea as a baby and even though her parents loved her, there was a part of her that felt the same loss I did from time to time. Her adoptive parents were so different from her physically that Ame often overcompensated by dressing even more alternatively, as if drawing attention to her clothes would draw people's focus away from her Asian features. It was only recently that she had stopped trying to—how did Donny say it?—*de-Asian* herself. I loved how she was starting to play up the shape of her eyes with eyeliner and no longer bleaching her hair to match her blond mom's.

Another long pause allowed me to take a huge drink. There

were no iced coffees in Under, at least none that I'd found. I was always very wary of what I ate and drank there anyway—it was a type of hell after all. The cuisine was often so fresh it still writhed on its serving platter.

"You're not mad at me that I went to prom with Haden while you were gone, are you?" Amelia blurted out, surprising me so that I almost spit out a mouthful of my drink. Apparently she'd been trying to keep that one in for a while.

"Of course not," I said. "Haden told me you went together. I just wish it had been more fun."

"Well," Donny said, "the whole night wasn't a waste. Gabe finally put out. He was so freaked out by that séance we had after the dance that he forgot he was being a prude. He was all 'Hold me, baby.'"

"There's something to be said for extreme fear," Ame said and then giggled.

Just then, Gabe, the boy who Donny pretended wasn't her boyfriend but most assuredly was, appeared. "Cheerios, Theia."

He hadn't heard us talking about him, thankfully, and had no idea why we were laughing so hard. When I was able to bring myself under control, I answered, "Cheerios, Gabe."

He'd mistakenly thought that all British people said "Cheerios" to one another in greeting, and I'd yet to bother correcting him. It was cute. *He* was cute. I don't remember Gabe ever going through an awkward phase during our freshman year when the rest of us did. He never needed braces, his sandy brown hair landed in perfect waves, his skin was always clear, and he was a natural athlete.

Everything about Gabe made him the wrong guy for Donny, except that he was perfect for her. Much to her chagrin.

Donny believed that variety was the spice of life—and she liked her love life very spicy indeed. She'd earned herself a reputation, but it had never bothered her. In fact, she was somewhat proud of it. If she'd been born a guy, she would have been known as a player. Since she'd been born a girl, instead they called her names like "slut."

Somehow, though, Gabe had managed to really get under her skin. And stay there. And he was a sneetch, of all things. Donny had nicknamed the popular crowd at our school "sneetches," from a Dr. Seuss book where the Star-Belly Sneetches thought they were better than the other sneetches born without stars. Donny had no use for the sneetches other than to mock them. And now she was dating one. Exclusively. It must be killing her a little.

A boy I didn't recognize stopped in front of us and stared at me. He looked younger—possibly a freshman, definitely not a sneetch. He worked his mouth open and closed a few times, as if searching for words that refused to come.

"Hello," I prompted.

He blinked hard and dropped the stack of papers in his hands. It looked like it was an essay or a report, something important, so I crouched down to help him collect the pages.

"You don't have to—I mean . . . it's okay. . . . I'm sorry," he rambled, trying to hide that he was shaking while he picked up his papers. We stood up and I handed him what I had gathered. He stammered some more. "It's just . . . you're nice . . . and I . . ."

"Are you all right, dude?" Donny asked.

"She's so pretty," he replied, his face turning beet red. "I'm so stupid." And then he ran.

We all looked at one another, dumbfounded. "Well, that was thirty-one flavors of weird," Ame said.

Donny slugged down the rest of her coffee. "I have to get to class. One more tardy and I have Saturday school." She squeezed my arm as she passed.

Haden texted me that he would be late, so Amelia and Gabe headed to class and I made my way to the admin office. By the time I got my paperwork signed and in order, the hall was empty but for one other student. I didn't recognize her at first. Brittany Blakely, one of Haden's admirers and homecoming queen three years in a row, ambled down the hall like a zombie. Her blond hair, normally bouncy and shiny, hung lankly in a messy ponytail. Instead of her normal cheer uniform or miniskirt, she wore a pair of sweatpants and an oversize T-shirt. Her skin looked sallow, and the dark circles under her eyes made her appear to be hollowing from the inside out.

She didn't look at me when we passed each other, which I suppose was no big surprise. The sneetches rarely deigned to notice anyone who was not in their social circle. I don't know why it bothered me that she hadn't even looked at me. I'd always been a doormat to the students at Serendipity High. The only time they'd cared was when my disappearance had become a juicy morsel of intrigue. The more I thought about the way she looked, the more satisfaction I felt. Good. She deserved to be sick. I may have been through hell, literally, but at least I didn't look like it.

The pattern of light on the opposite wall caught my eye as it became disordered from the shape of the windows. A shadow from nowhere stole across and ate the light, darkening the entire hall for a second. I blinked and a hunger pang began in my center and radiated out through my veins. My mouth filled with saliva and I felt weak. I leaned against the bank of lockers and tried to stop shaking. It wasn't like the pangs that twist the stomach . . . it came from a deeper place than that. A depth I hadn't possessed before the curse.

After I took a few deep breaths, the consuming hunger was gone as quickly as it had come upon me, leaving me breathless and clammy but otherwise back to normal. I splashed water on my face from the drinking fountain and tried to reason away the sense of impending doom that something wasn't right.

I leaned against the wall and tried to collect myself. I didn't really want Brittany to be sick—that was just my petty jealousy. It was only natural to feel jealous from time to time, I rationalized. Other girls said catty things about one another all the time. It didn't mean I really wished her harm. And the dizzy spell . . . Well, I hadn't eaten anything before school. I was a bundle of nerves before I had even added the caffeine. That was all.

Surely, that was all.

Looking forward to my trig class was a new experience for me, but it was the only class I had with Amelia, and I needed to see a friendly face.

She met me outside the door. One look at me and her sunny smile slid into a frown. "You okay?" she asked.

"Everyone is staring at me. I'm used to them ignoring me, but now they are staring and ignoring." I hated being the focal point. I preferred the background to the foreground. "Sometimes I hear whispering, but I can't make out what they're saying."

Ame shrugged. "They'll get bored soon."

"Is my seat still open?" I asked as we entered the room. Our seats weren't assigned in that class, but in the hierarchy of high school politics, there were still rules about seating. The last thing I needed was to anger someone by taking a chair that no longer belonged to me.

"Of course it is." She tugged my sleeve. "What kind of friend do you think I am? I saved your seat because I knew you would be back."

When class began, I opened my book and tried to follow along. Unfortunately, while I was a good student, I had just missed too much to pick up that day's lesson. Which meant that instead of concentrating on the law of tangents, my mind went off on a tangent of its own.

As always, my daydreams circled back to Haden. He'd found me between classes after first period and made it quite clear to anyone who saw us together that we were a couple. It wasn't like it was an extreme display of public affection either. It was the way he looked at me when he held my hand—as if I were the sun in his orbit.

Just thinking about him made me warm all over and I blinked myself back to the land of trig equations reluctantly. It was then that the sensation of being watched hit me again. I tried to ignore it, but the tension grew each minute like a balloon gathering more and more air. The feelings were overwhelming. The balloon was going to pop from all the pressure.

The heat grew over my right ear and I finally whirled in my seat to send a scathing look to the rude starer. Two rows away, Mike Matheny's eyes grew wide before he cast them down quickly to the open book in front of him.

Towards the end of class, we were released to work together on the next day's assignment. Brad Wickman approached my chair.

"I thought you might need this," he said shyly, handing me a spiral notebook.

"What is it?" I asked.

"Trig notes. The ones you missed are towards the end."

My brows knit together. "You're giving me your trig notes? Don't you need them? We still have a final coming up."

"I'll be okay." He smiled.

"Brad, I can't take your notes—"

"Wick," he interrupted.

"Excuse me?"

"Everyone calls me Wick."

"Erm . . . well, thank you, Wick. It's very sweet for you to share your notes, but I would feel really bad about keeping them. How about I copy them in the library and give you back your notebook tomorrow?"

He blushed a little. "That would be really great. You're the best, Theia."

Before I could respond, he bolted back to his seat. The tips of his ears were bright red. I knew a thing or two about blushing, but it was a strange experience to be on the other side of the flush. Had I made him nervous? Me? Perhaps he was embarrassed to be seen talking to the notorious girl on campus.

The bell rang and we all scattered to my next least favorite place on campus—the cafeteria. Maybe that was an exaggeration. There was nothing wrong with the cafeteria; in fact, I quite enjoyed the pizza and Tater Tots, since I didn't get that kind of food at home. I just wasn't in the mood to be in an enclosed space with everyone in the school and their gossip.

Amelia had to retrieve her cell phone from jail—her first-period teacher was well-known for confiscating them—so I went on to the lunchroom without her. I threaded my way between the tables in the cafeteria with my tray and waited for my friends at our old table. Mike Matheny, Amelia's unrequited crush and somewhat rude starer from trig, joined me. His presence was unexpected. For one thing, most of the school had always preferred to ignore me rather than acknowledge my existence. For another thing, he seemed to prefer to ignore *Amelia* rather than acknowledge *her* existence, and she was really the only thing we had in common besides our math class.

"Hey, Theia," he said. His tray was filled with what must have been two lunches.

"Hello, Mike."

Mike wore what most of the male population of Serendipity High sported in the late spring—board-length shorts and a T-shirt with a sports logo. Somehow, even though Haden shopped in the same stores, the clothes looked different on him. Mike, however, blended seamlessly into the fabric of our school.

He looked at me intently, as if he was expecting something. Only, I didn't know what. I lowered my eyes to my tray, hoping he'd get the hint, but I still felt his gaze on me, overwarm and awkward. You would think he'd have gotten the hint after I caught him staring in class.

To be fair, while he didn't know that Haden was born half-demon and that I had been cursed with demon blood, Mike had been part of our group briefly. I decided to give him the benefit of the doubt and assume that he was trying to be supportive and not just nosy. And Amelia still liked him, so if they ever dated, his presence would be normal at lunch every day. Still, he could have said something. Anything.

"Are you excited for the end of the year?" I asked, finally, to break up some of the strangeness. It's not as if I didn't know the answer to my question—everyone was, after all. "Do you have plans for the summer?"

"I'll be working for my dad," he answered. "I get to wash all the new cars on his lot." I gathered he wasn't very excited about it by the tone of his voice.

Amelia would be happy to know he would be staying in town for the break, though I still wished she'd give Varnie a better look. Mike was nice, but he would never understand the things that really made Ame happy. I didn't see Mike hanging out reading auras with her or casting spells. But Amelia had always liked Mike, so I guessed I had better at least make an effort.

"Do you like cars?" I asked, for lack of another subject.

"Yeah, I guess. I don't like working for my dad." He bit into his apple and spoke around the mouthful. "We're not close."

I looked away from his open mouth. "I'm sorry. I'm not very close with mine either."

"English," Gabe announced as he slid onto the bench next to me, nodding at Mike. "I need a favor." He looked over his shoulder at the students filtering in and then hunkered closer to my ear. "I need your help to—"

"Well, isn't this cozy?" Haden's cold, steely tone preceded him as he stopped at the end of the table. His posture was relaxed, but there was no mistaking the look on his face—his jaw clenched tightly and his brow drew down. Then he smiled.

"Relax, dude." Gabe rolled his eyes. "I have enough girl problems without adding your British babe to my stack."

"British babe?" I repeated. I liked the sound of that.

Haden sat on the other side of me. He wasn't *really* jealous, but I liked that maybe he was just a tiny bit. "You couldn't handle her anyway," he said to Gabe.

Haden held my hand under the table and we shared my lunch while Gabe explained that he needed help distracting Donny. Her birthday was coming up and he wanted to install a new stereo in her car. I really liked Gabe. He was everything Donny *never* wanted in a boy, which made him perfect for her.

Donny and Ame joined us, and Donny had to force Ame to take the seat next to Mike, who didn't seem to speak for the rest of the lunch period unless it was to ask, "Are you done with that?" before he helped himself to the rest of your lunch. He just sat there. Chewing.

Everything seemed fine until I looked at my pizza slice and realized it would never fill me up. Never. All of a sudden I was starving. I wanted . . . I wanted to eat something that wasn't on the menu. I realized I craved the light of a human soul. The force of the craving hit me like a blow to my stomach, and then, just as suddenly, it was gone.

Nobody seemed to notice that anything had been amiss, and I relaxed. I didn't hurt anyone. The craving came and went and everything was fine. I was in control.

"The end-of-the-year carnival is coming up," Donny said. "We should all go together."

"Okay," Mike answered, and I'm afraid we all stopped eating and looked at him for a moment. I'm not sure Donny had meant to include him, and it was strange that he accepted the invitation.

Amelia blushed and played with the ends of her braid. She hadn't touched her salad, but I didn't blame her. It didn't have dressing. I abhorred vegetables and could only eat them if they were drowning in some kind of sauce. Her reason for not eating had to do with nerves, though.

Haden scowled at Mike—a real frown, unlike the playful one he'd used on Gabe. I don't even think he knew he was doing it. Perhaps he was feeling a loyalty to Varnie and didn't want Mike getting too close to Amelia. Wouldn't that be something, if Mike and Varnie had to fight for her affections? I hoped Varnie would win too, but my loyalty was firmly bound to Amelia. She'd been in love with Mike Matheny since puberty; if she stood a chance at getting what she wanted, I wanted her to get it.

"Well, okay then. We'll all six of us go to the carnival together."

"We should invite Varnie," Amelia said.

Again, we all stopped in midbite.

What was going on? Amelia liked Varnie, as a friend, but why would she pass up the chance to be paired up with Mike?

"Seven is a lucky number, right?" said Gabe.

Haden looked at Ame for a long minute. "Maybe he'll want to bring a date."

I squeezed his hand. *What was he doing?*

Amelia crinkled her brow, like the thought hadn't occurred to her, and now that it had, she didn't much care for it. "Maybe," she said simply.

"I don't like carnivals," I said. And I didn't like Haden deliberately baiting my friend either. Though maybe he was right—maybe a little jealousy might spark her attention to Varnie.

Haden leaned into me. "I want to go on one of those rides in the dark with you."

"The only dark ride they have is that awful scary one."

"I'll keep you safe." His words were normal, but the low timbre of his voice reached inside me and played like a seductive song.

I leaned further into him. "Maybe you should be more worried about your safety."

Thankfully, the lunch period was almost over and Mike said he had to go. Ame made an excuse to go the same direction.

"I don't like him," Haden grumbled, turning over his shoulder and watching Mike all the way out the door.

"Matheny's all right," Gabe assured him. "Ame could do a lot worse."

"She could do a lot better. I don't know how to explain it, but something is off with that guy."

"He's not Varnie," Donny suggested. "I think that's what you mean."

I nodded. "Do you think Varnie will stick around, though? When we first met him, he was getting ready to move out of Serendipity Falls. Something about bad juju."

"He pretends he's all Cowardly Lion guy, but he hasn't backed down from anything that's threatened one of us." Donny bit her lip. "Look, she's never going to see Varnie as boyfriend material unless he makes the first move, so all this talk is getting us nowhere. They need to work it out on their own."

Gabe laughed. "You're so full of it."

"What?" she asked.

"The very last thing you're thinking about right now is letting them work it out on their own. You're already planning something this very minute."

"No, I'm not, pretty boy."

"Liar."

"You think you know me so well. You don't." She stood up. "I have to get a book out of my car."

Gabe flashed a grin at me while he gathered their garbage.

"That means she wants to make out with me before class. See you guys later."

She glared at him before she stomped away. Instead of barreling through it, she stopped and waited for Gabe to catch up, and they went out together. I guess he was right.

"Just you and me now," said Haden.

I turned my attention to him.

"You're so beautiful, Theia." He traced his finger down my jawline.

I shook my head. "Rather ordinary, actually."

"I'm never wrong, and I say beautiful. Do you know how many different shades of hair color you have?"

"Um . . . no." Most people call it dishwater blond. It wasn't quite blond, but it wasn't brown either.

"Neither do I. I counted seven once, but I think there are more than that. Each one catches the light differently. Some are gold, some are wheat, and you have a few stray coppers in there as well."

"You make my hair sound very interesting."

"I could write a sonnet about your lips too."

On cue, I licked them. I didn't think about it; it was just a natural reaction. Haden's natural reaction to that was a low growl that shocked us both.

And then the bell, which never rang when it was supposed to, shrilled loudly.

I sighed, blinking out of the spell he'd put on me. "I have to go to class. I keep hoping one of my teachers will take pity on me and pass me despite my absences. I don't think it's going to happen."

Haden walked me out, kissed the top of my head, and told me he'd see me in history.

When I got to class, I reached into my bag and found a note scrawled in handwriting I didn't recognize.

You're in danger.

CHAPTER THREE

Later that night, we all joined hands around a table in the room at Varnie's that Donny had dubbed "the war room." The war room was where he did all his psychic readings for clients as "Madame Varnie" and where my friends had done séances and spells to try to find me when I'd been abducted to Under. The ambience of the room was very clichéd, with red, purple, and gold scarves draped everywhere and white lights and candles illuminating the space. Incense burned in the corner and it made me feel as if I couldn't get a full breath of air.

I didn't tell anyone about the note.

I don't know why. After the cold dread flushed through my body, I crumpled it up and threw it away. I guess I just wanted to bury my head in the sand a little longer. After all, the warning was redundant. I was well aware that I was in danger and that at any given moment I *was* the danger. I shuddered at the memory of craving a human soul for lunch.

Instead of a crystal ball, a very old book, opened near the middle, graced the center of Varnie's table. The book itself didn't seem very mystical, the binding aged and scarred as if it had been passed around many times. The text was typed on very thin paper, but none of the letters was recognizable, forming nothing but gibberish. Before joining our hand-holding circle, Amelia scattered a dusting of glitter in a circle around the book.

Donny rolled her eyes. "That is leftover glitter from the craft store. You're not fooling anyone into thinking that's fairy dust or anything."

"Aesthetics are an important part of magic," Ame answered. "Your surroundings can help center you. Plus, I did purify the glitter with a crystal in the sun. So, bonus—pretty *and* practical."

"I'm just glad that we can go boy/girl on the hand-holding now. Thanks for coming back, Theia. I was getting tired of holding hands with your boyfriend." Gabe winked at me across the table.

I winked back. "I'm sorry my abduction to hell caused you so much strife, Gabe."

Donny's eyes widened before she laughed. "Theia, did you just wink at my boyfriend?"

"She totally did," Ame teased.

"Obviously, I'm going to need to keep a close eye on her."

Haden's tone was light, but I sensed an underlying tremor of something beneath it. Jealousy? Maybe.

Boys were confusing. Before I met Haden, I'd never been comfortable around them, thanks to my father's strict rules about me not associating with anyone male. Though I'd been tutored by Donny, who had been collecting boys for many years, I never had any reason to put flirting into practice until I met Haden, so it was a little strange that I winked at Gabe. I took it as a sign that I was maturing. It was harmless.

"Let's get this dish plated up," Varnie said. "I have an early-morning appointment with the surf tomorrow. Is everyone holding hands? Okay, so, we are going to use the bond that we all have with each other to strengthen the spell, but all you guys have to do is hold hands. Miss Amelia will do the actual spell casting."

"What are you going to do?" Donny wondered.

"Sit here and look pretty," Varnie answered.

Ame gave him the *You're joking, right?* stare. "Varnie's job is to help keep me centered. He's a strong psychic, but he's not really into practicing witchcraft."

"Or demon summoning, for that matter, but nobody ever listens to me about that," he interjected.

"The last one worked just fine," Amelia argued, gesturing her head towards me. "We got her back, didn't we?"

Donny sighed heavily. "Can we get started? Gabe hates these things and when he gets nervous, his hand gets sweaty."

Gabe glared at her. "Most girls just want me to take them

to the movies, a nice dinner now and then. You're the first one who makes me go to séances and exorcisms."

"I'm not any happier about it than you are. It's not my fault my best friends are nut jobs and demons."

"Focus, people," Varnie admonished.

Haden and I exchanged a glance. He didn't look as if he felt this was going to work, but I thought it was sweet that he went along with it anyway.

We all shushed. Varnie led us on a journey into our minds, where we were supposed to find a meditative, or at least calm, state. Amelia called that part of her brain the nougaty center, which was disgusting, but it wasn't surprising that she could find candy-bar symbolism in just about anything.

As we all settled into a strange quiet place, Amelia started chanting. It was hard to believe that just a few months ago we'd been teasing her about the Hello Kitty tarot cards she was no good at reading. She seemed so much more confident now.

The book in the center of the table jiggled and then tendrils of white and gold reached slowly towards the ceiling, curling and looping and glowing. I held my breath as the letters seemed to lift off the page, arranging themselves into new formations and then dissipating in puffs of smoke. Instead of stomach butterflies, an angry swarm of bees churned inside of me. Magic, even the kind Amelia performed, made me uneasy. The blur that marked the border between the illusion of reality of the world I wanted to live in and that of the realm I didn't want to remember was fraught with a magic that seduced before it bit.

I didn't understand the words Amelia was saying, but she

looked right at me and the letters lifted from the parchment again, only this time they floated across the table, stopping in front of my face. They began rearranging into new words, I guess, ones I couldn't read, and then into shapes. That's when things got chaotic.

They formed into what looked like several arrows and suddenly they speared themselves into my arm painfully. I yelped, but was transfixed. Time slowed to a crawl as the words of her spell pinched my flesh. I watched in horror, unable to stop the attack. Fear choked the air from my lungs, prohibiting anything but an impotent, silent scream from coming out. Haden tried to block the arrows, but they kept coming, sharply burying themselves into my skin.

Ame cried out, Varnie slapped the book closed, and Haden threw me to the ground and under the table. The letters were under my skin now, tattooing my forearm with symbols and unreadable words. The tattoos wound around my arm like word serpents, marking me inside and out. What did it mean? Why were they targeting me? Maybe Mara had somehow infiltrated the spell casting.

Ame joined me under the table. "Omigod, omigod."

"What's happening, Amelia? What are they doing?" My heart raced wildly, like a rabbit kicking my rib cage, pushing all of my senses into overload, and I clawed at my own skin trying to make the sensations stop. "I don't know," she said, grabbing my hands so I'd stop hurting myself. "This wasn't supposed to go like this."

Everyone crouched around us under the table, but I still

didn't feel safe. In fact, I felt trapped. My head filled with a high-pitched keening that I slowly realized was coming from me. Ame grasped my wrists and her eyes rolled back in her head. For a moment the Amelia I knew seemed gone. The one next to me was different, other. It chilled me. I watched, shocked, as all the words slithered from my arm to hers, and then disappeared.

Her eyes stayed open, but showed only whites for another few seconds, and then she blinked and came back to herself. I stared at her, mesmerized by the change. She brushed the hair out of my eyes. "I'm sorry, Theia. I didn't know it would do that. Are you okay?"

"Not really." I was upset, scared, and a little angry at being attacked. "What just happened? How did you know how to make it stop?"

She shrugged. "I've gotten really intuitive. I don't know . . . it's like everything clicked and magic just became easy to me."

"Amelia, you didn't pick up that kind of power from spending time in the metaphysical bookstore. Something has to have changed." I didn't trust it. It seemed too easy.

"Well, Varnie has taught me a lot. I think I'm just a natural." She shrugged again.

I didn't have the energy to explore the issue further. Ame and Haden helped me out from under the table. As I stood shakily, I noticed that everyone but Haden was surrounded by a different-colored glow. I blinked, but the image remained. "Everyone is glowing."

"Glowing how? Like an aura?" Varnie asked.

I blinked some more. "I guess. You are all different colors." I looked at my arm. I didn't see the light around me, but I was glad to find that I didn't see the strange letters and symbols either.

"Auras are so cool!" Ame exclaimed, rushing to help me back into a chair. "Some people say it's your human soul."

Souls. I didn't think it was necessarily a good thing that I could see the souls of my friends glowing around them. Not when a mare demon's power included the ability to absorb them.

I began trembling from coming down off the excitement and adrenaline. "Well, they are fading now, but they were really bright a few seconds ago."

Haden stood behind my chair, massaging the tops of my shoulders absently. His touch calmed me, though I felt light-headed. He asked, "What went wrong with that spell? I thought it was for protection, but it seemed more like an attack."

"It *was* a protection spell. I'm not sure . . ." Ame bit her lip.

"It wasn't your fault, Miss Amelia," Varnie reassured her. "We researched that spell really well. I don't know what went wrong, but I don't think it was anything you did."

My skin felt clammy and cold, and my vision blurred slightly. Nausea and hunger battled for attention in my stomach. Was I still coming down from the rush of fear? Because it felt suspiciously close to the low blood sugar problem I sometimes had when I skipped a meal. Only, I'd eaten a huge dinner before going to Varnie's.

Perhaps my body was telling me I needed to feed the unnatural hunger Mara had cursed me with. My heart began to break. "Maybe instead of protecting me, it was protecting all of you *from* me."

Amelia squeezed my hand. "We don't need protection from you, Theia."

"You don't know that, Ame. None of us knows what I'm capable of. You shouldn't have brought me back."

"Theia," Amelia said, her sweet voice making it even harder for me to accept the danger I put them all in just by being in the same room. What would happen if I lost control, even for one second?

I couldn't breathe. The weight of their expectations felt like an anvil pressing against my chest. I knew they just wanted to reassure me, but everything was so overwhelming. I needed to get out of there.

"I'm sorry," I managed as I pushed past all of them and ran to the door, ignoring their protests.

The cool evening air, thickening with fog, slapped me as soon as I got outside. I sat on the steps, hanging my head. Pins and needles in my limbs flared and then seemed to dissipate as I concentrated on deep breathing.

Haden came out with my sweatshirt and offered me a hand up. "Come on, let's go for a walk."

I nodded, letting him help me up, and turned so he could ease me into the sleeves of my hoodie. He held my hand as we walked, but didn't press me to talk until I was ready. When I began to feel more myself, I squeezed his hand. "I'm sorry about my outburst back there. I—"

He paused and turned me to him. "Don't apologize. It wouldn't be natural for you not to be affected. It was scary. We're all concerned about you."

There was the anvil again. "I'm fine."

Haden looked at me darkly. "You're fine."

I nodded.

"Theia, you were attacked by some kind of magic spell about ten minutes ago. It's okay to be upset."

I nodded again. "I hope Amelia doesn't blame herself."

"She probably does. The spell was likely reacting to Mara's blood inside you. She couldn't have known that would happen."

Now was my chance to tell him how I'd been worried about the hunger I'd felt. I tried to find the words, but before I could speak, Haden kissed my knuckles.

"Let's go back to the house. I'll make you some of that tea you like so much."

I swallowed the words I'd meant to say. "Tea sounds lovely."

By the time we got back, everyone had left. I had a couple of texts from Donny and Amelia to call them when I felt like talking. Varnie made an excuse to go to bed early so Haden and I could have some privacy.

I settled in on Varnie's ugly, lumpy couch. "You're getting quite good at making tea," I told Haden. "I think it's sweet that you keep PG Tips here for me."

He looked down slightly, adorably embarrassed to be complimented for being sweet. His dark briar of eyelashes swept across his eyes. "That's what you like. I want you to be comfortable here." He looked at me through those lashes. "This is where I live. My home. You need to feel welcome wherever I am, but especially here."

My heart clutched. He needed this life he'd found in Serendipity Falls. He'd been so alone for so long—but now he had a lumpy couch, and friends, and a home where he felt at peace. It would be selfish of me to tell him about my worries that I would lose the ability to stay in control of the demon urges. They could be just that—worries. I hadn't acted on the hunger. There was no need to make him worry too. Not yet.

He leaned back into the couch, so I curled into him and rested my cheek on his chest. "You and Varnie are odd roommates, you know."

Haden kissed the top of my head. "How so?"

"Well, he dresses like a woman, for one thing."

"Only for his clients. He still won't let me drink his beer, you know. Can you believe that? I'm technically older than him, in demon years, but he still says no."

"He feels responsible for you," I said. "I think it's sweet."

"You think everything is sweet."

"Did you figure out his real first name yet?" I asked.

"All the bills come to A. E. Varnie, and he refuses to tell me anything other than that it's awful and he considers legally changing it every day."

I pondered that. "So, it can't be something normal like Adam or Andrew."

"No. I bet his license has it . . . but I don't want to snoop. Do you need to go home soon?"

In the quiet of the room, the stillness between us, I felt like I could breathe again. I leaned back to look at Haden. "Probably. My father is still avoiding me, but I don't want to give him any reasons to swing back into overprotective mode either."

Haden got up first and pulled me after. We stared at each other for a long moment. The stress of the evening began to fade and I felt myself falling into the place where nothing mattered but the two of us.

He took my hands into his, the touch of his skin electrifying mine. He brought one hand to his lips and kissed the backs of my fingers, and the jolt of his touch thrummed as if on a direct wire to my center. I finally looked at him, his inky dark eyes full of mischief and desire.

"I can hear your pulse racing faster. Do I still make you nervous, love?"

"Yes," I admitted, thinking that I gave him more power than I wanted to as the word slipped out on a quick breath.

Instead, my truth seemed to do the opposite. Haden's expression softened and somehow, by admitting my weakness, I gained control. As I felt the shift of power come back to me, I brought his other hand to my chest, placing it over my wildly beating heart. He swallowed hard and pressed his hand more firmly against my skin.

We stood so close that we shared the same air, breathing each other in and out. My heart pounded beneath his fingers like it was trying to break free. The moment stretched, the corners of the room rounded, and the light around us seemed to sparkle and dance. A need took form in the center of my heart. It grew and spread, hollowing me until the only thing that would ease the growing ache was Haden.

"It's not safe to want you this badly," he said simply.

"I don't care," I said.

He closed his eyes, trying to find that reserve of control he kept deep inside. The one I'd found myself trying to crack since the night my dreams led me to his world. The atmosphere held a charge, each passing second threatening to detonate everything. "You should."

He was acting very strangely all of a sudden. "Haden? What is it? What's wrong?"

"Some days are harder than others," he said, as if that explained anything. "Come on, I'll take you home."

He had erected a wall between us and I could see no reason for it. But I was tired and worn out from the attack, so I pretended everything was fine.

I was getting pretty good at that.

A moon hung large and impossibly full in the purple sky as the wind moaned solemnly through winter trees barren of leaves. The trunks were bent and curved like old women and I shivered at the creepy mosaic of long shadows they created. And also at the bitter cold. I'd gone to bed wearing yoga pants and a T-shirt in case I woke up in Under, but it didn't change the outcome—I still awoke wearing my white nightgown. I shivered again.

The shadows danced without movement from their source, gyrating into complex patterns and then back to the shape of the trees. Around me were the crooked headstones of an uncared-for graveyard. Forgotten. No grass or flowers grew in the untended cemetery. The midnight chill felt like a permanent feature of the desolate burial ground.

I didn't think Haden would have arranged such a meeting, but I was unmistakably in Under. I tried to read the epitaphs on the gravestones, but most were worn away or cracks ran through the words, making them indecipherable. A crushed-rock path wove through the graves, I hoped leading out of the cemetery. The living in Under were scary enough; I didn't want to meet the dead.

While I knew better than to assume the trail was safe, it seemed preferable to walking over the graves, so I stepped carefully onto it, hoping the rocks wouldn't cut the bottom of my feet. I followed the winding path through the hilly yard with every hair on my neck prickling. The night was eerily serene despite the mournful wind, and moonlight illuminated my way. I kept looking over my shoulder, waiting for the doom I was sure to find at any moment.

I finally reached the end of the trail, its conclusion a black iron gate leading out of the graveyard. The tips of the fence spires were shaped into knife points, chilling my blood again. Were the blades to keep someone in or out? I wondered.

I opened the gate slowly, the creaks and groans lamenting how long it had been since the hinges were last used. Latching it back into place, I turned and found that the other side of the fence was rife with glimmering figures. Ghosts.

My heart thundered in my chest, but they didn't seem to notice me. They glowed phosphorescently white, transparent and yet not. The apparitions, all girls of varying ages with blond hair, were tending what looked like flower beds. As I peered closer, I realized they were gardens of bones.

Poking through the mulch of ash were joints and femurs and skulls . . . and more. Some of the ghosts held watering cans, while others were on their knees weeding through ash. One young girl holding a basket was picking the bones, depositing each piece of her harvest into the straw container.

She turned and looked at me and I lost the feeling in my limbs as I froze in horror. She was about ten years old. I recognized the dress. She was me.

I sucked in a breath and looked at the faces of each ghost— all of them were apparitions of my youth. They smiled and waved at me before returning to their work. Tending their dead blooms.

I backed into the gate, desperately wanting to get back to the other graveyard. The latch was stuck, so I turned to fiddle with it. A sensation of frost coated my back and I turned around to see that all of the ghosts had formed in a horizontal line behind me. There seemed to be one for every year of my life, the eldest holding a baby wearing a gown I recognized from my christening pictures.

I rattled the gate as they began to walk towards me. It wouldn't open. There was nowhere to run. The ghosts of me formed a semicircle, trapping me against the fence. The eldest— my current age—stood directly in front of me and held the baby towards me as if she wanted me to take it. I shook my head but her face melted into an angry expression, her lips pulling back into an evil snarl at my refusal. I held out my arms and she put the noncorporeal baby into my hands.

The child was weightless but cold. Freezing cold. I didn't want to hold her, but I couldn't put her down or give her back. From behind me a shadow loomed. I couldn't see what was blocking the moon, but as it edged over my shoulder, the darkness ate the luminosity of the baby in my hands until it disappeared completely into a pinpoint of black and I awoke shuddering.

My bed was covered in frost.

There would be no more sleep for me that night. I'd found I needed less since my return anyway.

Despite my attempts to distract myself with books or even homework, I remained haunted by the chill of Under and what I'd seen. The frost had burned off my bed in a hiss of smoke after I'd jumped out of it—but I was still unnaturally cold.

A warm bath helped, but I couldn't stop seeing the ghosts. Every time I closed my eyes, they were there—they were me. I finally gave up and went downstairs for tea. It was almost time to get up anyway.

I was surprised to see my father in the kitchen.

"Good morning, Theia."

I looked at the clock above his head. "Is everything all right? You're usually at the office by now."

"Everything is fine," his voice said, but his posture told another story.

My father was not a physically big man, but the way he carried himself made him seem to loom large over others despite his absence of height or girth. As I watched him rinse out his teacup, he seemed shrunken to me.

"Father, are you ill?"

He turned to look at me, surprised that I had asked. "Just a little tired."

"Something is going around my school," I said, thinking of the way Brittany had looked yesterday. "Perhaps you have a touch of it."

"Yes, that's possible."

And then there was the silence.

Why was it so hard for us to connect? We were so polite it was like living with a stranger. All these years, all we'd had was each other and yet we never did. We never had each other. How unbelievably sad.

I'd rather have had him explode with anger because he thought I'd run away than ignore the fact that I'd been gone.

The silence roared between us, louder than anything I'd ever heard. I wanted to grab him by the shoulders and shake him until he reacted to me. I wanted to tell him about the demon queen, Mara—how she'd kidnapped me and poisoned me. He needed to know about my strange trip to Under last night and how scared I was. I needed my father to comfort me as my life unraveled, but he was nowhere to be found despite standing directly in front of me. I searched his eyes for something, but the contact made him look away.

"I won't be home for dinner this evening," he said, reaching for his briefcase.

"What else is new?" I said softly to his back.

He paused at the door as if he were going to respond to my words, but changed his mind and left.

CHAPTER FOUR

School seemed pointless. I'd missed too much to make up, though they said if I took summer classes and an extra class period next year I could still graduate on time next spring. Everyone insisted that I still attend as if things were normal, so I went from class to class drowning in normal.

I was checking texts on my way to history class and didn't notice Haden was sitting in my seat until I reached it.

He smiled and pulled me into his lap. "You're very quiet today."

"You were very quiet last night," I countered.

He inspected my hand and kissed the back of it. "I'm sorry. I was in a foul mood. I didn't like what happened with that spell." He shifted so I was looking at him. "Are you all right?"

"I'm a little out of sorts myself." I shrugged. "Things are strained with my father and I went to Under last night. . . ."

Haden had stopped listening to me. Something seemed to have upset him, so I followed his gaze and saw Brittany walking down the aisle between chairs. She wasn't even in this class—what was she doing?

She clearly wasn't well, her eyes even more sunken than yesterday. She sat down and rested her head on her arms. The teacher had to tell her she had history next period and that she'd come to the wrong class.

After she left, the room buzzed with how weird she had been acting the last week or so. I heard someone say, "She looked like hell." I looked back at Haden. He was troubled by her appearance. I didn't want to feel jealous about that, but I did. I slid off his lap and he barely registered my absence.

And then it struck me. I wheezed on air and the anger dissipated into cold dread. *Brittany looked like hell*, I repeated to myself. A simple expression to most people—if they didn't live in Serendipity Falls, because in this town, hell literally came calling. I thought of my father, his still slightly gaunt face that resembled poor Brittany's. And I recalled Haden's distress at her appearance.

Brittany looked like hell. And Haden had looked guilty.

Between classes later that day, Mike Matheny stopped me at my locker. He asked me about the trig homework, but I was distracted by yet another girl walking down the hall who looked like she hadn't slept in months. She reminded me of Brittany, the way she moved as if every step was in a vat of molasses.

She was alone. People actually seemed to veer away from her as they went past, but they didn't look at her when they did it. It was like they were instinctually avoiding getting too close.

I was glad when she turned into the nurse's office. *Please be the flu.* If Haden were somehow responsible . . . no. No. He wouldn't do that.

"This is going to sound dumb," Mike said.

I blinked, bringing my attention back to him. "What is?"

He handed me a plastic bubble from a toy-vending machine. Inside was a fake gold chain with charms on it. "I want to give you this."

I rattled the container. "Why?"

"It's stupid. But my little sister wanted the pink heart diamond ring in the machine. I mean, she was psycho scary about it—I know you don't have a little sister, but they can be pretty nutty. Anyway, I put a bunch of quarters in until we got it, and, well . . . this stupid bracelet kinda made me think of you."

He kept looking from his feet to the bracelet and back to his feet.

I was curious, so I opened the plastic. The charms were a compass, a map, and a treasure box. I cocked my head and looked back at him for an explanation.

"I just thought . . . you know . . . if you get lost again."

My breath hitched. It was a bittersweet gesture. If I ever got abducted again, I wouldn't need a twenty-five-cent charm to remind me I wanted to go home, but he couldn't know. He thought only to let me know I was missed.

"Thank you."

Mike shook his head. "It's dumb. I know. I'll talk to you later."

"No, wait." I sent him a reassuring smile. "I really like it. Will you help me with the clasp?"

Mike smiled earnestly and dropped his books on the floor. His hands shook slightly as he put the bracelet on my wrist and a bead of sweat formed on his temple. Had I made him nervous? How strange.

"You have really pretty wrists," he said and then blushed.

"Um . . . thank you."

He scooped up his dropped books and was down the hall before I could tell him how much I appreciated it.

"Please tell me I don't have to kill him."

I hadn't even seen Haden arrive. It was like he materialized in front of me. I stretched and kissed his cheek.

"I wish you wouldn't," I said. "We have enough obstacles in our path already. Visiting you in prison would make things even more difficult."

He twirled a finger in my curls. "Are we okay? Things feel . . . strange."

I wanted things to be okay. I didn't like doubting Haden. Everything just seemed so overwhelming. "We're fine," I decided as I said it out loud. We had to be.

It was daunting, really, to try to understand love. Six months ago I hadn't known Haden existed. How did my heart recognize his so quickly? How did I go from not knowing him to risking my life for him? I used to think that love at first sight was ridiculous, but now I understood that it was never instantaneous. . . . Love was older than time. It wasn't ruled by logic or our concept of reality—it was the reason we had souls.

"You're deep in thought, love," Haden whispered in my ear. "Maybe I need to step up my game if you find it so easy to tune me out."

He nipped my earlobe and every nerve in my body fired a new rhythm. Haden tied me in knots and then loosened them at will. I was about to fall at his feet in a boneless heap.

He pulled back, pretending to be oblivious to my near state of Theia-puddle. "If you keep looking at me like that, we're going to have to skip class."

That sounded lovely to me. I never used to skip classes, but it hardly seemed like a big deal anymore. I was about to tell Haden we should go when I saw his expression change again.

I followed his gaze to see which girl was making his jaw tic this time and was surprised to see two sneetches in letter jackets standing behind me. Haden wasn't just upset; he was furious.

Not paying attention to the fuming demon next to me, one of them, who'd never spoken a word to me before, said, "Hey, Theia. We just wanted to let you know a bunch of us are going to Hootenany's after the baseball game. You should come."

The conversation had me wondering if there were hidden cameras in the hall. I'd never been invited to a sneetch gathering. Why would they start now? "Er . . ."

"She's busy." Haden finished for me as he slid his arm around my shoulder.

"But if I can stop by for a few minutes, maybe I will." I sent the sneetch a bright smile even as I felt the heat from Haden rising.

The boy smiled like I'd just given him a birthday cake. "That would be great." After a quick look at Haden, he offered, "You can come too, man."

Haden gave him a clipped nod, and as they walked away, he spun me around to look at him. "What the hell are you doing? Do you think that's funny?"

The sharp tone of his words slapped me. Before I could respond, he murmured something about forgetting a book and he left. Though he walked away, the sting of his jealousy remained, wrapping around me like a barbed vine.

Little needles of emotion filled my throat, but I couldn't let them out. I didn't want to cry, not in the hallway. Anger replaced my hurt feelings, and as my temper rose, so did my awareness. I stood in the sea of students, each of them shining with a slightly varied aura of color, and the more upset I got, the more vibrant their shades became. Sharp knives of hunger stabbed my insides. I drew in shaky breaths, counting to ten, and tried to ease the emotions rolling around inside of me at boiling point. I had to get myself under control before I became like the monster who made me.

Haden had made no attempt to see or call me to apologize for being such—what would Donny have called him?—an asshat. I got tired of waiting for him and decided to walk to Hootenany's. I realized, of course, that I had no business going. I wasn't friends with the sneetches and it made Haden jealous that the boy, whose name I'd figured out from a yearbook to be Pete Miller, had invited me. But I decided that I wasn't going to let my relationship with Haden resemble the one I used to have with my father. I could decide on my own where I wanted to go and who I wanted to be friends with.

Hootenany's was a restaurant/pub where all the popular kids hung out doing whatever it was the popular kids did. Maybe it was pretty much the same as what I did with my friends—well, aside from casting spells and summoning demons. When I pulled open the door to their hangout, I was so nervous it made me . . . giddy. Who would have thought that I would ever be brave enough to face the sneetch lair on my own?

The music was loud and very Top 40. Happy-people music, I supposed. I wandered in, suddenly unsure that it had been such a great idea. What was I to do, walk up to a table and introduce myself? I felt small. Smaller than small. What on earth was I doing there? I didn't belong with those kids. I was making up my mind to leave when I heard my name.

Pete nearly knocked over a waitress carrying a tray of drinks to get to me. "You came!"

I smiled at his enthusiasm, relieved to see a friendly face. "How was the game?"

"We won!" He smiled and I heard my name again.

Mike and a friend joined us. "You look pretty," Mike said.

I smiled, accepting the compliment awkwardly. I hadn't worn anything special and my hair was as disobedient as usual.

I certainly didn't feel pretty. The other boys nodded earnestly in agreement, though, which made me feel strange.

Someone handed me lemonade and Pete got us all a table. They were all amusing, or at least trying to be, and I began to relax and eventually even had fun. People stopped at our table every now and then and the atmosphere seemed miles away from all the angst I'd been getting so accustomed to in my real life.

"The soccer team had to forfeit a game today," Pete told me.

"Why?"

"A bunch of them missed school so they didn't have enough players. I think it's the flu," one boy said.

Pete shrugged. "I heard it was food poisoning. They all ate at the same restaurant on the bus ride home from their last away game. Coach told us we all have to bring sack lunches for the rest of the year for our away games, just in case. We're too close to the championship to chance it." Pete pulled a small flask from his pocket. "Can I freshen your drink for you, Theia?"

"What's that?" I asked.

"Vodka. It makes the lemonade much better, trust me." Without waiting for me to agree, he poured some into my glass.

"What if we get caught?" I was pretty sure the whole base-ball team was in the restaurant. Weren't they worried about the championship too?

"Relax," Pete assured me. "We do this all the time. If you don't want it, I'll get you another lemonade. Or whatever else you want. I'm not trying to pressure you."

Maybe he wasn't, but I sort of felt pressured anyway. "No, it's okay."

I sipped it slowly. I have to admit, the little rebellion felt fun.

While the boy sneetches were all proving to be friendlier than I had given them credit for, the girls at Hootenany's remained aloof and snobby, sending me barely concealed looks of annoyance. Well, too bad. I was enjoying myself and I really didn't care whether they liked it or not.

After another lemonade, more boys squished into the round booth. They were all so genuinely curious, asking me so many questions about everything but my disappearance, the time seemed to fly. They wanted to know my favorite sports, colors, food, and then one asked what was it that made girls go crazy for Haden Black.

A hush fell over the table as they all leaned in, eager to hear my wisdom. I thought for a moment before I spoke. "He's handsome. And charming. As are all of you, of course," I said, trying to be diplomatic.

Each boy smiled, a light pink tingeing his cheeks. And then they wanted more from me, shouldering each other aside to hear me better. I wasn't used to all the rapt attention. I tipped back my glass to give myself more time, and more liquid courage, and then coughed, as the content in the bottom of my glass was far more potent than the rest of the lemonade had been.

"But seriously," Pete said, leaning closer, patting my back. "What's his secret?"

"His secret?" I repeated, again stalling for time. I couldn't tell them that Haden had the Lure, a special demon trait he was born with that made him attractive to humans. And even that wasn't what had drawn me to him—the Lure actually repelled me from the start. I'd always been immune to his demon power . . . so what was it that had made me fall so hard so fast?

From our first meeting, Haden had unsettled me—no, he'd awakened me. He was exciting and dangerous, but at the same time protective and chivalrous. The desire between us grew more every day, and it was a robust and vital thing that often seemed to take on a life of its own. But to me, Haden was so much more than the way he looked or the way he charmed and seduced. He was vulnerable in ways that most people never saw; he'd been the loneliest person I'd ever met.

We'd known instantly that despite our many differences, we shared a sameness as well.

"C'mon, Theia, don't hold out on us. . . . What's Haden Black's secret?" another boy asked.

"It's . . . a mystery," I answered.

Pete rolled his eyes. "At least tell us where he gets his cologne. Because I think even the Old Spice Guy would switch if he heard how the girls went on and on about how good he smells."

"It's not Axe," one boy offered.

"No shit," another answered.

"I heard he gets it from France."

As they continued to argue about what the girls at school possibly saw in Haden, I began to feel a little lost. I hated the way Haden and I had left things. I missed him. Even worse, I felt awful that I had suspected him of being capable of draining Brittany's essence. Of course he would never do that. He'd already told me he didn't need to feed to survive. I'd let my jealousy get the best of me. I obviously needed to get a better handle on my emotions.

As I sat there, thinking about him, I began to really miss him. I wanted him. A new need clawed its way to the surface. I was done waiting. What exactly had I been waiting for anyway? We loved each other and it was time to take the next step in our relationship. Emboldened further by my spiked drink, I decided to do something about it.

I declined another "refresh" of my drink, but it took a while to get out of the restaurant. I got stopped several times on my way to the door with offers of rides home, a few welcome backs, and two boys who wanted me to watch them arm-wrestle. Honestly, they made me feel like I was some kind of celebrity or something.

The fresh air felt good when I finally got outside. I wasn't drunk—at least I didn't think I was. I'd had alcohol only one other time and it had made me dizzy and then sick. I didn't feel like that this time. I felt . . . a little wicked, though.

As I walked the dark streets of Serendipity Falls, I realized I wasn't afraid. That was probably stupid and I wondered if maybe that was a symptom of the vodka after all. I should have taken a ride home, but as I meandered through town I felt emboldened when I realized that I *was* one of the frightening things in the dark now.

Haden's bedroom light was on, but the rest of the house was dark. How long had I been at Hootenany's? I checked my clock. It was only nine. I had left a note for my father on my pillow, in case he happened to check on me when he got home.

I didn't hold out much hope for that. He would assume I was safely tucked away in bed. I think he thought I wouldn't run away again if I had no rules at all. Either that or he just really no longer cared.

I pushed that thought away and tapped on Haden's window.

His face was scrunched in annoyance as he pulled up his blinds and peered out through the glass. When he saw it was me, annoyance turned to confusion. He slid the window open. "Theia, what are you doing here?"

"Help me up," I answered, tucking my phone into my jeans pocket.

"Is something wrong with the door?" he asked as he leaned out and pulled me through as if I weighed nothing.

"I didn't want to wake Varnie."

He set me on my feet and I looped my arms around his neck. "I missed you."

"Have you been drinking?" He pulled back to look me in the eyes. "What is going on?"

I waved my hand. "Just one. It's not a big deal."

His eyebrows arched incredulously. *"Just one? Not a big deal?* What exactly is going on? The Theia I know doesn't drink or sneak out of her house, and she would never tap on people's windows in the middle of the night."

I rolled my eyes. "It's nine o'clock. It's the middle of the night only if you're seventy. Relax, I had one drink and I'm fine. I just missed you. You're my boyfriend, after all. And the last time I saw you, you yelled at me. I came here to make up." I poked my finger into his chest. "Even though *you* are the one who should be making up with me."

He angled his chin to send me one of his formidable don't-mess-with-the-demon looks. "Theia," he warned.

Instead of being chastened like he expected, I giggled. "Aren't you at least a little happy to see me?"

He narrowed his eyes. "I don't like that you've been drinking."

"That's very hypocritical of you. You drink." I had my hands on my hips like we were confronting each other on the playground and it was my turn for the swing. I felt a little foolish, actually. I'd been hoping for a warmer welcome.

"I'm quite a bit older than you, if you recall. Besides, this isn't about me. This is about you doing things out of character." He pried my hands off my hips and shook them gently to loosen me up. "You're being a little defensive right now."

I slipped from his grasp. "And you're being a little condescending right now."

He leaned against his dresser and tunneled his hands through his hair. "Let's start over, okay? I am, of course, happy to see you. I'm always happy to see you."

I realized I was pouting, so I relaxed my mouth just as I noticed a smile playing on his lips. "What?"

"You're adorable."

I groaned inwardly. "Stop being charming. I'm mad at you."

He took a step towards me. "I'm sorry."

I raised my eyebrows. "Do you even know what you're apologizing for?"

"Not exactly, but I assume it's the best way to get you to stop being mad at me." He took another step. "I don't want to fight. And I'm sorry, really I am. I shouldn't have snapped at you in the hallway today." His arm snaked around my waist, his fingers pressing into my back. "Forgive me?"

Hopeless. When he touched me, I was completely in his thrall. "I don't know. If I forgive you, what will we do instead of fight?"

"I'm sure we can find something to pass the time." His eyes darkened even more and my belly fluttered at his words.

He began at my shoulder and trailed soft kisses up the line of my neck and to my jawbone. I wanted . . . no, I *needed* Haden with a yearning so ferocious it scared me. It felt like he'd struck a match inside me and burned away everything that wasn't him. I clutched him tightly, afraid that if I let go I'd fall off the world.

The yearning had a will of its own and I trembled with its ache. I had no reserve of control left. I *wanted* to surrender completely to desire, to Haden. The roaring of my heartbeat filled my ears as I let my body brush more firmly against his.

Every cell blossomed with longing; there wasn't a part of me that wasn't aware of him. I craved Haden like oxygen, wanted him closer. I felt the searing brand of his lips and knew he touched my soul with them. We tumbled onto his bed, a jumble of arms and legs and lips. I just couldn't get close enough.

"Theia, stop."

I heard him, on some level, but not one that I heeded.

"Theia." Haden held my wrists together between us with one strong hand. His chest was heaving and his lips were swollen and stained pink. Mine must have looked the same. They felt so tender. Vulnerable. "We can't."

The words sounded as if they'd been torn from him.

"Why? Haden, why? Are you worried that I don't want to?"

"No." He laughed a little then, sitting up. "You're pretty clear about your signals right now."

I should have been embarrassed, but wasn't. "Then why?" He still grasped my wrists, so I curled up onto my knees and leaned towards him. "I want to. I'm not even scared." Well, okay, a little scared.

He groaned. "You're making this very difficult."

"Good." I tried to reach for a kiss, but he held me away.

The rejection felt like a blow to my chest. I eased back onto my calves, looking at him as the haze of desire cleared. "You don't want me?" I whispered.

Haden cut me off with a forceful kiss, stealing my breath. When he stopped, he rested his forehead to mine. "I *never* don't want you. I swear. I wanted you even when I couldn't remember who you were. Amnesia couldn't keep me from recognizing that you are the other half of me—nothing will ever make me not crave you."

We stayed like that for a moment. As in the past, I felt my heart skip and then resume a new rhythm, one that matched his. We both felt it. Our hearts synced in beat and yet I couldn't get close enough to him.

"Why can't we? Haven't we been through enough trials?

Nothing is promised to us, Haden. We need to take happiness where we can get it."

Tomorrow might be too late. A shadow might steal the light.

The muscle in his jaw twitched. "I can't make love to you, Theia. Not like this, and not now."

"What is standing between us now? You risked your life to save me."

He traced his finger down my cheek. "Don't think I've forgotten your sacrifice."

"Then what? What's keeping us apart now?"

"You're an innocent."

I rolled my eyes. "I took a blood oath with a mare demon. I have demon blood inside me now. That book Amelia used didn't think I was innocent."

"But you are." His voice lowered. "You aren't a demon, not really; you've only been poisoned by one. But I am, and you are an . . . *innocent.*"

A blush heated my skin and my cheeks felt too warm. Whatever words were coming next he didn't want to say and I certainly didn't want to hear.

Haden squeezed my hands. "If a demon takes a virgin . . ."

I couldn't look at him.

He let go of my hands and cupped my chin, bringing my gaze back to his. "If I take your virginity—" He bit off his words, though I hadn't stopped him.

"What? Is this like when you didn't want me to touch you, but when I did everything turned out fine?"

"Every time we touch, we get closer to the edge, and that is anything but fine." Haden rolled onto his back, raking his hands through his hair, disheveling the deep brown waves into an even more tempting state. "It's a ritual sacrifice when a demon and a virgin . . . It's not usually consensual."

"Okay, not usually, but for us, it is." It's not like I would fight him off.

"That doesn't matter. It's not the consent that is of importance to the ritual—it's the *innocence*."

I let his words drift over me, unable to make sense of them. It seemed so ludicrous to me. I had to fight to control my urges to eat mortal souls, but I was innocent somehow. And once again I was reminded of his sacrifice.

"If you had stayed human, we could have been together, couldn't we?"

"If I had stayed human, I couldn't have saved you, love."

I pushed off the bed, the need to move overwhelming. "All you ever wanted was to be completely human, to get rid of your demon half. Because of me, you had to take it back."

He blocked my pacing. "That was what I wanted before you. As soon as I laid eyes on you, you were all I wanted."

I shrugged. "So now you can't have either? What happens if we do it anyway?"

"I would go through a rite of passage of sorts, only instead of becoming a man, I'd become a beast, which may or may not be physical change. I would lose my grip on my humanity, maybe completely. I'd be more like Mara."

I shuddered. His mother's calling in life was to terrorize humanity. She was very, very good at it.

My heart sank. It just kept falling and falling. "I don't believe this."

"I should have told you sooner. There just was never a right time."

I wished I could argue, but he was right. There really hadn't been an opportune time to sit down and talk about why we could never consummate our relationship. He'd always been very adamant about not going too far. He hadn't even wanted to touch me at first. That reserve he struggled to hold on to, the one that infuriated me—I guess he had good reason for it.

I exhaled loudly, wishing to expel all my frustration but knowing it wasn't going to work. "Are you telling me that the only way we can be together is if I do it with someone else first?"

The temperature in the room shot up suddenly. "Absolutely not." His crisp words were delivered very carefully, but the vein in his temple throbbed. He looked very much on the edge of becoming a beast in front of my eyes. "That will *never* happen."

"I don't want to," I said quickly, trying to soothe him before his anger got the better of him, but the room got hotter and hotter. "I just can't believe that I'm being punished for being a virgin."

"Your purity isn't a burden, Theia."

"Isn't it? It feels like one to me."

"We will find a way. We just have to be patient. And careful."

I rubbed my temples. "I don't want to be careful anymore. I've been careful my whole life. I want to be reckless and heedless, and I want to show you how much I love you, and it's not fair that I can't."

Haden enveloped me in his arms, holding me close. "The best part of being human is loving you, Theia."

I let him hold me and tried to block the doubt that crept through the corners of my mind like a thief in the dark, stealthy and sly. Loving me could strip Haden of his humanity. I was far more dangerous to him than he'd been to me.

I sank further into his embrace, memorizing the thud of his heartbeat against my cheek, the way he smelled, the weight of his strong arms. I loved him so much that I couldn't imagine my life without him, especially now that I was changed—not human, not demon, something else entirely. We'd risked so much to be together, but his soul was the one thing I would never compromise.

Perhaps the truest test of my love would be whether I could be strong enough to let him go.

CHAPTER FIVE

After school the next day, Donny, Amelia, and I picked up coffees and cupcakes and took them to the park. We found a picnic table away from the playground area and Donny unpacked the caffeine while Ame doled out the sugar.

"You've been very quiet today, Theia." Donny straddled the bench next to me, scooping her hair into a messy ponytail. "Care to share?"

I choked on my coffee.

As she patted me on the back, Donny started laughing. "All righty, then. Theia got busy with her demon boyfriend, huh? I told you, Ame. You owe me five bucks." To me she added, "I bet Ame that you two would be horizontal before the weekend."

I continued coughing, Donny continued smacking me between the shoulder blades, and Ame said, "You are so crass." Then she looked at me. "But did you do it?"

My skin flushed cold and then furnace-hot. I had to put aside seventeen years of my father's training so I could speak frankly. I still had to close my eyes before I could begin. I cleared my throat and took a deep breath. "We can't."

Donny leaned towards me. "Define *can't*. Does he have . . . different demon bits or something?"

I slugged down some more coffee. "No, his bits are fine, as far as I know. But we can't shag, ever." I put my head down. This was not only humiliating; it also felt insurmountable when I said it out loud.

"Wait," Ame said. "'Shag' means 'do it,' right?"

"Yeah." Donny answered for me. Donny knew a thousand words for sex, including my British slang. "Are you going to get to the part where you tell us why?"

I raised my head up. "Apparently, by saving all my virtue for true love, I have doomed myself to being virtuous forever. If a demon has . . . If a demon . . . You know. . . ."

"Bumps uglies?" Donny offered.

I nodded. "If a demon and someone who has never had . . ." It was harder than I thought.

Donny patted me knowingly. "If a demon pops a virgin's cherry, what happens?"

I sat up and pinched the bridge of my nose. "Haden crosses through some ritualistic rite of passage into demon manhood. He'll lose his humanity. It's very bad."

"Wow," Ame said, stunned into grabbing another cupcake and shoving a huge bite into her mouth. "What if you did the deed with someone else first?"

I shook my head. "That is not an option." Even if I could, which I couldn't, Haden would tear the limbs from anyone who touched me.

"So, we need to figure out how to circumvent the ritual or get rid of Haden's demon side. Again." Ame pondered. "I'll talk to Varnie."

"No!" I shrieked. "I can't stomach the thought of everyone knowing. It's embarrassing. Besides, Haden doesn't think he should get rid of his demon side. He said that when he accepted who he was, the good and the bad, he was stronger. That's what saved me."

Amelia blew out a labored exhale. "Well, I can research some things on my own, but Varnie might know something I don't."

I shook my head. "Not yet, okay?"

Ame raised her eyebrows at me. "Okay. For now we will not speak of Theia's unsex life to anyone outside of our circle."

Donny sighed heavily. "Lucky for me, I've never had this problem."

"I have a hard time believing you were even born with your virginity," said Ame.

Donny snorted in agreement. And then we stuffed our faces with more chocolate.

"Was it different with Gabe?" I asked, licking the icing from my fingers.

"What do you mean?" Donny answered, but she didn't look at me. She traced the grains in the wood of the picnic table and tried to look busy.

"Because you care about him. Did it make it different?" She

didn't rush in with a response, so I overexplained. "Was having . . . sex . . . with Gabe different from the other guys?"

"Don't be stupid," she said. Then she bit her lip and closed her eyes before she said, "Yeah. It was."

"Mike hasn't even held my hand." Ame sighed and reached for her third cupcake. "I shouldn't eat this. He will never hold my hand if I eat this cupcake."

"You're not fat," Donny and I said at the same time.

"I'm not skinny either." She set the cake down and then picked it back up. "I don't understand what I'm doing wrong with him. I mean, I know that I used to just *wish* he would like me and didn't make any effort to get to know him, but I make efforts all the time now. I call him, I invite him along when we do stuff—what else do I need to do?"

Amelia's crush on Mike Matheny was nearing unfathomable lately. He was a nice enough bloke, but I didn't understand the attraction. I also didn't want to tell her that he'd given me a bracelet and told me I was pretty. "What advice do you think you're going to get from us?" Donny wondered. "I mean, you know I'm just going to tell you to do something you'll think is vile or crass. And this one—" She gestured at me. "This one only attracts demons. Besides, you never listen to us anyway."

Ame played with the pink ends of her hair. "I want to hear what you think. Really."

At the same time again, Donny and I both said, "I think you should go out with Varnie."

We looked at each other with a little surprise while Ame said, "You think that would make Mike jealous?"

"Gah, no." Donny smacked her lightly. "Forget Mike. Varnie totally has the hots for you."

Amelia made a face like she'd just realized she'd drunk curdled milk. "No, he doesn't. He's like . . . old."

"He's nineteen. He's like sixteen months older than you are. That's not old. That's perfect."

"I think Donny's right," I chimed in. "Even Haden noticed the way he looks at you. He told me so in Under."

"You guys are crazy." Ame began packing up our garbage. I knew she would rinse our plastic cups in the water fountain before she recycled them. "Varnie and I have nothing in common."

Donny's eyebrows arched higher than the Golden Gate Bridge. "What?"

Ame carried on very matter-of-factly. "He doesn't go to high school, he likes surfing—what do I know about surfing? Nothing."

"Have you hit your head? Who do you spend your every waking minute looking up all your hooey metaphysical stuff with? Not me, that's for sure."

Ame looked at the sky for guidance. "How can you still call it hooey? You're sitting at a table with a girl that might be part demon."

"How can you say you have nothing in common with the only person who understands half of what you say?" Donny argued.

They glared at each other for a minute until Ame broke

with her usual huge smile. And like always, that was all it took for them to be fine again.

It would have been a good time to tell the girls about the other things that were bothering me . . . the strange trip I'd taken to Under, the way my father ignored me, my bouts with painful hunger, and being invited to a sneetch gathering. . . . All were things I would have shared with them before I'd been abducted. For some reason, though, I didn't want them to know. I'm not sure if I just didn't want them to worry or if I was afraid they would judge me. Probably both.

I didn't want to delve into it too deeply. I needed time to sort things out, that was all. We weren't kids anymore. . . . I could figure some of my own life out without deciding by committee whether I should drink spiked lemonade with jocks if I wanted to.

"Are you okay?" Amelia asked.

"I'm just worried about Haden." It wasn't a lie. I was worried about him too. "You don't think he'll get tired of waiting, do you? Find someone else to be with?"

"What?" Donny sputtered. "No! Duh, he's way in love. He'd never cheat on you. And believe me, I don't have a lot of faith in guys. Haden is the real deal."

I eyed the cupcakes, finally giving in to temptation. "You all got very close while I was in Under, didn't you?"

"Well, yeah. It was awful—you were gone and Haden had zero memories. But even then, he knew he missed you—he just couldn't remember you."

Amelia nodded. "He was totally heartsick. That's when he and Varnie became so close, because Varnie took him in. I think they're like brothers now, you know? Varnie told me he'd never had a best friend before he met Haden. He was always too ready to run at the first sign of trouble to put down friendship roots. Varn thinks we ganged up on him and made him care about people again."

I was glad for that. "When Haden was growing up in Under, he didn't have anyone. I mean, I think he's sort of friends with some of the ghoulish things that live there, but he was the only one that was human. Nobody really understood him—and nobody loved him."

"Just the same," Donny said, "make sure he keeps it in his pants. I remember what he was like when he was all-demon-no-human Haden and I don't want a repeat."

Ame rolled her eyes. "*Keeps it in his pants?* Your parents are very nice people. I don't get how you turned out so warped."

A slinking shadow caught the corner of my eye, but when I turned, nothing was there. I shivered. It was probably my imagination. The girls hadn't noticed it or my strange reaction. They continued to bicker.

Ame actually growled. "Like I should take advice from you anyway. Gabe is only the best thing that ever happened to you and you won't even acknowledge that you're in love with him."

"Girls," I interrupted, vaguely creeped out. "I should probably get home soon." Though that was likely a lie. Father obviously didn't care where I was anymore. "I have homework." That I had no intention of doing. What was the point? But

leaving the park seemed paramount. My stomach felt unsettled
and I was uneasy. I wanted my friends someplace safer.

Which likely meant someplace without me.

Father was waiting for me when I got home from the park. He
was earlier than usual. I eyed him warily when he met me at the
door.

"I'd like to speak to you, Theia." He paced a little as he
directed me to a chair in the formal sitting room.

"Is everything all right, Father? I told Muriel I was going
to be late."

"Yes. Actually things are . . . wonderful."

I widened my eyes in shock. Father didn't say things like
that. Father said things like "pleasant" or "fair." "Wonderful"
seemed like the top of an emotional roller coaster on which my
father would never willingly ride. Much less purchase a ticket.

He still hadn't taken a seat. I began to dread his next words.
Perhaps he'd been promoted and we were moving. My stomach
clenched. I couldn't leave. I wouldn't leave. I'd run away for real
if he tried to make me, I resolved.

Father cleared his throat, oblivious to my growing distress.
"Theia, I haven't been very honest with you."

My stomach started tying itself in knots. "What is going
on? You're making me very nervous."

"Right. I should just say it and be done, stop hedging.
You're absolutely right." And then he paced some more.

"Father, I'm beginning to get worried."

He stopped in front of me and crouched to my level. My father didn't crouch, and he certainly didn't get this close unless it was for a perfunctory, mechanical hug. "You know I loved your mother. I loved her with all that I had, and when I lost her, I lost everything."

I nodded mutely. Here it was. The guilt was coming.

"I swore to never love again—and I know I hurt you by holding you at arm's length all these years. I know you think I never really loved you, but you're wrong. I was just afraid to express my feelings, afraid to open my heart."

What? Who was this man? Father didn't talk about feelings, much less fear. His eyes were a little crazy, like he was trying to make me infer his meaning so he wouldn't have to continue using the words.

"I met someone. A woman." He stood again. "I've been visiting her in the city for several weeks. Since you left, actually. She's . . . We're more than friends."

I let out a sigh. I'd never once considered my father dating again. Still, if he met someone in San Francisco, he wasn't planning on packing us back to England. "Okay," I said.

"It doesn't mean I love your mother less, you understand. But I'm a man. It's not good to be alone."

"Okay," I repeated.

He went to the window, looking out at his vast lawn with pride, I imagine. He sure loved that grass. "She's lovely. Smart and beautiful. It doesn't take away from what I felt for Jenny, you understand. This is different. She was there for me when I needed . . . well, when you were gone."

I joined him at the window. "Father, I never wanted you to be lonely. I'm glad you found someone, really."

He looked surprised. "Do you mean that?"

Probably not.

I'll admit it was a little strange to think of my father dating. Part of me knew everything was going to change, but part of me knew that it had to anyway. I was home for only one more year. Both of us would be dealing with new experiences. "You deserve to be happy. I mean that, Father."

He smiled. Father was very stingy with his smiles, but when he did smile I could see a person I barely knew inside him. A person I wished I knew better. "I want you to meet her."

The bottom of my stomach dropped a little. "Certainly." I could do this. I could be mature. She made him happy, after all. And my mother had been gone a long time.

"She's in the dining room," he said.

"What?"

"She's been patient for weeks, Theia, but she's right. There will never be a right time. She's having dinner with us this evening. She's waiting for us now."

I'd have liked a little time to prepare, get some advice from the girls at least. I suddenly felt like I was a child again. "All right," I said, feigning a bravery I didn't really feel.

Father led me to the dining room. "Darling," he called out, and I had to stifle a groan. *Darling? Ugh.* "Theia's here. She wants to meet you."

Pasting on my well-practiced smile-even-though-I-don't-feel-it smile, I followed him into the room and a woman stood gracefully, her smile even more fake than my own.

"Theia," she purred. "I'm so delighted to finally make your acquaintance."

I tried to swallow the lump that would not go down.

I'd met her before, as every hair on my arm rose to remind me. My father's new girlfriend was Mara.

Haden's mother.

The demon queen of Under.

CHAPTER SIX

Dread clogged my veins like sticky black tar. I couldn't move. She was here, in my house, and had involved my father in whatever evil scheme she was creating. Like a rabbit in the sight of a wolf, I froze, waiting for the inevitable creaking bones of her skeleton henchmen to materialize and take me away again.

Or worse.

Judging from her grin, Mara took great delight in my reaction. Father was right—she was indeed beautiful. Her unlined face looked like porcelain and her long dark hair hung like a sheet of midnight to her shoulders. Haden took his good looks from his mother, but he lacked the darkness that filled the space where her soul should have been.

Mara had seeded our realm with terror. It was Mara who stole into your sleep and gave you nightmares; it was her world,

Under, where nightmares were born. She didn't always kill her prey; sometimes she just drained a small amount of the human essence, leaving her victim with vague memories of a forbidden dream. Sometimes she played with the minds and souls of her victims until they were broken spirits in their torturously misformed bodies. Always, she used the Lure to enchant her prey so they didn't know they were feeding her never-ending hunger for our human essence.

And I had betrayed her and had been foolish enough to think I might get away with it.

"Theia," my father began as he rounded the table to take her side. "This is Mara, the woman I was telling you about. She's an interior designer in the city."

I closed my eyes, remembering that she decorated her home in Under with human bones.

"Theia?" my father asked, his mouth shaped in a quirky smile that was trying too hard.

I tried to remember to breathe. Mara was touching him, her arms wrapped around his in quiet but deadly possession. "Don't hurt him," I cried out.

My father's smile turned into a look of disappointment that I was well acquainted with. "Theia," he warned.

"Darling, it's all right. I think it's sweet that she's worried," Mara said to my father. To me, she said, "I wouldn't dream of hurting your father, lamb. Now, sit. If we're to become friends we must begin with this amazing meal Muriel prepared for us. We wouldn't want anyone to get hurt"—she paused—"feelings."

My heart galloped at her warning, so I slid into a chair. I

had to think. Though panic battled valiantly for the upper hand, I had to stay cool. So far, my father remained clueless that his girlfriend was a demon. I had to hope that was a positive thing. He'd become so gaunt while I was away that I'd originally assumed it was because my disappearance had crushed him. Perhaps, instead, Mara had been slowly draining him all this time. . . .

Play along. Stay calm.

"Forgive my manners," I said. "I'm understandably worried about my father."

He chuckled. "I'm a grown man, Theia. You needn't worry about me."

Mara winked at me, and I wanted to sob. The tension was so thick; I didn't understand how Father couldn't feel it, but he carried on serving from the warming dish as if nothing were amiss.

"Father, I need to go wash my hands. I just arrived home, remember? May I be excused?"

"Certainly." He nodded, obviously impressed with my concern about hygiene.

As I left the table, Mara sent me a warning, arching her brow dramatically. What was she so worried about? I couldn't do anything to her. And I could hardly flee and leave my father alone to deal with the mess I'd made.

I ran into the bathroom, shutting the door behind me forcefully. The sight of myself in the mirror gave me a fright. How could Father not sense something was amiss? I was pale as a ghost.

I fumbled for my phone. Haden barely had out "Hello" before I whispered wildly, "She's here. Oh, my God, Haden, she's in my house."

"Who is?" he asked, though I heard his keys jingle as if he were already on his way to the door. "Mara?"

"Yes. She's been *dating* my father. She's here for dinner. What do I do?"

"My mother and your father are dating?"

I didn't even want to think of that just yet. They weren't going to get married, after all. She was just using him to get to me. And it was working. But still—I didn't ever want to be Haden's sister, step- or not.

"Haden, focus. Mara is in my dining room. She's acting like she just met me. My father thinks she is an interior designer he met in San Francisco. I'm supposed to be washing my hands." I turned on the faucet.

I heard his truck start. "I'm on my way over. Just stay calm. She's dangerous, but not nearly as powerful here as she is in Under. She's still tricky, though. It's likely that she's playing with you right now, to scare you."

"It's working. I have to go back in there. What are you going to do?"

"I'll park down the street and skulk around the windows." Oddly, that made me feel better. "Honestly, if she was going to make a big power play, she wouldn't have given you any warning. She wants to jangle your nerves, Theia. Stay calm and try to figure out what she's after by coming here."

I didn't want to hang up the phone. I felt so much better

talking to Haden. Safer. But I had to return to the formal wainscoted dining room of death.

I hadn't noticed before, but Mara was sitting in my usual chair, a tactical move on her part to downplay my importance in my own home, I'm sure. As I sat across from her, she winked at me again. The weight of Father's earnest wish for me to like her felt like concrete blocks chained to my feet while I was trying to stay above water. She was evil incarnate, and he was pinning all his hopes on her. She was going to use him to control me, and what choice did I have but to let her?

I pushed the food around on my plate and listened to them talk, trying to decipher any hidden meaning in her side of the conversation. She seemed perfect for my father—cultured, pleasant, and intelligent. Mara was on her game, as Donny would say.

I knew when Haden arrived. I could feel his presence outside the window—our bond was getting stronger. Was it because of our love or because of the demon blood? Mara knew he was there too. The cold fire in her eyes ignited and she nodded her head towards me as if to say, "Touché."

Father gathered our dishes and talked of the dessert Muriel had left for us. I offered to get it, but Mara suggested that we use the reprieve for some girl talk. Father beamed at the idea, and I knew he would take twice as long to serve the cake as necessary so that we would have plenty of time to chat.

As soon as he was out of earshot, I said, "Why are you here?"

Mara sat back in her chair, looking so prim in her designer

suit, so unlike her true self. She even wore pearls, no doubt to impress upon my father how suitable they were for each other. "I made you a promise, dear. Don't you remember? I told you I would be the mother you never had."

I choked on a sob. Her words were so refined, yet the meaning was clear. I hadn't gotten away from Mara. She had no intention of letting me go, but she was a cat to my mouse; she intended to bat me around until I was too scared of my fate to run any longer. She wanted my heart to stop beating from fear before she devoured me.

"Let my father go. He has nothing to do with us. It's me you want."

She clucked her tongue at the suggestion. "I adore successful men, Theia. I can't just let him go now. Not before I've had my fill." She tipped her head. "I'm sure you know *exactly* what I'm talking about."

Mara knew the way her poisonous blood affected me. She knew I had urges because she put them there. Her wickedness flowed alongside my blood. I already belonged to her, much like the souls she kept for her whimsy in Under.

"Besides, Pussycat, I've missed you. You belong with us in the underworld. You know it, I know it, and Haden knows it. Let's just hope the rest of your friends don't learn it the hard way while the two of you muck around in all your well-intentioned denial."

Father returned with dessert, oblivious to the way her eyes had changed, the onyx pupils overtaking the white until they were like deep black pits of despair.

What she'd said was probably true. It had hurt to be away from my friends and family, but I couldn't deny that part of me was more comfortable in Under now. Maybe it was because I was less likely to hurt someone—or eat someone—there. My own realm was safer without me in it.

But if I were honest with myself, I'd admit to missing Under, even if only a little. Under was a frightening place, but it was also strangely beautiful in many ways. It had a Lure of its own.

Haden had courted me there. . . . It would always be special.

When I lived in Under, I'd found a book about portals in the massive library in the castle. The library was on a different floor every time I visited, but the book stayed the same. It told of many different worlds and realms that opened up from the portal. It seemed that none were inherently good or evil at their inception, but time and the inhabitants warped each to what it became.

The book may have been the history of the worlds or a fairy tale. It was always hard to tell, but it made me wonder what Under would have been if a different demon had reigned instead of the one now making eyes at my father across the table.

On cue, Mara spoke. "Darling, Theia was just telling me all about the nice young man she's been seeing."

My father and I both looked at her with equal alarm. *What is she doing?*

He spoke first. "Theia is not allowed to date. She needs to concentrate on school and her music."

"She's seventeen. It's unnatural to expect her to stay away from young men her own age."

"They are a distraction she doesn't need," he answered.

Mara actually engaged my father in an argument over the merits of allowing me to date Haden. What was she up to? After several minutes, Father began to relent. Mara smiled at me, like we were on the same side.

She set down her fork. "Let's all do something this weekend. Something fun. We'll invite her young man."

My father sputtered on his after-dinner coffee. "I'm not sure—"

"Don't you want to meet him? I think it would be far less pressure if she introduced him to you in a relaxed setting."

I hadn't said a word, not one. I didn't want to contribute to this conversation in any way.

Mara looked at me over the rim of her coffee cup, her pinkie curled slightly in a regal testament to how well she already knew my father. After she sipped, she said, "Then it is settled. The four of us will get together this weekend. Theia, I will leave it to you to convince your friend of the merit of this plan. We'll let the young people decide what we'll do."

I looked to my father for support, but he'd already given in to her whim. I faked yet another smile and agreed to the plan.

After supper, Father needed to drive Mara back to the city. She kept glancing at the window in a knowing way and reminded me to urge my *young man* to join us this weekend. It was important for all four of us. It was, in her words, *imperative*.

As soon as they pulled away from the drive, I ran to the kitchen, where Haden was already coming through the back door despite the lock. I meant to ask him how he did that, but instead I just propelled myself into his arms.

He wrapped around me securely, one hand holding the back of my head and the other on my waist. I wanted to crawl inside him where it was safe. Despite everything to the contrary, Haden was the safest place I knew.

His cheek brushed against mine, the stubble against my skin a reminder of our physical differences. Where I was soft, his body was taut, and the contrast spun little wheels of delight in my stomach. I pushed against Haden harder, wanting to feel every inch of him on me.

"I'm sorry I brought all this terror into your life," he murmured into my ear.

It wasn't his fault, I wanted to tell him, but first I needed to be closer to him. I pulled back just enough that I could look into his eyes, into the heat I always found there. They were dark, so very dark, and I felt like I could fall forever into the depths of them.

His gaze caressed me, soothing my fear while igniting something else. Something more primal than fear. He paused on my lips, and I couldn't help but lick them in response. Like tinder to a flame, the awareness sparked between us and he crushed my mouth to his.

Whenever Haden touched me, I lost the shy girl inside of me to the woman I was just getting to know. In conversation, the mere words that described kissing would cause me to blush, but when we collided into kisses, I was the opposite of bashful. Bold desires and yearning temptation overtook me every time.

Haden deepened the kiss, pulling sensation from the center of my soul. His lips left mine to smolder a line of hot kisses down my neck and onto my collarbone. We were losing control. When I felt his warm hands on the skin beneath my shirt, he groaned and wrenched away from me, his breath ragged.

He turned away, leaning heavily against the sink. His arms were shaking as he tried to gather his breath and his mind.

Haden was on the precipice of a hell of my making. I could push him all the way over; I knew that instinctively. He was strong, but I could take him. Have him. Part of me wanted the fall, the oblivion, the rapture. It wasn't even the demon blood inside me that craved it. No, it was the human.

I thought of the first time I'd seen him in Under, dressed in tails and a top hat. He'd shaken me loose from the foundation of my life in the time it took him to bow and remove his hat.

He turned on the water, splashed himself with it. Even then I knew I could slither across the kitchen and wind myself around him. I could whisper things into his ear—tell him what I wanted and give voice to what I knew he wanted too. It wouldn't take much to break the fragile hold he had on himself with the much stronger one I had on him.

I could have what I wanted so badly at that moment. But I would lose everything I wanted more.

Everything.

I let him leave the kitchen, giving him the space he needed to regain control while I tried to wheedle some sanity back into my own head. I hated stifling my desires after just recently finding the courage to be true to myself, but I couldn't go around doing whatever I wanted and ignoring the consequences. I needed to find the median between the old Theia who let the world walk over her and the new one who wanted to steamroll her way through.

Later, after we'd each found our quiet strength, I told him about his mother's fervent wish for us to double-date that weekend. He seemed to think we should go along with her, something about keeping your enemies close. The best way to protect my father was to keep him in the dark, Haden thought.

Before sleep that night I said a silent prayer that he was right.

The mist wrapped the world in cotton, muting all sound and color. I shivered from a chill that began deep in my bones and radiated through the rest of my body. I was awake in Under again.

My nightgown startled me, a red satin sheath that felt cool against my skin as I walked. It rippled like ruby water.

It wasn't mine.

I would never have chosen such a gown for myself—or the color. It was cut too low and held up by thin spaghetti straps. The shade, as red as blood, contrasted with my skin and the white mist. No, not something I would have chosen for myself.

There was no place to go but forward. I couldn't see much of the path ahead of me, but the trail was edged in barbed spikes, which I took as a warning, so I stayed in the middle. The wind whispered words, names, and they rushed past my ears like tickles. Names of people? Some of them were recognizable; others were strange to me.

My heart beat a tattoo of fear mingled with anticipation. Where would this path lead? Another garden of bones? Had Haden sent for me? I didn't feel the same sense of wonder that I did the night of the red and black petals. I didn't think he was there—I couldn't feel him at all. And while I was infused with a healthy dose of self-preservation fear, the sense of foreboding doom was also absent this trip.

As scared as I was, Under also made me feel curiously alive. My skin tingled, not unpleasantly. My senses seemed to open and each one heightened and became sharper. I smelled something sweet and fruity but like nothing I recognized.

The path began to curve. As I continued, I realized it was spiraling in on itself like a snail, the circle getting smaller and smaller until it turned me around and stopped abruptly. A wall of mist on all sides boxed me in, blinded me, and prevented me from going any farther. I slid my foot out in front of me slowly—an inch past my toes the path dropped into nothingness. Testing the area around me, I realized that there was no ground but that where I stood. I had no idea how far the drop would be if I stepped off, and there was no way to retrace my trail because it had disappeared behind me.

My pulse leaped in my throat. I was trapped in the realm of nightmares, and Haden probably didn't even know I was in danger. I'd gotten myself into a mess and I was going to have to find my own way out of it.

I reached my hand through the mist and it became substantial, not like mist at all. Like gelatin that hasn't thickened all the way. Convincing myself it was better than the alternative, I took a step into the abyss and hoped for . . . I don't know what I hoped for. I only knew I couldn't continue to stand in place and hope for rescue.

I didn't fall—but I did sink a bit. I took another step and another and, though it was slow going, I managed to move through the whiteness that surrounded me. One misstep caused me to tumble, but rather than fall down—as *down* seemed to be a murky concept wherever I was—I floated. I began to use my arms and legs to swim through my environment. A patch of blue caught my eye and I moved towards it and the whiteness around me became fluffier in appearance.

I was swimming in clouds.

It was like being underwater, but I could breathe. The red sheath I wore kept me from kicking as hard as I'd have liked, but I found a rhythm and began to enjoy the sensation of weightlessness. The blue opening in the clouds grew larger and when I poked my head through the clouds, I was dangling above the earth.

Below my perch, quite a ways down, was a beautiful patch of huge, bright flowers surrounded by the greenest of green grass. I wanted to get down there. It looked so beautiful. The cloud I was on began descending slowly towards the ground as if I had willed it. When I got close, I jumped off and it disappeared.

It took a few moments of walking on shaky legs to feel normal again. I had been weightless, after all. The grass beneath my bare feet was damp with dew, but the sun was shining brightly and kept me warm.

The flower bed drew my eye. The flowers were waist-high and each had a little smiling face. As I neared them, I realized they were what I had smelled up in the clouds. So sweet and fruity—almost like candy. Each color had its own unique scent. I held the stem of one and inhaled deeply, feeling the fragrance travel through my nasal passages and then through the rest of me. I tasted the sweet essence as much as I smelled it. A feeling of absolute tranquillity floated through me.

The flowers giggled when I smelled them, but didn't speak. The blue ones were my favorite. They smelled like cotton candy.

I wandered back into the grass and lay down in the warm sunshine. Several clouds returned, playing with each other and making shapes to amuse me. My eyes grew heavy and I drifted into a relaxing sleep.

When I woke up in my bedroom, the red nightgown was scratched and torn, though I had no recollection of how.

CHAPTER SEVEN

The next day passed in a blur. I looked for Mara around every corner—which was probably the reaction she was hoping for. I noticed that several boys from the soccer team were back in school, but they looked pretty tired.

Brittany was apparently at a doctor's appointment, I overheard in the washroom. Most people thought she had the flu, but the more vicious rumor, the one circulating here in the ladies' room, was that she was likely pregnant.

I waited until the girls had left before exiting my stall. Pregnant? I thought of Haden's guilty expression the other day and wondered just how close they had gotten while I was gone.

My hands shook under the water as I washed them. She'd been after him since he first enrolled at Serendipity High. And before we'd begun dating officially, I'd been pretty sure he and Brittany had some kind of a thing together. I couldn't know what had happened while I was in Under—but I did know that Haden hadn't remembered me. I wasn't even sure I could call that cheating.

But pregnant? I shook my head. I couldn't deal with the new threat to my relationship on top of everything else, so I had to try to put it out of my mind. If Haden thought Brittany was pregnant with his child, he would tell me. I had to believe that. The most important thing right now was figuring out what Mara's plan was and finding a way to stop her.

Haden was waiting for me in the otherwise empty hallway, leaning against a bank of lockers.

"Are you doing all right?" he asked.

I forced a smile and was about to say I was fine, but that wasn't true. "I'm jumpy. I'm distracted. I'm worried about my father and what Mara is going to do. I don't want my friends involved, but I don't want them blindsided either." And then I had an idea. "I think I should leave . . . we should leave. We could go somewhere. You could set up new identities for us like you did when you came here. We could build a new life."

He shook his head. "Mara's already taken too much from you, Theia. Don't let her have your identity too."

It occurred to me then that asking Haden to leave with me might be selfish. For the first time in his life, he had friends. He wasn't the only human in a world of monsters anymore. All his life, he'd longed for human companionship. I wanted that for him—I wanted his happiness more than my own.

"Have you talked your father out of this weekend's double date?" he asked.

"I wish." I had suggested bowling, assuming that neither Mara nor my father would agree to it. I was wrong. My father, taking his cue from Mara, had agreed wholeheartedly to the disastrous plan, going so far as to instruct his personal shopper to buy him bowling shoes, a suitable outfit, and his own ball and bag. He was accessorizing—even if Mara weren't a soul eater, this date would have certainly qualified as a hellish undertaking.

"Relax, Theia." Haden cupped my cheeks in his palms and kissed me. White stars blanketed my vision. He smelled wonderful, a combination of spices and vanilla that reminded me of a chai latte.

He continued to kiss me until I was breathless. As he pulled away, my heart tripped as if it weren't sure how to beat on its own anymore.

His Cheshire cat grin was firmly in place, but his eyes told me he was as gone as I was. He blinked a few times and said, "Oh, I'm supposed to tell you that we have a meeting at dawn at the bowling alley. Amelia wants to try to ward the building to nullify anything that Mara tries to do."

"Do you think it will work?"

He shrugged. "Likely not, but it makes everyone feel less powerless."

"It feels more like we're putting on a bulletproof vest to face cannon." I checked the time on my phone. "I'm supposed to be taking a quiz that I'm not prepared for right now. I have to go."

He kissed me one more time and I felt the weight of it all like stones lining my pockets before a dive into a lake.

*　　*　　*

He'd always known it was a mistake. It didn't stop him from racing to make it, but he'd always known their love story was a tragedy, not a happily-ever-after.

He didn't go to class; instead he peered at her for a few minutes through the window of her classroom door. He watched her smile at a boy he didn't know, reducing the poor kid to a puddle in his seat. He watched her puzzle over her test until she finally leaned over and copied the answers from someone else.

Haden closed his eyes. Theia was tiptoeing around the edges of her own boundaries. Before he'd come into her life, she'd navigated the gray areas of life much better. She knew what was right and what was wrong, what was black and white. And now—now he watched her struggle to find parts of herself not touched by the demon blood and not finding many. All because of him.

She would hate him when she found out what he'd been doing behind her back. He told himself it was better this way. He was doing it for her. But knowing he had to hurt her, that he was hurting her every day, left scars on his heart.

He'd known better, but he'd hoped he would be stronger, because it was his weaknesses and his yearnings that threatened to destroy the thing he wanted most to protect.

Friday morning we gathered behind the bowling alley to do what we could to prepare it for that night's expected ambush from a demon, a half-demon, and a demon-poisoned girl.

Still mostly dark, the sky was just starting to pinken and the edge between night and day seemed cold and hard. A bitter breeze swirled and eddied like whispers of fated danger. To say that we were all grumpy would have been an understatement. The only morning people in the bunch were Ame and Varnie, but Varnie was mopey about the epic waves on the coast that he was going to miss, and Amelia was upset with him about a witch ball . . . or something; the details were murky on that one. Gabe was barely awake, his eyes heavily hooded, and Donny hated every day until at least nine a.m.

Ame began giving us directions as to how we were to use the smudging sticks of white sage. I tried to follow along, but my mind was working overtime on everything but the sage. The fact that I was to face Mara filled me with fear.

I'd visited the flower garden in Under again last night. I wondered if I should tell Haden about it, but I was afraid he would say it was too dangerous for me to go to Under without him. The garden replaced so much of my anxiety with peace. And I needed that peace to face whatever was coming next.

"Penny for your thoughts," Haden said, interrupting my soul-searching.

I pulled his arms around me and snuggled my back against his chest. It was hard to think anything bad could happen when Haden held me.

He whispered sweet words into my ear and I was lost until Ame interrupted. "You two might want to pay attention. Some of the stuff we're using this morning could have an adverse effect on both of you if you do it wrong. Especially since we're trying to protect this place from demons like, you know . . . the two of you."

She was wearing her vintage Doc Martens. If I'd realized that earlier, I would have paid better attention. When Amelia pulled those on, she meant business. Most of the time she was fairly goth lite. She liked subcultures well enough, but she liked to mix them with her own brand of optimism. All her skulls had pink bows, and all her spiderwebs glittered. Unrelieved black was not her style, and she saved the Docs for when she was particularly determined. I pulled out of Haden's arms and stood at attention.

Gabe, on the other hand, was air-drumming with two white-sage smudge sticks, which annoyed Donny, so she snatched them from his hands and tried to give them to Haden. Haden stared at them dubiously, looking for confirmation from Varnie that they were safe for demon use.

Ame rolled her eyes. "You really haven't been listening, have you? The sage is fine. You and Theia will be in charge of smudging. It's the petroleum jelly you need to stay away from."

"Wait, what?" I asked. "I can't touch Vaseline?"

Varnie shook his head and made a face. "Nobody should, really. But especially not demons. It's like holy water."

Was he serious? I looked at Haden.

"This is the first I've heard of it too," he said. "Though frankly, the sight of it has always made me nauseated. I don't even know what it's used for."

Donny pulled out her hair band to redo her ponytail. Her cola brown hair always made me so jealous of the way it was shiny and not uncontrollable. "Is there a reason we had to meet here in the middle of the night to discuss personal lubricant? I mean, this could have waited until noon."

"It's morning, not the middle of the night. And we're trying to be covert, which is harder at noon than it is at five a.m. It's not the Vaseline that's harmful, people; it's the herbs we're going to put *in* the Vaseline. Quit teasing them, Varnie." Ame pulled a huge jar of it from her tote bag and gave it to Donny.

"What am I supposed to do with this?" Donny asked.

Gabe leered at her. "I have a few ideas."

Donny glared at him, but didn't retort. It was then I realized she wasn't wearing any makeup. Donny, in all the years I had known her, did not go anyplace a boy might be without putting her "face" on. Consequently, because Donny could find a boy just about anywhere, she was always perfectly made up.

It was early, really early, but the Donny I knew would never have let Gabe see her so undone. I wanted to hug Gabe. He'd done something no other boy had accomplished. He'd gotten past the Maybelline Great Lash.

Amelia, however, wasn't as amused. She rolled her eyes at Gabe and pulled out a baggie of dried herbs and a mortar and pestle, handing them to him reluctantly. "You two mix the Vaseline with the herbs, and then smear some in the four corners of each window. Just a dollop. We don't want anyone to notice it's there." Then she sent me a look that reminded me of my father. "And anyone with demon blood should remember not to touch the windows."

I nodded. "Okay, we won't touch the windows. Haden and I will do the . . . um . . . what was the word?"

"Smudging," Varnie answered. I noticed that despite the chill, he was wearing sandals and long shorts.

"What are the two of you going to be doing?" Haden asked.

"I'm not peeing in Miss Amelia's mason jar. That is a promise."

Everyone stopped what they were doing and got quiet.

Well, except for Donny, who snorted.

I looked at Amelia, who was pinkening like the sunrise. "Why do you want Varnie to . . . do that in your jar?"

Amelia pulled a jar full of sharp things from her bag. In it appeared to be bits of razor wire, rusty nails, thorny sticks, and shards of glass. They rattled against the sides of the jar in a disturbing anthem of cacophony. The sound made me wince, as if someone had grabbed my hand and raked my fingernails down a chalkboard.

She flashed her eyes at my disturbed reaction, and then sent Varnie an *I told you so* look. "This is a variation of a witch ball. It's a protection against Mara's magic. I've put all sorts of things in here, but it needs more organic matter."

Donny peered closer and then pulled back abruptly. "There are bones in there. That is so skeezy-looking."

"Well, it needs more." Amelia rattled the jar at Varnie, who shook his head in defiance. "It would be easier for him to pee in it than for me, but no, he's too prissy."

"Prissy but not pissy," Donny joked.

"I'm not prissy," he argued. "Besides, you have plenty of organic matter in there." He took it from her hand, the sound of the objects grinding against each other making me ill. "There's hair and bone. Is that blood?"

As she snatched it back, the clatter weakened my knees. "Please stop making it rattle. I think I'm going to throw up."

Instead of the Ame I was used to, the one who would have run to my aid and mothered me until I felt better, this new Amelia ignored my plea and argued with Varnie, her jerky movements sending little earthquakes of nausea through my body. "See? It wasn't stupid. It's already working on Theia. If you would just do your business in this jar, we could bury it in the bushes by the door. But no, you have to make everything difficult."

Varnie, noticing my distress, grasped Amelia's wrists so she'd stop shaking the jar. "I never said it was stupid. I just have a shy bladder."

"Oh, for God sakes, *I'll* pee in the jar," said Donny.

Ame shook her head, but thankfully not the witch ball. "It will be stronger if Varnie does it. Or me. I don't have a shy bladder, but I don't have a pen—"

Varnie let go of her wrists and covered her mouth before she finished her sentence. "Okay, I'll do it. God. Just stop talking about my . . . junk."

Donny's eyes took on the look that always meant trouble was about to happen. "Why can't we just kill Mara somehow?"

"Donny! I can't believe you just said that. She's Haden's mother. We can't just kill her." I was incensed that she would even suggest it.

"I don't see why not," Haden said. He ignored my gasp. "She wouldn't think twice about killing any of you. She doesn't love me, Theia. Not like a mother loves a son. She's not capable."

He said the words, but his face looked pained. I grasped his hand.

"It doesn't matter. You love her."

He wanted to deny it, but couldn't.

Varnie patted Haden's shoulder in a brisk, manly show of affection. "Killing Mara is a bad idea anyway. The human race actually needs her."

Even Haden looked confused at that. "Why?"

"Look, I don't know if we have time for a philosophical discussion here—" Varnie began.

"We don't," Donny interjected quickly.

Varnie fixed her with a pointed look. "But nightmares are important. They help us function—they pass down primal instincts through a sort of collective unconscious."

"Right," said Gabe, clearly not understanding. And probably not caring that he didn't understand. That was one of the best things about him—he would support Donny in whatever she needed without questioning or needing to understand.

"There are some things we need to be afraid of. Things that threaten our safety—like poisonous spiders, fire, drowning, predators . . ."

Amelia spoke up. "Clowns."

Varnie ignored her. "Nightmares are a necessary part of the continuation of our species. Our subconscious taps into that collective. We *need* those instinctive fears. Under is supposed to be the conduit, but Mara just gathered too much power. She's warped, but she provides a function pivotal to our psyches."

Ame chewed on the end of her braid. "Can't we just keep a *Big Book of Scary Things* to pass down to each generation instead?" She looked at her watches—she was wearing three that morning. "We need to get out of here soon."

Donny gave Varnie a sympathetic smile and the rest of her coffee to drink to encourage his bladder, and he went around the corner to fill the jar. Haden and I couldn't start smudging the perimeter until he finished, so I rested on the bumper of Donny's car. It really began to sink in that I was different from my friends. I couldn't touch certain herbs, and the witch jar made me seriously queasy. It was unnerving to be confronted with proof that I was not exactly human any longer. I was . . . Other.

Haden joined me. "You okay?"

"Did that jar make you sick?" I asked.

"A little. I guess I'm used to the feeling more than you are, though. There are lots of things in this realm that make me sick."

"Really? Like what?"

Haden traced a loopy pattern on the leg of my jeans while he thought of his answer. "Horseshoes, especially above doors, pure silver, some herbs . . ."

"So, we're evil then? That's what this means. The same things that ward off evil things like Mara make us sick too."

"I have spent most of my life believing that, Theia. That I was marked, corrupted by my birth. And then I met this girl." He paused, his fingers finding mine in a tight squeeze. "And she made all my dark corners light. And I realized that the measure of who I am doesn't have to be the way I physically react to St. John's wort. I'm going to make something of myself because you showed me I'm capable of it."

I rested my head on his shoulder and tried to make sense of

my new lot in life. "Maybe it's more like an allergy. Donny is allergic to strawberries; I'm allergic to pure silver."

"Exactly," he said, kissing the top of my head.

"Do you really think you could kill Mara? I know Varnie said that we needed her . . . services or whatever, but if we didn't?"

Haden chewed on that thought for a long time, staring into the distance far away from me even while he was so close. "She's not the only mare demon. Humans need Under, but I don't think they need Mara—she's carrying the torch, but it's the torch, not the runner, that is necessary."

"She's still your mom."

"She wouldn't give a second thought to killing me."

I squeezed his hand. "I think we both know that's not true. I don't blame you for not trusting her, but if she wanted you dead, you'd be dead, Haden. She must feel something for you, even if it's not what we equate with love."

He drew me in close. "If I have to end her life, I will. If I have to take her place . . ."

"No! Don't say that. You can't go back there. Being human is too important to you."

He pressed his lips to my temple. "You heard Varnie."

"Let's just get through this double date, okay?" I vowed that I would do everything in my power to keep Haden from taking Mara's place.

And we said nothing else while we waited for Varnie's coy bladder to finish its job.

CHAPTER EIGHT

☞

The Salad Bowl was already a gaping maw into hell before any of us set foot in it that night, but I don't think our presence helped it any.

A few years ago, the bowling alley's owners had taken out the liquor bar and replaced it with a salad bar. Unfortunately, being a bowling establishment, the place had always smelled like feet; now it smelled like feet and blue cheese dressing.

Varnie, Ame, Donny, and Gabe were camped out at Lane 1. We'd asked them to stay home, just in case there was trouble, but they refused. Haden and I arrived early to secure a lane and try to settle in before the big show. Haden looked ridiculous in rented shoes, but rather than them making him uncomfortable, I think he was happy to have such a silly human experience.

Several lanes were still empty, but it was by no means quiet. The constant rumble of the balls before the thunderclap of their crash against the pins set me on edge. So did the continuous electronic music of the video games in the arcade. The loud children's party a few lanes away was annoying, but it was also frightening. They were just kids. What if they were harmed by Mara's malevolence?

"Theia, relax. If you don't breathe, this night will be a lot worse."

I nodded, my fingers shaking as I tried to unknot the laces of my shoes. Haden put a stilling hand on mine and I met his steady gaze. He took the shoes from my lap and worked on the knots while I concentrated on breathing.

"Tell me what's on your mind. Talking about it will help."

I shot him an incredulous glance. "Are you being serious?"

"Yes."

"I wouldn't know where to start. This night is going to be a huge disaster."

"I disagree," he said simply.

I took a deep breath. "You want me to talk, fine. First of all, my father is going to meet you for the first time. This will not go well. This would not go well if we were thirty and you were a successful neurosurgeon. He doesn't want me to date. He won't like you."

"I'm not that bad." Haden smirked and I wanted to hit him.

"You're a demon."

"Half."

"You want to shag me," I argued.

"Well, it's not like I'm going to tell *him* that." He handed me back my bowling shoes with the laces unknotted and ready.

"Okay, so let's pretend that my father is a normal bloke and move on to the fact that he's *dating* your mother."

An involuntary shudder racked Haden. "Okay, yeah, I don't really want to go there right now."

"Now let's tack on that she's here to wreak havoc on our lives. She's an angry demon and we don't know how to stop her. We don't even know what she wants."

Haden put his arm around me. "And that is the bright spot here. By participating in this double date"—he paused to shudder again—"we have the opportunity to find out what she wants. The more information we can get, the better we can prepare ourselves. It's the *not* knowing that's scary."

"I'm pretty sure the *knowing* will be just as frightening. What if she hurts our friends? Or the children over there? What if she's already been snacking on my father? He looks very tired."

He squeezed my shoulder. "You're not exactly defenseless, lamb."

I shifted so I could look into his eyes again. "What do you mean?"

"You have a little something extra in your veins now."

"Don't remind me."

"There's power there, Theia. You could explore that, find out what you're capable of."

I was capable of draining the life out of people. That was more power than I wanted.

Haden sighed heavily, as if reading my mind. "You might surprise yourself. Have you tried running or moving something heavy?"

I shook my head. I'd never even thought of testing my limits.

"You may have heightened physical abilities. Or maybe mental ones. Try bending a spoon with your mind or something."

I sent him a wry look, unable to figure out if he was being serious. Bending spoons wouldn't exactly stop Mara from destroying my father. Before I had a chance to find out if he was teasing me, the temperature of the room dropped ten degrees instantly. Haden and I looked at each other rather than the door. We didn't need to see it to know she'd arrived.

"Showtime," he said, squeezing my shoulder once more before we faced our nightmare.

The unnatural chill that accompanied Mara's entrance into the bowling alley caused everyone to rub their arms absentmindedly while they carried on laughing, talking, and throwing balls down the lanes, oblivious to the dangerous predator in their midst. Haden stood like a gentleman, forcing manners and etiquette like a veneer atop his wary stance. As I joined him in getting to my feet, suddenly I was smacked with awareness of all the human essence glowing around the hapless prey in the room. The shine of souls was beautiful—the luminous colors were brilliant in shades of jewel tones and pastels. Some sparkled with vibrancy while others seemed muted and dull. They were captivating until they became intoxicating. I drew in a sharp breath as a knife of longing stabbed me everywhere at once.

I was hungry. So very hungry.

Mara smiled prettily as she saw my reaction, knowing that her presence amped up my awareness of my demon urges. The backs of my knees shook and threatened to buckle me to the floor, but Haden's low voice reassured me. "She's throwing everything she can at you right now, lamb. That's all the power she has here—at least tonight. If you can fight it now, it won't get worse."

The steadiness of his words and the timbre of his voice penetrated the gnawing ache to absorb the lights around me until I could make sense of what he'd said. I just had to gain control—Mara was strong, but I could be stronger. I lived with her in Under for a long time and I lived to tell about it. At least in this realm, she had to pretend to be civilized.

As she and my father approached, I concentrated very hard on putting the ravenous, throbbing urges behind a steel door in my mind. Mara arched a brow and she and my father stopped at our lane.

Father looked ridiculously perfect in ironed jeans and a sweater that tried too hard to be casual. The aura of his soul startled me—it was dim, far too dim—and I wanted to pounce on Mara for leaching his soul while he was trying to be happy for the first time since my mother had died. But instead of attacking her, I had to make nice.

"Father, Mara," I said, "I'd like to introduce you to my friend Haden Black." An awkwardness of epic proportions ensued, though Haden remained unruffled despite shaking hands with my stern, overprotective father and then his own mother, who was pretending she was delighted to meet him. My father watched Haden very closely. Had it been up to him, I would never date while in high school—or likely college—but he handled it better than I anticipated. Had I been a stronger girl, I would have forced this issue long ago. I'd assumed the confrontation would have been more explosive, but perhaps I underestimated my father's ability to be reasonable.

Then again, everything had changed since my return. My father treated me like I might run off again at any moment because of something he said or did. Though I'd never been a fan of his stern demeanor before, I missed the security of our old relationship. I'm sure it's something that happens to all children when they grow up and leave home—but I hadn't left and I certainly didn't feel grown up. Mostly I felt lost and confused.

Mara, the only one of us who seemed comfortable at all, made small talk. My father offered to get "refreshments," and had a normal boy my own age been with us, I'd have been mortified trying to explain why my parent couldn't say "snacks" like a normal dad would have. Luckily, Haden spoke even more formally than my father at times. When my father suggested that Haden accompany him, dread coiled in my stomach like a serpent. Haden shot me a cautious glance and I pretended I was going to be all right without him. I stole a look at our friends to make sure they were still safely a few lanes away.

Once the men were out of earshot, Mara cackled lightly. "Oh, Pussycat. The smell of your fear is still the sweetest ambrosia. And how nice of you to bring your darling friends along for added entertainment."

"What do you want?" I watched my father and Haden take

the long way to the snack counter, each of them wearing masks of grave seriousness while my father appeared to be the only one speaking.

"I want a lot of things, Theia. And when I want something, I take it. Like your father."

I whipped my head back towards her. "Leave him alone." A pressure began building inside me and my voice roughened with quills of anger, but Mara simply laughed at me. "He's done nothing to you," I argued. "He's not part of this."

She scoffed, fingering her pearls and ignoring the bowling shoes I knew she had no intention of putting on. "He's quite savory, darling. I'm trying to control my nibbles, but it's getting more and more difficult. Part of me wants to consume him entirely."

I closed my eyes. "You're killing him."

"I've a ways to go yet. I suppose what's left of your father will depend on you, won't it?"

How could anyone look at her and not see the ugliness that tendriled around her like thick ribbons of rancid smoke? People see what they want to see. I'd never realized how often we make excuses for the unexplainable or the unthinkable until I met Haden and found out that our world is made up of smoke and mirrors.

How had we survived so long against evil when we refused to see it?

I glared at Mara. "What do you want from me? What must I do to save my father?"

"Oh, you can't save him; I didn't mean to be ambiguous

about that. He'll belong to me, just like everything and everyone you care about will belong to me. You can't save any of them. But I'll let you destroy yourself trying to mitigate their damage." She touched my arm and the ice of her hatred froze my bones. "Crossing me was a terrible, terrible mistake. Remember that when your world falls apart."

Mara removed her hand and winked at me as the woman in the next lane screamed. Though I knew better, I turned my back on Mara to see what was happening to the woman.

I didn't recognize her, but her fear was a pretty aquamarine color—and it looked and smelled like spun sugar. I took a step towards her without thinking. It was then, as I shook myself out of my hungry stupor, that I realized she was in distress about the bowling ball she'd put her fingers into. Instead of a normal ball, it looked like it was made of flesh missing the top layer of skin. I'd barely registered how disgusting it looked when another rolled out of the return, veiny and moist with God-knew-what oozing from it.

The woman didn't drop it, as one would have expected; she just stood there screaming while the bloody discharge trickled down her arms. I couldn't move either. I just stared at the pulsing orb in her hands. Other people looked to see why she had screamed and gasped before they started bolting towards the door.

The crowd panicked, ratcheting up the tension. Mara disappeared and I tried to find our friends and my father, but Haden swooped me into his arms, ready to rush the door. "Come on."

He didn't look like a boy anymore; his preternatural *other-*

ness outshone all his human qualities when I was in danger. His demon speed made me close my eyes and get motion sickness. As he set me down, someone pushed into me and I was flattened against a window. I felt the effects of the protected casement even though it was on the other side of the glass. It burned and the flesh of my right hand began to blister. As the pain registered, I felt something inside push out of me like a huge exhale and the glass window blew out in shards—as did all the windows in the building.

Haden covered my head, but the damage was done as the glass was blowing out, not in. Everyone around us was afraid and it electrified me. Even though I knew it was wrong, I enjoyed their panic. It made me feel stronger, more powerful.

And very, very ashamed.

"Save my father," I pleaded with him, holding my burned hand to my chest.

He shook his head. "I'm not leaving you." He began pushing against the mob, trying to ease me through, but I resisted, ducking under his arm and turning back towards the lanes.

"Damn it, Theia!" Haden pulled me against his chest. "I'm taking you out of here. I'll come back for them."

Haden tried to tug me away, but I refused to run. I saw Amelia standing on a bench with Varnie. She turned her head sharply and was staring with intensity at the snack counter, so I followed her gaze as it landed on Mara. A look passed between Mara and Ame, and then Mara grabbed my father's face and appeared to kiss him before she disappeared as if she'd never been there.

"No!" I cried, knowing that it wasn't a simple kiss and running towards my father even as he fell to the floor.

Hours later, in the hall of the ICU in Serendipity Falls's only hospital, the cloying odor of disinfectant mixed with the scent of disease blanketed my sinuses. And yes, apparently I could smell disease. It was not delicious like fear; rather it was unappetizing, like sour milk. My father slept in the room across the hall, attached now to machines that breathed for him and monitored his vital signs. The unnaturally bright lights of the hallway seemed to bore into my skull through my itchy eyes.

The doctors couldn't tell me why he wouldn't wake up. But I knew.

There was nothing I could do for him by keeping vigil in the corridor, but still, I couldn't go home. I was afraid to leave him alone, unguarded, and afraid to be alone with my own fears too. So I sat there holding my bandaged hand and waiting for nothing to happen.

"You should eat something," Haden suggested.

"I'm not hungry."

"You can't help him by not taking care of yourself."

I closed my eyes, close to snapping at him. "I can't help him anyway." I didn't want to say something I would regret, but I was close to my breaking point. Guilt weighed so heavily on me. It was all my fault that my father lay unconscious in a hospital bed. "I can't even see the aura of his soul. I tried, but it's not there."

Then again, I had no control over when the auras appeared. I'd purposely been trying to block them from my vision since I'd returned, so maybe he still had one. Maybe.

Haden was quiet for a few moments more. I could feel him staring at my profile, but instead of turning to him, I stared at the curtain across the door to my father's room. I didn't want comfort; I wanted pain. I wanted to hurt as much on the outside as I did on the inside.

"Do you hate me for this?" Haden finally asked, his voice as harsh as the fluorescent spotlight beaming on my head.

"What?"

"I wouldn't blame you if you did. God knows I've caused enough damage in your life."

"I don't hate you," I answered. "This isn't your fault; it's mine."

"I will never understand why you don't wish I'd never come. I'm a bringer of doom, Theia. I've brought you nothing but—" He stopped when I put my hand on his knee to quiet him.

Haden hung his head, raking his fingers through his inky locks. He wore rings on each of his fingers and his nails were painted black. I wondered what my father thought of that. I liked it that Haden didn't try to camouflage himself, even though it might have made for a smoother first meeting. I'd spent my whole life trying to smooth everyone else's way; it never occurred to me that I could just . . . not.

"What did my father say to you when you were alone? Before everything went crazy at the bowling alley?"

Haden turned his head to look at me sideways. Deepening

his voice to match my father's serious tone, he said, "Your father would prefer that you concentrate on school and the violin. He feels that I may be a bad influence on you. He wonders if your rebellious attitude recently has something to do with my appearance in Serendipity Falls." Haden smiled very wryly. "Oh, and he's keeping a very close eye on me."

I winced. "What did you say to him?"

Haden sat up, rolling the kinks from his shoulders. "I said, 'I understand your concerns, sir,' and I told him that I hoped he'd give me a chance to prove him wrong."

"How did he take that?"

"He asked me if you'd told me about his rare-weapon collection."

I blinked. "He did not. You're teasing me."

"No. He told me all about the jewel of his collection—a katana so sharp—"

"My father doesn't have a weapon collection."

Haden shoulder-bumped me gently. "Let me take you home for a rest. You can take a nap, maybe grab some breakfast. I'll bring you back in a few hours, I promise." His voice was gravelly and tired.

I nodded and let him help me up. When we got to the door leading out of ICU, I paused and looked over my shoulder. "I don't know if I should leave him. What if Mara comes back?"

"Theia, you need your strength."

I met his eyes. "Will you stay with me? I'm afraid. . . . I don't think I can be alone right now."

"Of course."

I looked over my shoulder again. "Do you think he will ever wake up?"

"I don't know," Haden answered grimly.

And I knew at that moment that Haden didn't think he would.

While my house has never felt exactly warm and welcoming to me, the Victorian replica seemed even more forbidding than usual when we returned from the hospital. It wasn't scary so much as . . . bereft.

"Why is it so cold in here?" Haden wondered aloud.

"Maybe the heating unit is broken." The entryway echoed as if the house was empty and it was at least ten degrees cooler inside than it had been outside.

Haden gestured to the fireplace as we moved through the house. "Shall I build a fire?"

He sounded so formal, like he was a character from a Jane Austen novel, instead of a teenaged guy. "You don't really think my father would have a messy wood-burning fireplace, do you?" I crossed the room and flipped the switch, the gas flames coming to life with a *foomp*.

He looked sheepish and adorable. And then he looked wolfish quite suddenly. "You look amazing in firelight."

The roller coaster of emotions Haden kept me on dipped suddenly, leaving my stomach behind me. I hadn't looked in a mirror in about eight hours—I'm sure my appearance was anything but amazing, considering the night we'd had—but the way he looked at me took my breath. "Are you hungry?" I asked, my voice huskier than it should have been.

Haden's eyebrows raised in question and then he winked at me. "Famished. I've been trying to get you to eat something all night."

We warmed leftovers and ate in front of the fire. Haden distracted me by summarizing his favorite alien movies and at some point I began to feel . . . normal again. He made a nest for us with pillows and afghans from the couch, and I curled into his side to get a short nap before going back to the hospital. I fell asleep quickly, my exhaustion winning the battle over worrying—at least temporarily.

I dreamt of the place Haden had taken me where rose petals fell like snow from the sky. It was easier now to tell the difference between my dreams and my nocturnal traveling to other realms, though that razor's edge between sleep and dreams would always keep me wary.

In my dream, I climbed the steps into the candlelit gazebo. In the middle, a large bed covered in yards of white fabric and pillows beckoned to me invitingly. I had to use the two-step riser because the mattress was so high off the ground. I sank into the fluffy softness, pulling the quilt around my shoulders. It was heaven. My limbs grew heavy and I drifted peacefully, aware somehow that I was so tired, I was even dreaming about falling asleep.

At some point, I rolled to the center of my dream bed, surprised to feel Haden's bare chest against my cheek. Even in my dream I blushed furiously. He smelled delicious, like the spices of a fine tea shop and vanilla. His chest was firm and warm and his arm slid around me, pulling me tighter into him. I felt safe, cherished, and love blossomed from my heart, growing into concentric circles until I tingled everywhere.

I rubbed my cheek against his skin. It was my dream, after all—I could do whatever I wanted. My innate shyness faded as new, daring feelings sparked. I traced his skin with my finger, bolder than I'd ever been. He groaned appreciatively. I rose to an elbow to find him looking at me.

"Don't stop," he said. "You're the most wonderful dream in the world."

"You're still wearing the talisman I gave you." I touched the stone with the pad of my finger. It had been my mother's necklace once, but we'd used a spell to turn it into a talisman based on a cryptic vision of Varnie's before I'd gone to Under. I'd given it to Haden, not knowing if I'd ever see him again.

"I've only taken it off once." He captured my hand and kissed my fingers. "I'm sentimental." He grinned and telegraphed some very lascivious thoughts at me with his eyes. "It makes me feel close to you, like I'm wearing you against my skin."

That sounded like a very good idea to me. Haden rolled me to my back, covering me with his body, the weight of him so foreign, but familiar. I ached for him, feeling hollow wherever he wasn't touching me.

He kissed me, thorough kisses that ignited every nerve with need. I sank deeper into the mattress, pulling him closer and closer. His eyes were impossibly dark, predatory in the assessment of his quarry.

I blinked lazily and the candles flickered, bringing a new focus to my surroundings. The bed was gone, the gazebo faded, reality surfaced. Once again I was back in my house, covered by Haden's body and little else.

I gasped, shocked, and whispered his name hoarsely.

He shook himself out of his sleepy state and threw himself off me. I snatched a cast-off afghan to cover myself. My top was gone.

We stared at each other, both of us panting and wild-eyed. We'd come very close, too close, to letting loose a dangerous demon.

He crab-walked a few feet farther from me. "I'm so sorry. . . . Did I? Did we?"

I shook my head.

"It was close. God, I was practically forcing myself on you."

I shook my head again. "No, you weren't. I thought I was dreaming. I was . . . You were . . . Well, I wasn't trying to push you away. Let's just leave it at that."

He laughed harshly. "So we had the same dream, then."

Haden still looked a little wild, like he wasn't all the way back from the dream. His hair stood up in places. His aura glowed a bright crimson, pulsing with energy.

His aura.

"Haden!" I exclaimed. "I can see your soul!"

He'd wondered and worried, at times, about his soul. We knew he had one from his experience of being separated from his demon side—but it was still a constant anxiety for him. It was the thing he wanted most—to be human—and he clung to it, grasped at it. He could lose it, I thought. If his demon side ever took over completely, his grasp on his soul could slip.

I crawled to him, carefully holding the blanket to my chest with one hand and tracing the outline of his essence with the other. "It's beautiful," I said, in awe.

It mesmerized me. No wonder demons coveted our souls so much.

"You're crying," he said, wiping a tear from my cheek.

I couldn't actually touch the color that surrounded him, but I ran my hand over the outline of it, feeling a small vibration of energy. "Haden, it's just so extraordinary."

"This is the first time you've seen it?" He swallowed hard. I could tell he was trying to suppress his reaction, but he trembled slightly and his gaze practically burned holes into mine.

I nodded. "My vision of auras comes and goes. Do you see them all the time?"

"No—I don't see them at all. I don't need to see souls to . . . well, feed from them. Tell me about mine? Please?"

I studied the glow around his head. "It's a very bright red, flecked with gold. Not a yellow gold but metallic shards of light. It's very strong, Haden. You definitely have a soul." I met his eyes again. "It's beautiful. . . . Did I already say that?"

Haden hooked his hand behind my neck and pulled me towards him, resting his forehead against mine. We both closed our eyes, and I'd never felt so in-the-moment in my life.

My mother had been a reckless girl. Her spirit was indomitable, but her body hadn't been. As much as my father loved her, he'd never forgiven her for putting herself at risk without thinking things through. I used to long to break free from his domination and be more like the mother I never knew—but now I understood consequences.

From the start, it had all been leading up to this moment—this bleak, bittersweet moment in which I realized the depth of my heart, the weight of my love, and the harsh reality of my life.

"I think you should go," I said, every word struggling to get past my lips because I didn't want to say them.

He pulled back and looked at me, confusion on his face. "I'm not leaving you alone. We'll be stronger—it will be fine."

I pulled back, putting more distance between us. We would never be strong enough—I knew that now. The consequences of following my desires with abandon had already cost too much. "I won't be responsible for you losing your human soul, not after everything we've been through. We can't be together, Haden. It's not going to get easier the longer we're together; it's just going to continue getting more and more difficult until we bend so far that we break. I won't be the weapon Mara uses to destroy you."

He reached out, but I jerked away. The smolder in his eyes warned me of his unhappiness. "Stop it. This is ludicrous. We haven't been to hell and back for you to get scared and cut loose now."

"I'm not the same girl you fell in love with, Haden."

"What are you talking about?"

My father already paid with his life. . . . I wouldn't take anyone else with me on my descent. "I've changed. I'm changing more every day. I'm not *good* anymore."

"Sweetheart, you are good. It's not you. . . . It's what she did to you. But we can get through this."

I shook my head. "I think we should break up."

His eyebrows raised in question. "Are you insane?"

"We can't take any more chances. I know we can't cut all ties until we've figured out what to do about Mara and my father . . . but we need to be strictly platonic from here on out. We can't be together alone ever again." I stifled a sob. "We were never going to make it as a couple, Haden. You know that. You tried to tell me from the beginning, but I was too hardheaded to listen. You were right all along."

His eyes searched mine as if he was looking for a crack in my resolve, but I remained firm. I packed ice around my heart, feeling it get cooler and cooler as I retreated into my self-imposed isolation. The cold burned and bit harshly, but I knew I'd survive it. After all, I'd watched my father do it all my life.

"Theia," Haden pleaded, "I agree that we shouldn't be alone for a while, but I'll never accept that we aren't meant to be together. We're *not* breaking up."

I shook my head and crossed my arms over my chest to keep them from reaching out. "We have to, Haden." It was the only way I could make sure I didn't ruin his life. I didn't trust myself anymore. "It's not going to work between us. It's better to break up now, get it over with, than to drag it out and cause more heartbreak."

"More heartbreak? You think you could hurt me more than you are right now?" His eyes were wet with unshed tears. "You really believe that we can just turn off our feelings. Just like that." He paused. "Maybe you can. Maybe you're more like your father than I thought."

I let the sting find its mark. The burn made it easier to stay the course. "Just go, Haden. I'll be fine alone."

He slipped his shoes on, shaking his head at me. "I don't know how you can be so cold to me after what we were just doing. But I get the message. You don't think we're worth fighting for."

I wanted to take it back, to throw myself into his arms and to believe the lie that it would all work out. But I could never chance his soul, not again, so I stayed quiet.

He left without another word and the house grew colder and colder. I found my violin and played until dawn, until the muscles in my neck and shoulders felt like lead. Until my body ached as much as my heart.

A girl doesn't escape a blood oath with a demon. I understood that now. I might not be trapped in Under, but Under would always be trapped within me.

CHAPTER NINE

I roamed Under alone.

It was dark and quiet and I waded, nightgown and all, into the river of tears wondering why my own failed to fall. Oh, I missed Haden. It ached around the hole in my heart until I thought I would split open, but I didn't cry.

I didn't cry for my father, who didn't wake, who probably never would.

I didn't cry for the pieces of me I was sloughing off as I became more and more aware of the awakening demon inside.

I had no tears of my own, it seemed, and so I waded farther into the river that was fed by weeping mothers and let their tears seep into me from the outside in. I began to float on my back and watched the stars dance above me, forming intricate flights of fancy as they dashed across the night. The burns on my hand healed in the water, leaving no scars. I didn't expect the same for my heart.

When I'd had enough of floating, I walked the darkness; it too seeped into my skin. The shadows didn't scare me, even when they drew away from the objects they were meant to shade and stretched towards me in menace. The night flowers on the ground, huge and lush with calyxes in colors of magenta and amethyst, were carnivorous, with razor-sharp petals. They blatantly tried to lure me near them and leered at me as I passed. I walked across a path of broken glass as if it were nothing but a pretty trail that glittered under the double moons.

Like a butterfly emerging from a cocoon, I began to sense all the ways I'd been made new. I was timeless and strong, and I could feel my untapped power coursing through me as I walked through a forest of trees so monstrous that their tops could not be seen.

I came across a girl in the wooded glen. She was maybe ten years old. Her pajamas had pictures of sheep and her hair was a nest of tangles. I wondered if she twisted the locks around her finger in her sleep, like I did at her age.

"What are you doing here?" I asked.

She swallowed hard; there was a faint pattern from her pillow left on her cheek. Her slumber had been deep before she arrived here. "I don't know." She looked me up and down a few times. "Are you a princess?"

"Why would you say that?"

"You're so beautiful and shiny," she answered, so seriously that I was taken aback. "Your hair is pretty."

I looked at my clothes, amazed to see that I was wearing

the ball gown Mara had chosen for me the night she tried to wed me to Haden against both our wills.

"What's your name?"

"Veronica," she answered.

"I don't think you should be here, Veronica."

"Why?"

"It's not safe."

"But you're here."

I chuckled. "It's not safe for me either."

"I don't know how to get home," she said, squeezing her teddy bear tighter. "I don't like it here."

"You have to wake up to go home."

Her large eyes looked at me with such trust, as if I could send her home.

And I could. I knew in my bones that I could do it, and how. I didn't want to. But I knew that if I didn't, Mara would. And there would be no tender mercy for the small child.

I closed my eyes and Veronica shrieked as her teddy bear in her arms turned into a huge rat. It had beady red eyes and a sickening long tail. Veronica screamed for her mother and she disappeared like an extinguished flame. She woke up.

I'd fed my first nightmare.

The rest of the weekend passed with no change in my father's condition.

I knew I should tell my friends about going to Under, but I didn't even tell them about breaking up with Haden. I felt so alone, so confused, but I didn't want to drag them into my shame. And I was so very ashamed. What had I become?

I'd frightened that child. Given her a fear that might change her forever. Would she be unnaturally terrified of rodents now? Would her teddy bear cease to bring her any comfort after I'd tainted it with a nightmare? What had possessed me to . . . no, I knew what possessed me. But why hadn't I fought it? Why had I succumbed as if it were my duty somehow? Maybe . . . it was?

When they kicked me out of the waiting room Saturday night, I couldn't force myself to go back to the big, empty house. There were several texts on my phone from Pete inviting me to a party. I really wasn't in the mood for one, but I knew that if I went home I would call Haden. I needed to find a way to break myself of that habit, so I met Pete outside a house I didn't recognize, not too far from my own.

He met me out front so I wouldn't have to walk in alone. I looked at the front door dubiously. "It sounds pretty wild in there."

He put his arm around me—in a friendly way—and led me up the walk. "It's been a great party. A bunch of our parents went on a cruise together, so . . . we decided to have a progressive dinner."

"Progressive dinner?"

Pete laughed. "We have a different course at each house. We had salad at my house a little while ago—Bloody Marys. This is Jake's house. You met him the other night. We're having Beefeater gin here for the main course. Dessert is Jell-O shooters at Noelle's."

"Wow," I said. "Is it wise to mix alcohol like that?"

"I don't plan on being wise until I'm at least thirty," Pete answered and led me into the house.

The bass was so loud that the walls were vibrating. Someone walked by passing out red cups. I sniffed and made a face, which made Pete laugh. He said something that I couldn't hear, so he pulled me through the rest of the house until we got farther away from the speakers.

"Is it too much?" he asked.

"A little," I admitted. "I'm not really in the mood for a party. I shouldn't have come."

"I'm glad you did." He reached to touch my cheek, but I backed up. "You're different. I don't know—I never really noticed you before, but now it's like I can't stop thinking about you."

The blood left my face in a cold rush. "Pete . . . I hope you didn't think— I just want to be friends."

"I was afraid of that."

I set my drink down. There was no way I was drinking whatever Beefeater gin was. "I should go. It was a mistake coming here."

"No . . . wait. Stay. I'll keep my hands to myself—I promise. You really look like you need to have a good time. Come on. I'll teach you how to play quarters. You'll probably beat everyone, since you're the only sober person here. It'll be fun. Stay?"

I nodded and Pete took me into the dining room, where everyone was bouncing coins off a sticky table that probably cost more than Donny's car. He was right—I was good. And whenever someone chose me to drink on their turn, I sipped from a water bottle. They thought I was amusing, not boring as I'd feared, even though I wasn't getting drunk.

Suddenly, although the music still played, it felt like a hush had come over the room. Haden stood in the entryway. I'd wondered how it would feel, the first time we saw each other after the breakup. My heart kicked as it always did when I saw him, but the set of his features froze me in place. His eyes found mine and I raised my chin. I wasn't doing anything wrong. He squared his jaw and smiled at me, though it wasn't a real smile. It was the one he used on other people, people he didn't know or care for.

The boys around me shifted in their chairs nervously. It seemed as if they were each fighting an inner battle to stay or go. Haden was scarier than they knew and it wasn't fair of me to put them in a bad position.

I wasn't doing anything wrong and yet somehow I felt guilty. Haden and I continued our wordless staring while the fear in those around us became stronger. I could smell it.

He finally shook his head in disgust at me and turned around.

"Excuse me," I told the blokes at the table. "I really should go."

Pete stood. "Haden seems kind of mad, Theia. Maybe you should let me walk you home."

I had to laugh at the idea that Pete thought he could protect me from Haden. "I'm fine, but thank you. I just need to be alone."

"Did you guys break up?" he asked, hopefully.

It occurred to me that the pass he'd tried to make earlier

had come before he thought I was even unattached. Pete seemed like a nice boy, but I didn't like it that he would put moves on a girl he thought had a boyfriend. He was still waiting for an answer, so I just told him, "It's complicated."

I pushed my way back to the front room, the bass throbbing uncomfortably in my belly. The party had seemed fun at first, but now it was assaulting all my senses. A whiff of brimstone tickled my nose. I raised my eyes in alarm.

Haden was talking to a girl in the arched doorway, only he was looking right at me. The girl was beaming at him as if he'd given her a dozen roses. She leaned against the framework while Haden had one arm over her head, caging her in slightly. He looked back at her and I thought she would swoon.

He was using the Lure on her.

Whenever he used his demon charm, something passed over his face that only I could see. He ceased to be handsome to me in those seconds—instead it brought out his demon looks and I always smelled the sulfur scent of brimstone when he changed. And that was when the other human women liked him best. They didn't know how vulnerable they were—they knew only that he was impossibly charming and handsome.

I glared at him until he looked at me. There was a time when I would have meekly shied away from an altercation. The girl raised by my father wanted to go home and hide her head under a pillow, but the girl who shared her mother's wild heart and the cursed blood of a demon was in control these days . . . for better or worse.

I ignored the way that everyone's auras began to shine again and I pushed my way between Haden and the hapless girl. "May I see you outside, please?" I inquired sweetly, but I felt the blade of tension in my throat like a knife.

"Certainly. If you'll excuse me," he said to his newest victim. I half expected him to bow.

As soon as we were in the yard, I spun on him. "Turn it off, Haden."

"What, you don't care for it?"

I ground my teeth. "You know I hate it."

He shook his head as if he was disappointed in me. "Don't be such a hypocrite."

"What are you talking about?"

"Why is it okay for you to set your beacon to high but not for me to employ the same?"

I rubbed my temples but found no relief from the tension. He wasn't making sense. "You shouldn't use the Lure. You've got a better handle on your demon side than that. You're mad at me, but it doesn't excuse your behavior."

Two of the streetlights popped and burned out. Haden was struggling to keep his emotions in check. "Excuse my behavior? What about yours?"

"What about mine?"

"You can't be serious."

My mind retraced the beginning of the conversation. "What did you mean about my beacon?"

"Are you going to continue to play the innocent?" He was accusing me.

"I don't understand."

"You don't understand?" He closed his eyes, scrubbing his hands through his hair. He looked back at me. "Oh, God. You don't know, do you?"

"Know what?"

He swore. "In the hallway at school . . . just now at the party . . . you were luring them to you."

I sucked in a shocked breath. "No, I wasn't. I don't even have the Lure."

"You were employing the Lure. You may not know you have it, but you do."

"I don't believe that. How is that even possible? Wouldn't I know?"

"It may be that you can't control it . . . though I hope that's not the case. It's something we will need to work on."

Is that why those boys were so interested in talking to me all of a sudden? Because I was using demon powers? I thought—I *had* thought—that I was just coming out of my shell and that my new confidence made me seem more open. I sat on the curb. "I feel sick."

And stupid.

Haden joined me and put his arm around me, drawing me in. "I'm so sorry."

"I don't know how to do this."

"Do what?"

"Navigate my life. Everything is upended. I have no control over my new demon attributes that seem to crop up daily. . . . It's just that everything is so mixed-up." I leaned on his shoulder. *Just for a minute*, I promised myself.

"I handled it all wrong. I'm not good at controlling my jealousy, and when I saw you enticing them . . . it untied every tether I have on my emotions."

"Not every tether. A few months ago, when you got jealous, you set the school bell to a hell noise pitch and deafened the school for a few hours. This is progress."

He snorted. "Ah, the glass is half full, I see."

We were quiet for a few minutes, though the party in the house behind us remained raucous.

"How is your father?" he finally asked.

I sat up straight. "The same. I should go."

"I'll take you home."

I shook my head. "I don't think that's a good idea. I need to learn how to handle things without you, Haden."

"You can't be serious." He reached for my hand, but I moved away from him. "Damn it. You know we need each other now more than ever. I can't believe you're being so stubborn. This breakup is ridiculous."

"It's not. It's what I have to do."

His eyes blazed. "Fine. I'm going back to the party then."

I swallowed the tears. "Good. Have a nice time."

"Theia . . ."

But I turned and ran. As it turned out, I had one more demon attribute I hadn't yet known about until I felt the wind rush through my hair. I had demon speed now too.

CHAPTER TEN

Sunday was another afternoon at the hospital, and I had the joy of dealing with a social worker. Her original plan was to put me in a foster home, but I was able to get through to my father's assistant, who was able to put the social worker in touch with Father's own legal counsel.

My father had planned well for many eventualities—just not this one. The social worker was satisfied that Muriel would be a suitable temporary caregiver for me until the doctors had a prognosis. The alternative was unthinkable. Father's will dictated that I be sent back to England in the event of his death, to be raised by his cousin and her husband. His will didn't address what should happen to me if he was in a coma of unknown origin when I was almost done with my schooling.

I couldn't leave Serendipity Falls. Not until I'd put back together all the damage I'd caused.

On Monday morning, Muriel talked me into going to school. I'd assumed I would spend the day at the hospital, willing my father to wake up, but she felt I should try to get back into a normal routine. Donny agreed with her, which is why she was in my bedroom shoving my backpack straps over my arm and pushing me out the door at seven thirty in the morning.

"You have your phone," she said. "If there is a change in his condition, they will call you. Plus, I bought you a coffee but I left it in the car. You can't have it unless you get in."

It wasn't just that I worried about my father. I worried about running into Haden and I worried about accidentally using the Lure on my classmates and stealing their souls. My life was so out of control, and the more I worried about it the more stressed out I got and the more likely I was to lose containment of my emotions.

But Donny was stubborn.

"All right. You're so pushy." I got into the car and waited until she got into the driver's seat. "Also, your skirt is too short."

She winked at me.

I sipped at the now-less-than-piping-hot brew. "I saw the newspaper reported that a woman had a psychotic breakdown at the bowling alley. They said her screaming caused a mob effect but everything was fine now."

"Yeah, I saw that. Everyone is buying it too. They don't want to see the scary stuff, so they just won't, I guess."

The small town whizzed by as Donny drove too fast through the streets. It all looked so cozy and quaint—it was hard to believe that the dark secrets could stay so well hidden.

"Do you ever think we should try to make people understand about the dangers of living in Serendipity Falls? Tell them about the things Varnie talks about and Mara . . . and that demons go to their school and various other assorted horrors?"

Donny checked her face in the rearview mirror. "Nope. Nobody would believe us anyway."

"But don't they deserve to know?"

"Look, I don't know all the lore that Varnie refers to, but he says it's been going on for centuries. If we're all supposed to know, I'm thinking we would have figured it out by now. Especially with all the collective-unconscious stuff he was rambling about."

It was a great time to open up to her about my part in that over the weekend, that I had participated in a young girl's nightmare, but I didn't. I tried to. I wanted to. But I just couldn't.

I also didn't tell her that Haden and I had broken up.

If she could tell that I was hiding something, she didn't let on. "Besides, Theia, if you started telling people what you know, they would medicate you and lock you up. You can't help anyone that way."

I bit the inside of my cheek until it bled.

I didn't think we were early, but Donny got a prime parking spot. The hallway wasn't nearly as crowded as it should have been either—and the students that were left seemed . . . tired.

"Something isn't right."

"What do you mean?"

We stopped at my locker. "Look around." She shrugged and waited for me to explain. "It's the sneetches, mostly. They look . . . sick or something."

Donny rolled her eyes. "They had a banner weekend. Some of their parents went on a cruise together, so there were parties all weekend. I'm sure their hangovers will be legendary."

I didn't tell her that I already knew that because I had been to one of the parties. Instead, I watched Noelle, one of Haden's admirers and Brittany's best friend, groggily make her way down the hall. Like Brittany the other day, Noelle looked like she'd rolled out of bed and gone straight to school. No carefully choreographed outfit, no shampoo-commercial hair—it didn't even look like she'd bothered with a bra.

Other sneetches shuffled along looking more than hungover. The corridor also smelled wrong to me. I couldn't put my finger on it.

Gabe and Mike joined us, but after he got a look at Donny's skirt, Gabe stuttered a few times and pushed her towards the janitor closet. Which left Mike and me blushing and awkwardly alone together.

Mike rubbed the back of his neck with one hand, trying to look at ease. "How was your weekend, Theia?" he asked.

My upbringing required me to answer with a polite, pleasant reply. But that was ridiculous, given the circumstances. "It was awful, actually. My father is in the hospital. He's in a coma." I left out *And Haden and I broke up, so I went to the underworld and fed nightmares to a child as if they were candy, and then I found out I have demon powers that I don't know how to control.*

He seemed shocked by the news of my father. "Wow, sorry. That sucks. Hey, do you want to go do something tonight? Coffee or something?"

"What?" I asked, stunned. Surely I wasn't using the Lure just then.

"I mean, you know. . . . I just thought . . ."

The muscles between my eyebrows pinched painfully. Was he serious? "No, sorry. I can't. I have to stay at the hospital with my father."

He nodded, oblivious. "Maybe some other time." Then he ducked into class.

I stood there for another moment, trying to figure out what had just happened. Had Mike meant to ask me on a date? Was my use of the Lure that strong? I couldn't even tell when I was doing it.

"You okay, Thei?" Ame said from behind me.

"Yeah, sure." I tried to shake it off. I didn't tell Ame about Mike. There was no point in hurting her feelings. She'd spent years waiting for him to invite her to coffee . . . or anything, really. "I have to get to class. See you later?"

I hadn't seen Haden yet, and I was grateful. I didn't want to face how awkward it would be. We had only one class together and he often skipped it.

I was one of the last students to take my chair—but I noticed that Brittany's seat was still empty. One of her sneetchy "friends" told another one how she wasn't surprised by her absence—Brittany had really looked awful that weekend. The other girl barely looked up from her phone but made a comment about it not stopping Britt from getting laid Saturday night, which apparently was just gross since Brittany hadn't even washed her hair.

I didn't understand their friendships. If one of my friends was sick, we'd be worried, not snarking about how bad she looked. Of course, I had little room to talk about being a good friend. I hadn't been honest with my friends lately.

The teacher was taking her time starting class. We were so close to the end of the year, it really didn't matter anyway, so I doodled while trying to listen to the conversations around me without *looking* like I was listening. It wasn't difficult—my classmates had been ignoring me for years. Once they'd settled down from my reappearance, their interest in me had dwindled back to normal except for the odd moments when I employed the Lure without my knowledge.

I heard snippets about the parties, complaints of feeling groggy still, horror stories about vomiting, and one hushed whisper that Haden Black had looked really good Saturday night.

My stomach flipped.

I felt sick.

The bell rang and I packed up my backpack. A piece of notebook paper was hanging out of the zippered pocket. I pulled it out and had begun to unfold it when a girl I barely knew stopped at my desk.

"You're holding up really well," she said.

"Excuse me?" I answered.

She blushed. "I didn't mean it in a bad way." Her voice was rushed and the rest of her words tumbled out like a river breaking over a dam. "I just mean, like, I know you and Haden were really tight and it sucks that you guys broke up." I swallowed hard, trying to find words, so she filled the silence some more. "I was kind of rooting for you. I mean, you kind of gave the rest of us hope. If you could hook a guy like that, then there's hope for us all, you know? And it wasn't cool that he moved on to Brittany so quickly after you left on Saturday."

The world stopped moving. He'd already moved on to Brittany?

"Theia!" Donny charged into the room, grabbing me before I could respond. "We need to talk." She said something to the girl that made her run off—scurrying like her life depended on it. Donny had that effect on people. She then turned me to face her. "Where's Haden?"

All I could do was shrug while burning tears threatened. I was upset and I was angry. I forced myself to speak. "I don't know. We broke up."

"Yeah, I heard. Thanks for sharing with your best friends."

My emotions were swirling in a soup of ugliness in my stomach. Kids were filtering back into class for second period. Auras became more pronounced as my emotions became more confused. This couldn't be a good thing. I really didn't want to become aware of my unnatural hungers in the middle of a classroom full of students.

Donny didn't realize my dilemma, though. "Why didn't you tell me?"

She shone a royal blue color today. It was lovely. I wanted to touch the color and wrap it around—"Earth to Theia," she said, exasperated, as she waved her hand in front of my face. "So the rumors might be true? Everyone is saying he took a very drunk Brittany home Saturday night and neither of them has been seen since."

My thoughts began to jumble and my body temperature rose uncomfortably. In between spikes of anger and confusion, pangs of hunger stabbed me from the inside out. I clutched her arm fiercely. "Get me out of here, Donny."

"Jesus, Theia. Your eyes are black."

She pulled a pair of sunglasses out of her purse and pushed them haphazardly onto my face. When we got to the hall, the sensory overload was worse. With the sunglasses covering my eyes, the hall seemed so dark, and yet the darkness seemed to move, as if it was gathering into a shadow. Whispers assailed me from every direction, mocking and disorienting me. Some were the kids in the hall, but some—some came from some-place dark and evil, someplace inside me.

"Make them stop," I whimpered.

"Make who stop?" she asked. "Thei, you're scaring the crap out of me. Are you about to get all wear-a-hockey-mask-and-kill-my-classmates?"

I was sucking in air, but it wasn't going to my lungs. People were staring at me—I could feel their eyes on me. I was scaring them—I was scaring Donny too. That much I could smell.

She pulled me down the hall, and people parted to let us through. She was dialing with one hand. "I got one whacked-out demoness on my hands. Meet me at my car. And find Ame," she said into her phone while I continued to wheeze.

The more I tried not to lose control, the more I felt my grasp on it loosening. "Go faster," I urged between clenched teeth. The whispers grew louder. *Make them pay. Ease the hunger. Do it.*

We skidded around a corner and out the door, but Donny didn't stop until we got to her car. "Are you going to try to eat me?" she asked. "Because I have to tell you, I'm totally freaked out right now. Your pupils took over most of your eyeballs in there and it's not an attractive look. Also, I don't have a problem punching you in the throat if you try to absorb my essence or whatever—just so we're clear."

I saw Gabe running towards us, and Donny looked relieved. Was it because she was happy to see him or because she didn't want to be alone with me?

I inhaled deeply, trying to recover. My whole body hurt as I was racked with tremor after tremor of need. Donny tried to put her arm around me, but I skittered away from her, not trusting myself to touch her.

I concentrated on the repetition of breathing. I tried to bring back that peaceful feeling from the morning after I smelled those beautiful flowers in Under. After what seemed like an eternity, the pangs lessened and the fog in my head began to clear.

"Oh, God," I said.

They both looked at me as if I'd . . . well, as if I'd just about turned into a demon in front of their eyes.

"Are you . . ."

"I think I'll be okay," I said. "But it was a very close thing. I'm losing control, Donny. I'm not sure how much longer I can do this."

Gabe ran his worried fingers through his wavy hair, making it even more perfect instead of disheveling it. "Ame said take her to Varnie's and she'll join us as soon as she can."

"Not Varnie's." I couldn't chance running into Haden. I was all over the place emotionally and he would put me over the edge.

Donny opened the passenger door for me. "Why not Varnie's?"

"Haden might be there."

"So? Then you can confront him about the Brittany rumors."

My gaze flitted all around the parking lot but wouldn't settle on any one thing. Like a frightened animal, I sensed danger everywhere. "You don't understand. It's not just about Brittany."

She put her hand on her hip. "Then make me understand, Thei. What is going on with you?"

"I think I need to feed." It was the first honest thing I'd said all day. "That's what is wrong with me. It's worse when I'm upset . . . and frankly the idea of seeing Haden right now . . ." I slid into the car without finishing. I didn't want to give voice to my thoughts. They were ugly and they made me feel unstable—something I couldn't afford to be.

She got into the driver's seat. It seemed like so much time had passed since we'd pulled into the lot.

"Look," she said, "I know you don't want to see him, but he's the only one who knows what you are going through right now. He might be able to help."

"I can't. Donny, my control is precarious. Thinking about Haden makes it worse. . . . Seeing him might do me in."

"Okay, but seriously. It's not like I can go through the drive-thru at Souls-to-Go and pick you up a snack. Whether or not you and Haden have an uncomfortable relationship, you know he'll help us. And he might not even be there, in which case Varnie is the next best thing."

I nodded. She was right.

Haden would know what I was going through because maybe he really did need to feed. Maybe that was what was happening with Brittany and the others.

We went straight to Varnie's. Haden wasn't at the house. I alternated between fear, anger, and numbness. It was the numbness I tried to hold on to since it seemed to dissipate my unnatural cravings. Thankfully, my eyes returned to normal and I wasn't drowning in a vortex of emotion any longer. The pangs of hunger subsided, and the whispers faded into silence. I was still very wary, though.

Gabe had a final in third period, so we sent him back to school, even though he didn't want to leave us. He was really the only one of us with direct access to the sneetches anyway, so his job was "recon." Donny's nervous energy got the best of her, so she went for a drive to scout for Haden's truck. Ame stayed with me and insisted on holding my hand even though I asked her not to touch me. I didn't want to accidentally absorb her essence. She patted me and told me I was being silly.

How awful to be afraid of being alone with my best friend.

My heart hurt too. I was really trying to hold it together, but I was scared that the last band of my control was about to snap. I concentrated on centering myself, something that Amelia always talked about. I used to ignore her ramblings—what did I care about being "grounded" or "centered" metaphysically? Now it was a lifeline.

She suggested that I imagine a place where I was at peace, and my mind immediately pictured my favorite spot at the riverbank in Under.

The underworld was my happy place?

I loved that riverbank. The water reflected the rock bed beneath it—a crystallike stone that reminded me of highly polished lapis lazuli. The river flowed contentedly, never rushing, never stagnating . . . just a steady current around bends and turns. On the bank, a proud willow tree stood guard. And comforted me . . . literally. It never spoke, but I knew there was a gentle entity of some kind inside it. I spent a lot of time there, beside the tree, playing my violin while the breeze feathered the leaves gently. For those moments I was happy in Under, a thought that shocked me now.

Happy. In Under.

Just thinking about my river spot soothed me, though. I smiled at Amelia. I almost felt whole for a minute.

I remembered the unread note I'd stuffed back into my bag when everything fell apart at school. The paper had been torn from a spiral notebook, but it felt ominously heavy in my hand. I didn't want to alert anyone yet, so I waited until Ame went to the bathroom to read it. I opened it slowly.

Be careful. You're too trusting.

Who would have given it to me? Mike? He'd been talking to me in the hall before I found the note—but why would he warn me secretly? It made no sense.

Was someone trying to mess with me? Play games with my head? Maybe it was one of the girls who wanted Haden for herself. I balled it up and thrust it back into my bag. It didn't matter who wrote it, or even why. They weren't telling me anything I didn't already know.

Varnie finally opened his office door, ushering his client gently towards the front door. His eyebrows shot up when he noticed us. "Oh, hello, dearies," he said, his voice a terrible imitation of Mrs. Doubtfire. "What a lovely surprise."

Varnie did most of his psychic work in drag as Madame Varnie because his clients seemed to trust him more when he was a middle-aged woman than when he was a young surfer. Today he wore a red muumuu and a matching turban. His face was under layers and layers of thick makeup, and the bodice of his dress was stuffed full of who-knew-what to give him huge, pillowy breasts.

"Hello, Madame Varnie," Ame said in a singsong tone, teasing him.

Varnie glared at us from behind his client's back. Then to her he said, "Same time next week?"

As soon as she was out the door, he swept the turban off and slid down the back of the door to a sitting position on the floor. "Duck my life." He banged his head on the door to punctuate every word.

"*Duck* your life?" I asked.

He gestured to Ame with a chin nod. "Miss Amelia doesn't like it when I swear."

Amelia grinned back at him, her dimples on display, and she was positively beaming. I looked back at Varnie, who had dipped his head and was smiling shyly back at her. They were absolutely adorable. How could Ame still be blind to the chemistry they shared?

"Not that I'm not happy to see you, but what are you two doing here? Shouldn't you be at school?"

"Theia's having an exceptionally bad day. Have you seen Haden?"

He shook his head. "I thought he stayed with Theia this weekend."

Ame and I shared a look. "They broke up," she said, so I wouldn't have to.

Varnie looked shocked. "Are you sure?" he asked me.

"I was there," I said blandly. "The kids at school say he spent the weekend with"—I couldn't say her name—"sneetches."

Varnie grimaced. "That makes no sense. He doesn't like those people you call sneetches. He says most of them are boring because they all try to be like each other. He says Gabe is the only one he'll voluntarily spend time with."

"And Gabe hardly hangs out with them anymore," Ame said.

I tried to rub the chill off my arms. "Brittany and Haden haven't been seen since Saturday night."

"What's really going on?" Varnie wondered. "You sound jealous. . . . Are you jealous?" He looked at Ame. "Is she jealous?"

"No!" I protested, a little too loudly. "I'm worried. That's all. And . . . just worried. I should go to the hospital to check on my father."

Amelia yanked my sleeve. "Not so fast. You have your cell. If there is a change they will call you. Right now we need to figure out how to keep you from wanting to eat your classmates every time you get your feelings hurt, and we need to find your boyfriend, ex-boyfriend, whatever, and figure out why the sneetches are all zombified lately."

I bit my lip. "Do you think something is happening to them? Other than being knackered?"

Varnie squinted in a look of confusion.

"She means tired," Ame explained to him. Then to me she said, "It's a little coincidental that the people you dislike the most are suddenly shambling to class with pasty skin and bruised-looking eyes."

"Wait. You think *I'm* draining their essence?"

Amelia looked at Varnie nervously. He quirked his eyebrows at her, but didn't say anything. "Well, you have the ability." She winced. "I mean, maybe it's not you, but it's possible, right? You don't have much control over your demony urges, and you *are* jealous of Brittany."

"I am certainly *not* jealous of Brittany. I can't believe you'd accuse me of that."

"Hey, now," Varnie broke in, "nobody's accusing anyone of anything."

My temples throbbed. "It's not me."

Amelia put on her best super-sunshine smile. "You're probably right. I'm sure you are—really, I am. But it would be really foolish of us not to look at all the possibilities."

"Fine. What are the other possibilities? Let's look at some of those."

I should have told them right then about the Lure and the little girl's nightmare. I just couldn't say the damning words. They would think that I was like Mara then . . . and they wouldn't believe me that I wasn't the one taking souls.

The front door opened an inch into Varnie's back and he groaned.

"What the hell?" we heard Donny say from the other side as she continued to shove the door into Varnie.

It went on for another few seconds until Varnie moved away so she could get in. "How come you don't get mad at Donny when she swears?"

Ame shrugged, and just as Varnie sat back against the door it opened another inch into him. "Ducking A," he moaned. "Nobody knows how to knock?"

"Sorry, dude," said Gabe.

"Gabe, tell us what's going on with your people," Donny said as she plopped onto the couch.

"They're not my people. *You* are my people," he told her as he popped a kiss on the top of her head and sat next to her.

"Don't get all sweet with me. You know I don't like it."

"Whatever. I know for a fact that you do. Anyway, you guys aren't going to like hearing what I learned. Maybe we should just wait until we find Haden and let him explain. That seems fair."

Donny rolled her eyes. "We're not concerned with good

sportsmanship. The entire school is saying that Haden is cheating on Thei and now he's gone MIE."

Varnie decided to sit in a folding canvas chair instead of in front of the door. While he spoke, he removed his turban and unzipped his caftan to reveal a Dead Kennedys T-shirt and board shorts. "What is MIE?"

"Missing in Evil. Gabe, tell us what the sneetches know." Donny impatiently prodded him with her finger. "Like now."

"Fine." Gabe looked at me, then averted his eyes, choosing a spot on the carpet to focus on. "There was a series of parties on Saturday." He raised his eyebrows at me, but didn't tell the others he'd heard I had been to one. "Haden showed up kinda late to the last one and while he was there, they say he stuck close to Brittany. She was plastered and they left together. Nobody has seen either one of them since."

Varnie snorted. "Well, that doesn't mean he cheated on Theia. Besides, according to Theia, they broke up." He removed his clip-on earrings. "I agree it looks bad, but he might have a good reason."

"Dude, your breasts are really distracting me," Gabe said.

Varnie crossed his arms over his chest protectively.

Ame sat up a little straighter in her chair. "What could possibly qualify as a good reason for cheating on Theia?" Her eyes were shooting daggers at Varnie. "Even if they'd had a fight, he shouldn't have gone off with another girl the same night."

Something in his expression softened and then solidified into an almost grim determination. I thought for sure he was about to stalk across the room and kiss her. I wished he would. I think Ame deserved to be kissed really soundly.

And it was past time for Varnie to tell her how he felt.

"Why are you staring at me?" Ame asked him. I wanted to pinch her.

There was a high current of tension in the room. I knew for a fact it wasn't doing me any good. The air crackled with the weight of all the emotion that was pulling and pushing us in opposing directions. It was like we knew we were just one misstep away from chaos.

Varnie blinked, pulling his gaze from her. "He's not cheating on Theia," he argued.

"How do you know that?" I asked.

"The guy is completely in love with you. I'd lay odds that you were the one to break up with him, because no way in hell or Under would he ever break up with you. Am I right?" He saw the answer in my eyes. "He's not cheating. Whatever is going on, I'm sure he thinks that he's handling it the best way he can to protect Theia and the rest of us."

Gabe nodded, but Donny folded her arms across her chest like Varnie. "Wow, I feel so much safer knowing Haden is keeping the world safe by sacrificing himself one cheerleader at a time."

I slammed my eyelids closed and sucked in a breath. The thought of Haden kissing her . . .

The sound of glass breaking startled me. Varnie got up and followed the sound to the kitchen. "Huh," he said, in a characteristically subdued tone.

"What happened?" Amelia asked, following him. "Whoa."

The rest of us got up to find out what had both of them

awed. Varnie stood in front of an open cupboard. Every drinking glass in it was shattered into jagged shards.

"Sorry," I said. "I think I did that." I blushed. I could feel it heating my whole face. "I'm pretty sure it was me that blew out the windows at the Salad Bowl the other night too. When I get stressed, glass starts exploding and I see auras."

Nobody even seemed surprised. That's how crazy our lives had become. Donny just sighed as if she was getting accustomed to her friends adding strange things to their personality.

"Psychokinesis. Cool," Gabe said, patting me on the back.

"How do you know about psychokinesis?" Varnie asked.

"Video games."

"What exactly is it?" I asked, unsure if I wanted to know. I didn't want any more demon powers.

"Basically, it's moving or controlling things with the power of your mind." Varnie rubbed his face, forgetting he was wearing makeup, so he wiped his hand on his muumuu. "There are lots of different manifestations of it. Blowing things up is a pretty cool one."

"Except I have no control over it," I added.

"Yet," said Ame.

Gabe's phone buzzed and he handed it to Donny after he read the message. "Holy shit. Gabe just got a text from the sneetch party line. Nobody's seen Haden yet, but Brittany was just admitted to the hospital. Sources say she's in a coma."

CHAPTER ELEVEN

The nurses wouldn't tell us anything about Brittany's condition since we weren't related, and then they kicked my friends off the hospital floor too. Since Brittany was in the same wing in the ICU as my father was, I was able to monitor her condition by the expressions of her family while I sat in the lonely hall outside his room.

Her parents' faces were drawn and pinched underneath their fabulous vacation tans. What a terrible way to end a vacation—though they all should have known it was ill-advised to leave Brittany unsupervised. What had they been thinking? It's not like Brittany and the other sneetches were usually examples of good behavior. They were overprivileged at best and spoiled rotten at worst. Few of them had real responsibilities and fewer had ever experienced repercussions.

I would know—I'd been one of them for a few hours.

Brittany, who now lay comatose, suffering the same condition as my father, was not pregnant. I felt a little relieved at that, but then I felt worse. Yes, I was glad she wasn't carrying Haden's baby, but there was no known cure for what she and my father were fighting. The doctors hadn't come up with anything, and Amelia and Varnie were stumped as well.

Was Haden responsible for her coma? I didn't want to think it was possible for him to have been draining her slowly all this time—especially since we'd still been together for most of it. I hated doubting him, but I knew firsthand how difficult it was to resist the urge to feed.

I listened for more clues in the hall. Brittany's family was so different from mine. Her dad golfed with my father sometimes. That was all the two of them had in common personality-wise. Whereas my father was formal and distant, Mr. Blakely was funny and casual. My father worked all the time, seven days a week; Brittany's family was always going on vacations to expensive resorts.

Mrs. Blakely was an older version of Brittany—their sisterly image most likely helped along with Botox. Under the harsh fluorescent lights, though, she'd aged considerably. She and her husband both had. I tried not to be alarmed by that. Nobody looks good in hospital lighting, and they were under a great deal of emotional stress. I hoped that was all it was. I didn't see their auras, and I didn't want to, even though it might have helped me diagnose whether their pallor was related to demon activity or my own anxiety. I didn't feel strong enough to go *looking* for human essence. None of my friends were around to bail me out of trouble if my eyes turned black like Mara's and I lost control again.

A doctor came out of Brittany's room and began talking in hushed tones to Mr. and Mrs. Blakely. Focusing very hard, I hoped for extrasensory hearing, but unfortunately my ears were not affected by the demon curse in my blood and I couldn't hear a word. I left the uncomfortable plastic chair and meandered slowly past them, making a big show of counting change in my hand as if I was headed to the vending machines.

"She's in stable condition. We still haven't isolated the illness that brought this on, but hopefully the lab in San Francisco will have better luck. The courier is en route, but the lab will still need to perform the tests and receive the results," the doctor said. "Unlike the medical dramas on television, lab work takes time."

I dropped some of my change as I got just past them so I could hear more.

Mrs. Blakely sobbed into her husband's shoulder while he addressed the doctor. "I don't understand. How can she be in a coma with no reason? She's been sick for weeks and no one has been able to find anything wrong with her. It makes no sense."

"I understand your frustration, Mr. Blakely. We're all working very hard to bring your daughter safely out of this. It's just that every test result has pointed to a very healthy young woman. There is no medical reason that we can find for your daughter to be wasting away like this."

At his words, Mrs. Blakely sobbed harder, and I had to get up off the floor and go to the snack machine to avoid getting caught eavesdropping.

Though not from the same doctor, I had been given a similar diagnosis for my father. They hadn't had any luck from the lab in the city either. There was no head trauma, no disease, no medical ailment. My father, and now Brittany, were just withering, like cut flowers in a vase with no water. Their bodies were drying up, not because they were ill but because their souls had been leached out until only the husks remained.

At the machine, I pondered the snack choices absently. I wasn't hungry. Not even junk food sounded appealing. I just kept turning the last few days over in my head.

A couple of hospital employees wearing scrubs got behind me, so I pushed a random button and took the trail mix it offered me back to the plastic chair. The Blakelys were no longer in the hall. They'd either gone home or were in Brittany's room. I thought about going back into my father's room to sit with him for a bit. The nurses said it was fine for short periods, but seeing him that way frightened me, and the tubes and machines made me uneasy. I wished I'd fought harder to keep at least one of the girls with me. They'd let Haden stay with me that first night, but maybe he'd used the Lure to convince them without my notice.

It was getting late and I'd promised Muriel I would be home before eleven. I allowed myself a count to ten and then I crossed the hall and pushed back the curtain that had been acting not unlike a portal between two worlds. On the one side, I could only speculate about what damage might be done, might still be being done, to my world. On the other was confirmation I didn't want to face. My father's condition couldn't be explained away or looked at with rose-colored glasses.

I'd already lost one parent and I feared very much that I'd lost the other.

I hated the smell of the room—sickness and disease, and not just from my father. It was as if every infection that had ever been in the room had left a trace of odor behind. My father's skin was an aberrant shade of gray. It wrinkled unnaturally and was mottled with spots that seemed to lack the energy to be any color at all—more like shadows of blemishes. Challenging my fear, I focused very hard to see any light surrounding him. There was none, though whether I could see it on command had yet to be determined.

I walked slowly to my father's side, remembering that Amelia had told me to try talking to him, because maybe on some level he could hear me. He appeared shrunken, almost brittle. "Hello, Father," I said. I had to clear my throat. "It's me, Theia."

I winced. Of course it was me. Who else would call him Father?

"I just wanted to say that I'm not giving up hope." I blew out a long breath. "And I love you."

I wished it had been easier to say that to him when it mattered more, when he was healthy. I stared at the stranger in the hospital bed, wondering if he could hear me, wondering if the specialists would deem his medical condition beyond repair. My father had a living will—there were going to be some difficult decisions to be made. I doubted I would have the authority to make them, since I was just seventeen—and I was glad for it. That kind of responsibility was too much for me to handle.

Funny how a few months ago I'd argued that I was old enough to make my own choices. Seventeen had felt like *almost* eighteen, *almost* an adult. Standing at the hospital bed of my dying father, seventeen felt aeons closer to childhood.

I pulled up a chair alongside his bed. I was afraid to touch him. I inched my hand across the stark white sheets but never made contact. He looked so brittle.

Sitting back in the lumpy hospital chair, I tried to think of more that I could say to him, if he really could hear me. Did he understand that Mara had done this to him? Did he know that I was the one who had brought her into his life?

I closed my eyes. What a mess. A few minutes later, I felt myself tumbling into the place between sleep and awake. I fought it, despite how tired I felt. I didn't want to be vulnerable at that moment. I patted my cheeks and blinked briskly. I should go. Muriel had made me promise to take a taxi home, but a walk would do me good. Clear my head. Wake me up.

A movement caught my eye. The tubes running in and out of my father's body jumped. I leaned closer to see if they would do it again. Had he moved his arm? Hope filled me, stirring my heart. If he moved his arm, he could be waking up. What I wouldn't give to see him open his eyes.

There again, the tubes moved. Only my father was still . . . still as death. It was just the tubes. They began to ripple, morphing suddenly from clear to shiny black. From the ends of the tubing grew sharp metallic pincers and thorny, gruesome-looking attachments. I gasped as little needles dug into my father's flesh, lancing and lacing his flesh in crisscross stitches of black thread. I screamed, but no sound came out. No matter how hard I yelled, nothing happened.

To my disbelief, the ventilator and monitors grew into a hulking, demonic machine and I could feel its sentience and malevolence as it sewed itself onto my father's body.

"No," I cried, reaching towards it until one of the black tubes lashed back at me.

I darted back and forth, trying to stay out of its grasp and trying to reach my father. His eyes opened in horror and the oxygen tube that had been keeping him alive choked him and he rasped with what sounded like an alarming amount of liquid in his throat. The tentaclelike tubing snapped and coiled around my wrist, drawing me sharply towards the machine that tortured my father. I struggled, but other tubes tangled around my waist and legs, holding me in place helplessly while my father's tortured gurgles of pain and fear riveted my attention. His eyes were unseeing and full of terror. I don't know if he even knew I was there.

I thrashed against the evil, trying to pull it off me and get to my father. The stitches were causing his skin to pucker and swell in some places, and in others they were being systematically ripped out, only to be redone. The machine was sewing my father to the hospital mattress too.

I finally got hold of one tube and yanked it violently.

"What the hell are you doing?"

My world tilted as I was pushed to the floor by someone in purple scrubs. I blinked as the rest of the room came back into focus and the hospital machines returned to normal, sounding an alarm. Several other nurses ran in, crowding my father's bed.

"Get security up here. She was pulling out his IV when I walked in."

"No," I protested, my voice raspy as if I'd been screaming. "That's not how it happened."

I got back to my feet. My father, though still unwell, had no trace of stitching or wounds. His eyes were closed, his breathing measured and normal, thanks to the tube. *My God.* What was happening to me? To him?

Every time I blinked, I saw his eyes, full of panic. How could I have imagined the whole thing? It had seemed so real. Was I going crazy? Had the nurses been right? Was I trying to yank out the tubes that were keeping him alive?

I used the distraction of the medical crisis to sneak out of his room and then the hospital. When I got outside, I reached into the pocket of my hoodie to turn my phone back on, but something poked my finger sharply.

"Ouch!" I brought the injured digit to my mouth while gingerly using my other hand to find what had poked me.

A corsage?

A black rose corsage with spiny, barbed thorns that circled the stem like teeth. The lace was tied to it with the same black thread that had been stitching my father.

I hadn't imagined it.

Somehow, I had gone to Under for those few moments. That machine, that torture, was what my father was living every second he was in the coma. I'd been in Under for only a few minutes. My father was still there. I could feel it. And it was up to me to get him back.

*   *   *

Everything was nearly in place.

He'd hoped for more time, more stolen moments of a life he should never really have had, but that was over now. Theia had made it clear that they were better off apart. Why he had tried to argue with her was a mystery. It was what he wanted as well.

No, not what he wanted. Never what he wanted.

But for now it had to be this way. Haden felt the screw turning in his heart with every passing minute. Soon she would know what he'd set into motion. She would be hurt and angry—that couldn't be helped. He'd never meant to betray her, but that was how she'd see it. She should have known better than to fall for him anyway. And he never should have let her. No matter how fast he ran, his destiny always found him.

He ached from a place that didn't exist before he'd met her.

If only they'd had more time.

I stole a car.

Muriel's car.

She was sound asleep when I got home. Nobody from the hospital had called her yet, to let her know that her court-appointed ward had tried to pull the plug on her father's life support. I had a feeling she wouldn't have believed them anyway.

When I was younger, I used to wish Muriel was my mother. I'd never told anyone that. She was so warm and my father so cold—she made life bearable in that house. I repaid her in kind by stealing her car.

I grabbed only my violin and her keys from the house.

The road was unfamiliar and poorly lit. I had very little experience driving anyway, as Father had elected not to let me get my license. My hands gripped the steering wheel so tightly that they were damp with sweat but I was too nervous to remove them long enough to wipe them on my pants. I hoped I wouldn't get lost; I'd been to the cabin in the woods only a few times.

The shack belonged to Gabe and his older brother, and it wasn't pretty. They'd built it themselves, adding things like rudimentary plumbing and electricity as they grew up. A lot had happened in the cabin, though—it was where I'd been abducted and where I'd been returned. As I turned onto the rocky driveway, I hoped that the remoteness of it would be an asset to me. I needed someplace to go where no one would think to look for me for a while. I left my phone in the car—there was never any cell service in the cabin and I didn't want to talk to anyone anyway.

I let myself in, locking the door behind me, but I didn't bother trying to build a fire to warm it up. The musty smell of the room wasn't overpowering, but it certainly wasn't pleasant. Someone had put down a new floor rug recently. Donny and Gabe sometimes used the place to be alone. . . . I wondered if Gabe was trying to fix it up for her. It seemed like something he would do.

I opened my case and pulled out my neglected instrument. The familiar weight of my violin settled into the place on my body where it had always belonged, but I hesitated. Before I'd known what Under was, I had played a song that transported me there against my will.

This time I would take myself there.

My trips to Under had never been in my control. Often I'd been a pawn in a game I didn't understand. The conflicting desires of Haden and Mara brought me in and out of their world on their whims. Back and forth, I'd been urged and repelled.

And where was Haden now? I wondered as I sat in a scarred wooden chair. I readied my bow. Did he miss me? Or was he filling his time with pursuits of other girls? Girls less complicated. Girls who could feed his appetites.

I closed my eyes and pulled an age-old tune from my soul, twisting and turning it around until I found just the right notes. In my head, I could hear the rest of the orchestra joining me. It was a song I'd heard only once, but such was my gift that once was all I ever needed to translate what I heard to my bow and strings.

Father had always pushed me to use my gifts to study and play classical music. I think it had been his dream that I play in a renowned symphony, but it was never mine. I heard a different kind of music in my soul—I always had. The kind of songs they played in Under. Perhaps I'd lured the underworld to me all along and not the reverse.

I didn't need to open my eyes to feel the change. The atmosphere was thicker in Under, as if the air coated my skin. The music played on, though I no longer held my violin. I opened my eyes.

The ground below me was parched and cracked, so devoid of color I couldn't even call it gray. All around me it hinted at

once being resplendent by how desolate it now appeared—
nothing grew, but in place of vegetation, the stalks of dead
plants withered in the bleakness. The wasteland seemed to
stretch for miles around me in every direction. On the horizon,
bolts of lightning cracked the sky and the beyond rumbled back
as if in protest for the deep crevices the lightning left behind.

The whole place felt lonely.

A splash of color caught my eye. I couldn't tell how far it
was from me, but I started towards it. My legs grew heavier the
farther I walked, but the colors were so beautiful in the middle
of the barren earth that I pushed myself to slog ahead even
when they seemed to be getting no closer as I walked towards
them.

In the distance, dark clouds gathered ominously. The thun-
der clapped louder, followed by long sizzles that echoed as if I
were standing in a cavern instead of on the flat ground. I didn't
like the noise; it sounded as if the sky was being torn at the
seams.

I kept moving, knowing that standing still would be no
safer, despite the part of me that wanted to cover my head and
hide. Finally I looked down at myself and realized I was wearing a large, heavy coat. Strange. While I walked, I unbuttoned
it, shrugging out of it and letting it fall to the ground. I felt a
little lighter, but I was still wearing another coat. I kept shuck-
ing off layer after layer of restricting jackets and coats, getting
lighter and lighter until finally I was down to a nightgown, red
again.

Without the bulky clothing, I moved with ease and sprinted

to the colorful spot in the desolate landscape. As I neared it, I realized it was the flowers that I had liked so much. Strange that they could grow where nothing else survived, here in the middle of nowhere. I smiled when I could smell them—so sweet, like fruit.

I needed to go find my father, but first I rubbed the soft petals of the yellow bloom across my cheek, inhaling deeply at its fresh scent. The pink one was next and then the blue. I felt giddy, despite my surroundings. If my flowers were here, it couldn't be that bad.

"Theia!"

Haden's voice startled me and I turned abruptly towards him, surprised to see him. He wore faded jeans and one of his white button-up shirts with an untied cravat under the collar. His face was covered in stubble and his hair was rakishly mussed. His black eyes made him appear more demon than human at that moment, and he reeked of the sulfur that accompanied his use of the Lure. His face was stretched tight and I couldn't decide if he looked tired or angry or both.

He looked behind me and then back at my face. "My God, what have you done?"

Confused, I turned to the flower bed. The yellow flower had lost its color and its stalk bent sadly. "I don't understand," I said, looking back at him. "I was just smelling the flowers."

I looked behind me again, and the flowers were all drooping. Dying.

"Oh, Theia." He looked crushed. More so even than the night I had broken up with him. "Those aren't flowers."

CHAPTER TWELVE

M y eyes snapped open. Someone was pounding at the door.

I was back in the cabin, still playing the song on my violin that had carried me Under. I had to concentrate to pull my arm away from my instrument, my body still a little possessed with the aftereffects. The pounding on the door continued, but I couldn't seem to move from my chair. I was paralyzed with grief. I hadn't found my father. A blade of guilt slashed my stomach. I'd been distracted by the flowers.

The flowers.

Every time I'd touched them or inhaled their pleasing fragrance, I'd been draining them. Their scents had filled me with a sense of well-being. I'd taken such pleasure from them.

The shame overwhelmed me. Not flowers . . . souls. I'd been feeding from human souls.

"Theia, I know you are in there. Open up. It's Mike."

Why in the world was Mike at the cabin?

The oddity of his presence startled me out of my numbed state. I crossed the room, aware for the first time that it had begun to rain while I'd been gone, the sound of it like falling nails on the tin roof. I opened the door with trepidation. "Mike?"

He dripped all over the stoop, water running down his face in rivulets. He was breathing heavily and looked agitated. He folded me into his wet embrace, squeezing harder when I stiffened in his arms. "It's okay. It will all be okay now," he assured me.

He didn't loosen his hold on me, but instead pushed into the cabin with me in his arms. Unease shot arrows down my spine. I tried to shove away from his chest, but his arms didn't relent. Years of wrestling made him strong. "I promise it will be okay now. You don't have to worry anymore."

I panicked and struggled vainly in his viselike hold. "Let go of me!"

He released me and looked surprised at my vehemence. "I'm sorry, Theia. I got you all wet. I shouldn't have grabbed you like that." He shook his head, chastising himself. "You're shivering. I'll make a fire, okay?"

Something was so wrong with his presence, but I didn't know where to begin. "What are you doing here?"

He went about laying kindling in the ancient woodstove. "I came to save you."

My arms erupted in goose bumps. "Save me? Save me from what?"

He didn't answer me. He methodically built a fire, as if we'd been in this situation a thousand times.

I wrapped my arms around myself, but my chill went further than my damp skin. "Mike, what is going on? You're acting so strangely. How did you even know I was here?"

"You don't need to worry anymore. It's all taken care of." He sat back on his haunches. "That should warm you up in a few minutes." He looked up and pinned me with his gaze. His eyes were filled with an earnest fervor that I'd never seen him express before. Not even for French fries. "There is still hope for us all, Theia. But you need to turn away from the evil that has infected you."

I stared back, the hairs on my neck standing up like a porcupine's quills. "Mike, what are you talking about?"

He stood and stepped towards me, not seeming to care that I backed away. "He's used the powers of evil to turn you from your true nature. Renounce the evil demon and all will be won." Mike's vehemence shone in his eyes. "He's brainwashed you, Theia. Just like he's done to everyone. But you know, deep inside, that staying with him is wrong. You're holding the hand of the devil, but it's not too late."

"Too late for what, Mike? Who are you talking about?"

"Haden is a scourge, a plague, on earth. We must unite and defeat his evil. We must wipe him off our world. He is a demon and must be killed."

My knees turned to jelly. He sounded like he was on a street corner citing Bible verses at random passersby. Not the easygoing wrestler I was used to, the one with a huge appetite and very little to say. What had happened to him? "Mike, you don't understand."

"Theia," Mike pleaded, "you know the right path. He's led you astray, but you know the truth. You know what you must do. It's not too late. I forgive you."

"Forgive me?" He kept moving slowly towards me, so I moved away, putting a chair between us. I aimed my voice for cheerfulness, but it came out sounding thin and reedy. "Where did you get the idea that Haden is a demon? Surely you know that sounds crazy."

"I know all about Haden. I know how he's tricked everyone into thinking he's such a great guy. I know he's an evil incubus. It's disgusting." Instead of closing the distance between us, Mike crossed the room and threw the bolt on the door, locking us in. "We'll wait until the rain lets up, okay?"

My heart pounded dangerously. My natural instincts warned me that I was in some kind of peril, but I couldn't afford to lose control of my emotions. The last thing this situation needed was my demon side making an appearance. I had to keep myself calm; I had to keep Mike calm. I thought to play along. "What will we do then, Mike? When the rain lets up?"

He took off his jacket and laid it over the back of a chair near the fire. Not answering my question, he said, "I tried to warn you about Haden. The notes . . ."

"I didn't realize that was you." Had he been putting some kind of plan in motion? "Why did you—"

"You're wearing the bracelet I gave you."

I looked down at my wrist. I'd forgotten it was there.

"Mike, I have to go. My father is at the hospital, remember? I have to go to him."

"You can't go right now. The roads are terrible. It's my job to keep you safe now."

He stood in front of a window and looked into the dark, though I was sure he couldn't see anything. I felt his craziness coming off him in waves.

"Just the same, I think I'll go. I'd feel better if I were closer to my father."

He stepped in front of me, blocking my path. "He's coming for you, you know."

"My father?"

Mike smiled, but his eyes were serious. Deadly so. "No, of course not. Haden."

"Haden doesn't know I'm here."

The door shook from a sudden pounding and I jumped. Mike just smiled at my reaction. "I told you."

"Theia!" Haden yelled through the door.

Mike clapped his hand over my mouth and turned me so my back was to his chest. I stopped struggling when he flashed a knife in his other hand. "Not a word, Theia. You just let me handle this. It ends tonight."

Haden banged on the door a few more times and then he crashed through it, dead bolt and all. It didn't take him long to assess the situation. "Let her go, Matheny," he growled.

I could smell Mike's fear and agitation. "You should have let her go a long time ago. You're an abomination."

Haden spread his hands to show he was unarmed. "You're

not wrong about that. But let Theia go and we can settle this between ourselves. She's an innocent girl."

Mike squeezed me tighter. "She used to be innocent until you ruined her. But once you're gone, I can save her. I *will* save her."

"We both know you're not going to use the knife on Theia, so let her go."

Haden sent me a look that told me more than words could ever have said. It was comforting, but more, it reached down to my very soul.

I needed to find a way to distract Mike. I wasn't helpless and the situation needed to be defused quickly before anyone got hurt. Mike wasn't thinking clearly, if he was thinking at all. He was so unlike himself that it was frightening.

The windows. I'd been making glass explode for a while without thinking about it. I wondered whether I could do it on purpose. I concentrated very hard on one across the room. At first nothing happened. I let myself absorb some of the tension in the room, and something broke free deep inside me. It felt like a warm ball of light gathering around my breastbone, and then it funneled into a stream directed by my will and burst out of me.

The window began to shift in its casement. I had no idea what I was doing, but I kept thinking about it shattering. I saw it over and over in my mind. The pressure built inside me and I tuned out the argument between Haden and Mike. A final push, and several windows shattered, spraying shards of glass into the room, like water from a hose nozzle.

Everyone instinctively ducked to avoid the spray and I used

the distraction to wrench out of Mike's arms. Haden leaped on him, yelling, "Theia, get out of here. Now. The keys are still in the ignition."

I started to run, making it all the way to his truck before I remembered that I didn't know how to drive a stick shift. The keys to Muriel's car were still in the cabin. As I started to go back, the boys rolled out onto the porch and then into the grass. I knew Haden was holding back because he didn't want to kill Mike, but Mike was an all-star wrestler and he wasn't holding back.

The rain came down in sheets, soaking us all. Haden and Mike continued grappling and a glint of silver slashed into the air. "Watch out for the knife, Haden!"

I grabbed a nearby stick and got up, holding it like a baseball bat. It was a sturdy branch but I wasn't sure how much damage I could really do with it. I held the stick firmly, feeling the bark roughen the skin on my palms.

Time rearranged itself, playing the scene in slow motion and yet somehow, at the same time, very quickly. The knife gouged into Haden's side. Haden gasped once and stopped moving, but Mike continued to pummel him with his fist. He kept grunting and yelling out nonsensical words. When he raised his arm to stab Haden again, I swung with all my might. I'd never hit anyone before. I wasn't prepared for the give of his skin or the sound of bone meeting wood.

Mike collapsed on top of Haden. I fell to my knees and rolled him off. They were both lying so still. *This can't be happening.* I began trembling from head to toe, my teeth chattering, my heart stuttering. The rain poured over me as if dumped from a bucket.

I leaned over Haden's mouth and felt his breath on my ear. "Thank God. Please wake up."

I pulled off my hoodie and held it to his side to stanch the blood. I had to get him to the car, unless my phone got magical cellular reception.

The sound of gravel crunching under the wheels of a car preceded the headlights on the dirt drive leading to the cabin. *Now who was here?* "Haden, please wake up."

I recognized the car to be Donny's and relief flooded through me. "It's going to be okay, Haden. We'll get you to the hospital."

Donny, Ame, Gabe, and Varnie ran to us and stopped short when they saw the boys on the ground.

"What the hell happened?" Donny asked, and then looked at the other unconscious boy. "Mike?"

As soon as Amelia saw Mike, she squeaked and collapsed. Varnie scooped her into his arms before she hit the ground. "We need to dial 911. Donny, can you—?"

"There's no cell service. What the hell happened?" Gabe asked, echoing Donny.

"Mike stabbed Haden, so I hit him and knocked him unconscious."

"I'm taking Amelia inside," Varnie said. "She's unconscious too."

"What is going on?" asked Donny.

"I don't know exactly. We need to get Haden to the hospital." There were far too many unconscious people in my life. "How did you know I was here?"

"Varnie had a vision right in the middle of the *American Idol* finale," Donny answered.

Haden groaned. "Theia."

I touched his face. "I'm right here."

"It's raining, you'll catch cold," he mumbled.

I laughed a little. The sniffles weren't high on my priority list. "We need to get you to the emergency room. Do you remember what happened?"

"Matheny." He blinked. "Where is he?"

"I hit him. Our friends are here. We're going to take you both to the hospital." I didn't tell him about Amelia.

"I don't need a hospital. I'm already healing. It's just going to take a little longer. He must have used a pure silver blade."

"You're bleeding from a knife wound. You need a doctor."

He winced as he sat up very slowly. "I'll be fine."

He obviously wasn't going to agree with me. Donny and Gabe were carrying Mike into the cabin, though I'm not sure if we should have moved him. I helped Haden up. He leaned on me but was able to walk back inside.

"What happened to Amelia?" I asked.

Varnie sat on a chair with Ame curled like a small child in his lap. She whimpered while he reassured her, stroking her hair and lying to her that everything would be fine. "I wish I knew. She's awake, but she's not all there."

I settled Haden into a chair, trying not to panic at all the blood on his shirt, and went to find the first-aid kit, crunching across all the glass. The place was a mess.

"We need to tie him up," Haden directed the others, pointing to Mike's prone body on the couch.

"Dude," Gabe said, "he's unconscious. We need to get him a doctor."

"When I got here, he was holding a knife on Theia." Haden's voice was deceptively calm. "He's lucky I didn't kill him."

Ame began sobbing inconsolably. It was actually more than a little strange. Donny and I looked at each other. We didn't know where to go first. Ame? Mike? Haden? They all needed help.

Donny sent me an exasperated sigh and then rolled up her sleeves. "Okay, English. Give us the short-story version so we can fix this."

Where to begin? She took the kit and held it open while I pulled out some bandages and antiseptic. "You and Gabe check out Mike, I'll look at Haden's wound, and Varnie can take care of Ame," I said. "We'll get Mike to a doctor as soon as I know Haden isn't going to die on the way. The short story is that Mike somehow knows Haden is a demon and wants to save me by killing him. He also kept me here against my will." I snapped the box closed. "He stabbed Haden and I knocked him unconscious." I looked at Haden to fill him in. "Oh, and my father is being tortured by Mara in Under, so I have to go back as soon as possible." Returning my gaze to a wide-eyed Donny, I said, "I don't know the rest of the story."

She raised her eyebrows. "Why is Ame having a melt-down?"

"I don't know that either."

"All righty then."

The wind blew rain in through the open windows. Our shelter wasn't much of one anymore.

Haden tried to take the bandages from me, but I just pushed him towards the small bathroom. "You're not going to Under," he said as I closed the door behind us.

"Just take your shirt off," I answered.

He paused, blinking at me, and then he began unbuttoning. As he stretched his arms back to remove the sleeves, he doubled over. "Son of a—"

"Easy," I murmured, and eased the shirt past his shoulders. The intimacy of removing his clothes painted a hot stroke of embarrassment over my face, but it was quickly replaced by a flush of cold horror. "Oh, Haden."

He looked down at the wound. "I do believe that is going to leave a scar."

I didn't appreciate his sarcasm. The wound was festering and mottled. Dried blood, as well as fresh, covered the purplish mass. I saw his aura flare around him. Where his wound was, however, there was an absence of its glow. The gap was alarming, though I couldn't say for certain why I knew it was a bad thing. The knife had broken his spirit, literally. It reminded me of an unfinished bridge, a breach that shouldn't be.

I took a deep breath and wet down a cloth with warm water. I longed for a good old-fashioned fainting spell, but there was no getting out of this. "You're probably going to hate me for a few minutes. This is going to hurt."

He didn't answer, so I met his eyes with mine. They were fathomless. I ached with how much I'd missed him.

"I don't think I could ever hate you," he said simply. He looked at my arm and wrinkled his forehead. "He bruised you."

I brought my arm up and inspected the blue and purple skin. "It's nothing."

He took my hand. "You have such fragile skin." He pressed a kiss to the inside of my wrist.

I shivered. Why was he making this so hard? "I'm not fragile, Haden."

"No, you're not. You certainly proved that today."

I looked away, but he gently cupped my chin and brought my gaze back to his. "We need to talk about what happened in Under. How did you get there?"

Looking into his eyes hurt too much, so I avoided the contact and inspected his injury. "I don't know, really." I began pressing the cloth to the outside of the stab wound, getting most of the dried blood worked away so I had a better idea of the damage. His abdominal muscles twitched and tensed under my hand. I dabbed around the wound and then rinsed the cloth. "I played the song . . . the one from the first night in Under. The one they played in the labyrinth. Somehow I knew it would work. I was trying to find my father."

"You should have come to me."

I pressed too hard and his face screwed up in pain. "You weren't around."

"Theia . . ."

"Nobody had seen you since you left the party with Brittany." I paused. "I know I shouldn't be jealous. I'm the one that broke up with you. I just didn't expect you to replace me so quickly."

"Replace you? Now I *am* angry. I didn't replace you. How could you even think that? I went home shortly after you left the party on Saturday night, but a few hours later Brittany called me. She was drunk. She told me she'd been having nightmares about you every night."

"Me?"

Haden hissed as the cloth got closer to the open wound. "She said the weird part was that several other people at the party said they'd been having the same dream. The last few nights, just as they began to fall asleep, you would show up with glowing red eyes. They couldn't move or breathe or wake up. Brittany was getting more and more agitated, so I drove back to the party, which had moved to Noelle's."

His voice got tighter the closer I got to the wound. "She was already mostly unconscious when I arrived. She'd been so sick, it didn't take much booze to put her over the edge. I offered to take her home, hoping to get the rest of the story. People saw us leaving. She was belligerent and out of it, so I carried her. I suppose they assumed we were hooking up."

"Where did you take her?" My own voice was tight as well. The wound was angry and ugly. It made me queasy and lightheaded.

"I took her home. Jesus, that stings."

"I'm sorry. I'm being as gentle as I can." I bit my lip and concentrated on not showing my revulsion. "What happened then?"

Haden dropped his head back and stared at the ceiling. His chest rose and fell heavily. "Her parents were still out of town, so I carried her all the way into the house. I tried talking to her, but most of what she said was gibberish."

"Did she say anything more about me?" Was I really making nocturnal visits to the sneetches?

"No. Not a word. I even tried to bring you up. She was too far gone. I put her to bed." He paused. "Fully clothed, mind you. And then I left. That was the last time I saw Brittany." He lifted his head and fixed me with a look that reminded me he was still a demon, albeit a very charismatic one. "Are you satisfied?"

"I believe you," was all I'd admit to.

"And then I went to Under."

"Why?"

"I've been forming an army." Before I could ask, he continued. "We're staging a coup. I didn't tell you about it because . . . well, you wouldn't like it. I'm going back, Theia. I've been planning this for a while, actually."

"Haden, no." All the reasons that was a bad idea began ricocheting through my head. I'd broken my heart so he could have a normal human life and all the while he'd been planning to return to Under? "Why didn't you tell me? Were you just going to disappear?"

"You broke up with me, remember?" It was an accusation posed as a question.

"It sounds to me like you were planning this before we broke up."

He held his jaw so tautly it must have ached. "Mara has to be stopped. It's my job to keep you safe."

I threw one of the rags into the sink. "Your job? I'm not a responsibility, Haden." My outrage was quickly boiling over. I took a deep breath, trying to stay in control. "What happens if you win . . . or, God forbid, lose? It's not fair that you kept this from me."

"Like you came to me when you started worrying that your demon side was getting stronger? Don't look at me like that. Of course I knew. I kept waiting for you to ask me for help, but instead you pushed me away. Look, I don't want to fight. We both should have been more honest."

"You didn't answer my question. If you win?"

"Then I take my place in Under."

I sucked in a breath. "No." A shock of cold froze my blood at the thought. "Haden, you can't do that."

"I have to. I was hoping that someday, somehow, I could find a way we could be together—but it has to be after the danger is gone. You already compromised your soul for me once. I need to make sure Mara can't hurt you again. So, yes, I was going behind your back because I knew you would try to talk me out of it."

It felt like a betrayal to know that he'd been plotting a course of leaving me without my knowledge. "So it's okay to lie to me if it makes me easier to live with?"

"Of course not. I've known all along it wasn't okay. It doesn't change the fact that I have to do it. Do you think I enjoyed knowing how much I was going to hurt you by leaving? But then, I guess it doesn't matter anyway, since you left me first—right?"

Anger warmed my face and I turned away. "It sounds like you're just mad that I beat you to it."

Haden grasped my wrist, pulling my attention back to him. "I would have come back to you."

I twisted from his hand. "Unless you died." He wanted to look away then, but I silently dared him to keep the eye contact. "You were going to rush headlong into some kind of war. What would happen to me—to all of us—if you didn't come back?"

"It's a chance I have to take."

He hadn't used past tense. "You're still going through with it?"

He closed his eyes. Getting that small distance from me made his words seem sharper, more forceful. "I will make sure she can no longer threaten you or those you care about. If it's the last thing I do, I promise you that."

I wanted to throw something, hit something. "I hate that you lied to me . . . that you've been lying." I thought about how hard it had been to break ties with him when all along he'd been planning on doing the same.

"I lied because I love you. Everything I do is because I love you."

Though I knew he meant the words, they felt hollow. What good was love now? I shook my head. "Did you see my father . . . when you were in Under?"

"No, I didn't know he was there."

Something else niggled at my brain as I returned to dabbing the cloth around his cut. "How did you find me tonight? If you were in Under, how did you know to find me here?"

"I listened to my heart," he answered, very softly.

His words made my own heart trip and stumble over all the blocks I'd tried to put between us. I felt the pull and I wanted to fall back under his spell as if I'd never left it. No. That. couldn't happen. I had to be stronger. I tried to find the anger I had felt only a moment before and held tightly to it. I stepped back, trying to put some distance between us. The wound was as clean as I could get it.

He was right—it was healing already.

Which meant it was on to the next impossible thing on my to-do list. It was hard to believe it was still the same day. Every time I came up for air, my head got plunged back into the icy water. "If the sneetches are all dreaming about me, then I must be the one feeding from them. I thought they were flowers, Haden. I swear to God I thought they were flowers."

"Tonight wasn't the first time?"

I shook my head slowly.

"How did you get there the other times?"

I washed my shaking hands, all the words from our conversation finally sinking in and making a home in my brain. "I don't know. I just kept waking up there."

I looked into the mirror above the sink, surprised to see Haden's reflection behind my own. His face was bruised from the fight outside and he was tired, so tired. But he rested his hand on my shoulder and kissed my messy curls. "Are we done with the stupid breakup now?"

I wanted that more than anything. I wanted to rest. I wanted to feel the peace I always felt in his arms, but how could I? How could I lead him down the path of his own destruction? Especially now, knowing how out of control I'd been without even knowing it. "How can you still want to be with me?" And how could I trust him?

He turned me around to face him, his hands on my shoulders. "You were tricked into smelling the flowers, Theia. Why would that make me want you less?"

I swallowed the tears. "I've been slowly killing my classmates. I need to be locked up or something."

"I'm not convinced you're to blame."

"You heard what Brittany said . . . and you saw me do it."

He squeezed my shoulders gently. "Brittany was out of her mind. She'd been sick and then she added alcohol and who knows what else at that party. Just like you were deceived by the flowers, it's possible she and the others were deceived by Mara. She feeds nightmares, remember? She could have planted those dreams in their heads."

My chin trembled; the tears were imminent. I felt like there was no place to step that didn't turn my world upside down. "Do you really think I could be innocent? Oh, Haden, I feel so terrible. I had begun to think it was you and it was probably me all along."

"You were definitely draining souls when I found you, but I don't think you're strong enough yet to be the one responsible for all the sickness in Serendipity Falls. And I can assure you it wasn't me."

Though I should have put a stop to it, the weight of his hands on my shoulders felt good. I brought a shaky hand up to wipe at the tears gathering in my eyes. I didn't understand how I could be so angry with him and want him at the same time. "How have you been able to fight the urges all this time? It's so hard. I'm afraid that part of me knew what I was doing, but I didn't want to stop, so I pretended not to know."

Haden exhaled a sigh that seemed bottomless. "The urges are powerful. We both know that. But there is something more powerful and you have to believe that. The thing that you will do anything to protect, anything to save . . . that is the thing that will keep you strong. For me, it's you."

He tucked a curl behind my ear and I was suddenly quite aware that he was shirtless. The intimacy, the sense of the forbidden, the ache in my chest—all conspired against me. It would be so easy to fall back into his arms, to let him comfort me, to forget the lies and the hurt. But my father was still a captive, Mike Matheny had suddenly become a problem, Amelia needed our help, the passion I felt for Haden would destroy him if we gave in to it, and I was dangerous to my friends and family and every soul I encountered. They never should have brought me back from Under. I should have stayed below and been stronger. I was guilty no matter who was actually consuming the souls.

"I can't do this," I whispered.

"You're where I find my strength, Theia. Your love changed me. I will always come back for you."

"I'm more like Mara than you think," I argued.

"You are nothing like Mara."

I thought of that little girl and her teddy bear. "You don't know what I'm capable of. I'm not even sure I know. I can't be your girlfriend right now. I can't be counted on to be anything to anyone."

I brushed past him to get out of the small bathroom. Everywhere we touched sparked, singeing me with longing. He held me gently inside the door and leaned down to whisper into my ear. "You don't have to do this alone. When you're ready, I'll still be here. I will *always* be here."

The moment was the edge of a cliff. I wanted to let him hold me back from the fall. My traitorous heart skipped a beat in order to sync to the rhythm of his. I had to give him up, though. I had to give all of them up. I imagined the looks on their faces when I told them that I had slipped into the sleep of a child to give her a night terror. How would I explain to Donny and Amelia that I relished the scent of human fear? How could they ever trust me after they learned that I felt so good after I took the essence from the souls of the "flowers" I had found in Under.

They were better off without me and all my failings. Once they were all safely home again and we figured out what was wrong with Mike Matheny, I would return to Under and free my father. Then I would disappear for good.

And then Donny screamed.

CHAPTER THIRTEEN

We rushed out of the bathroom to see Mike on his feet in the corner and Gabe and Varnie standing in front of him trying to stay between him and the girls. The mood was definitely tense.

"What's going on?" Mike asked. "Why won't you let me out of here?"

"What happened?" I asked.

Donny leaned on the broom she was holding. "I might have overreacted. I'm a little jumpy. I was sweeping and Mike regained consciousness, sitting up and rambling like a crazy person, and I screamed. He startled me, plus he's all whackadoo."

Mike looked up, his eyes red and glassy, his upper lip puffy from the fight outside. "Look out!" Mike shouted. "Haden's behind you!"

We all looked at one another like *Yeah, and . . . ?* Haden

was with us the whole time. At any rate, he moved in front of us and stood directly before Mike, waiting for another fight.

"He's a demon," Mike explained.

"No shit, Sherlock." Donny, of course.

Gabe and Varnie closed in on him and "convinced" him to sit in a chair.

I looked to Ame for advice on how to proceed. "Amelia?" She stood transfixed. Just staring at Mike. "Sweetie, are you all right?"

Donny let go of me and we put Amelia between us like we were bookends.

Donny said, "She hasn't said a word since we got in here. After she stopped crying she just stopped making any noise at all. It's like she's catatonic. Varnie has been trying to get through to her, but she's someplace else."

To prove her point, she waved her hand in front of Amelia's face. Nothing registered. Amelia was in a trance of some kind and that really scared me. Ame was our solid ground, our group mother and the expert on all things paranormal as well as all things Mike Matheny. I didn't like seeing her "there" but gone. Selfishly, I needed her sweetness and boundless enthusiasm more than ever.

I looked back at Mike and noticed a strange trail of light between him and Amelia. It wasn't bright like a healthy aura, but rather an almost sickly color of gray. It roped like a fleshy intestine and was pockmarked in some places with odd fungus-like growths in others.

I pointed to it. "Does anybody else see that?"

Everybody looked in the direction I pointed, but nobody jumped in with an affirmative answer. Great. My jolly good day just continued with all the fun.

"What do you see, love?" Haden asked.

"There is something connecting Amelia and Mike. It's like an aura of some kind, only it's really unhealthy-looking." Unnatural.

"Describe 'unhealthy,'" Varnie said.

I nodded to him. I had to hope that he would understand. Without Ame contributing to our cause, we were quite short on expert opinions. "Okay, it's a gray . . . -ish light that extends between the two of them like a cord. Almost . . . um . . . gelatinous-looking. It reminds me of when we looked at different germs under a microscope in biology."

"Fantastic." Donny threw her arms up. "Is it too much to ask that you guys attach yourself to normal boys? Who would have guessed I'd have the only normal boyfriend?"

Mike got my attention. "It's not your fault what you've been doing." He jutted his chin out at Haden. "If you turn from him and come back to where you belong, I swear I can get you the help you need to stop. The kids are dying. You're killing them a little more every night—"

"Shut up!" Haden yelled, lunging at Mike, but Varnie stepped between them. "I should have killed you when I had the chance, you lying piece of—"

Mike shook his head in disgust, but before he could say another word, Donny wanted to know what he meant by me killing them every night.

I took a deep breath. "You saw me today, Donny. It's possible that all the sneetches are sick because of me . . . because I can't control what changed in me when Mara gave me her blood."

Mike shook his head. "Theia, it's not your fault. Haden brought this on you, on all of us. But we can stop it. We have to kill him. It's the only way."

My blood ran cold.

Before I could respond, Varnie had already begun. "Whoa, dude. Chill out. That's my best friend you're talking about. How about you tell us about whatever fleshy trail thing you've got attached to Miss Amelia and lay off the demon rhetoric."

"I don't know what you're talking about," Mike answered. "I hardly know Amelia. I don't have anything attached to her."

Varnie looked at me and I pointed to it again. "I know you can't see it, but it's still there. Pulsing."

"Gross," Donny said.

"Don't you understand?" Mike began again, and we all rolled our eyes. "You're special. I'm special. We're meant to bring the worlds together. The queen told me so."

"The queen?" We all looked at one another when we asked the same question.

"The Queen of England?" Gabe asked.

"No, of course not," Mike said. He glared at Haden, but hardly managed to look menacing. "He could have been a prince, but he chose the path of evil. She gave him everything, but instead he took what was forbidden."

"Excuse me," Donny said, "but who the hell are you talking about? Who is the queen?"

"She goes by many names, but we know her as Queen Mara, and she's asked me to save this world and her own, which I will do. Salvation will be ours when I kill the demon."

We all looked at one another again. Dumbfounded.

"She comes to me in my dreams. She tells me stories of her kingdom. How beautiful it is." Mike smiled. "She told me I was brave and strong and had a destiny to fulfill."

"This is getting creepier every second," Donny said.

"I agree," Varnie said. "Let's get back to Amelia. What is the thing attached to you both, Mike?"

"I told you I don't know," Mike answered sullenly. "Ask the demon. He probably did some perverted spell."

Gabe scratched the back of his neck in a gesture that looked nonchalant, but I realized he was pointing his head at the knife on the table, warning me, since I was closest to it. I moved it to a drawer. Mike had been thoroughly brainwashed and we didn't need any more violence.

"Mara is a demon too, dude," Donny offered, perhaps trying to lure Mike back to normal logic.

"She's not a demon," he protested. "Mara is a queen. Haden's father was the soulless monster that raped her. He was the demon. She had too big a heart to blame Haden for his father's sins, so she tried to raise him with love. This is how he repays her."

Haden snorted. "Ah, yes. Love. She baked cookies and read me bedtime stories every night." He shook his head ruefully. "You imbecile. You believe every lie that comes from her mouth. My father was a human. Mara took him from this realm and forced him to stay in Under. She doesn't have a maternal instinct in her body."

"You liar," Mike spat.

Varnie wrapped his jacket around Ame's shoulders. "All this is fascinating, really, but Amelia is catatonic and Mr. Alderson is being tortured. Should we—I don't know—leave or something?"

"I'm here to save you all," Mike said. "The sooner we kill Haden the—"

"Enough," I interrupted him, my voice gritty with anger and exhaustion. "If you don't stop threatening to kill Haden we're going to gag you when we tie you up."

"Theia, you're making a mistake," he said. "I'm not the one you should tie up. Haden is the dangerous one. He stole you. Mara has plans for us."

I held up my hand, the trinket he gave me jingling on my wrist. "Stop right there. I know exactly what kind of plans Mara has for me. She's ripping apart the fabric of my life because I betrayed her, and all of you get to come along for the ride. She's no benevolent queen. She's a killer and worse."

Gabe grabbed the rope, sensing that things were going to get dicey. "Sorry, dude, but Theia is right. You're usually an okay guy, but I was at the bowling alley the night Mara came to town. Your queen is totally psycho."

Fatigue overwhelmed me, but something kept poking at my subconscious. Something that wasn't right. "Mike, how did you know I would be here tonight?"

He smiled and it chilled me. There wasn't any happiness in

it—whatever he was seeing in his mind was something completely different from the world the rest of us lived in. "We're supposed to be together, Theia. I told you. You can't hide from destiny. You'll never be lost again."

I looked at my wrist. My skin was suddenly hot underneath the bracelet. *The bracelet.*

My fingers itched to remove it, but the clasp wouldn't come undone. "Get this off me." It should have broken easily, but I suspected it wasn't a cheap toy from an innocent vending machine after all.

"Calm down, Thei." Donny tried to work the clasp, but it zapped her. She shook her hand and paled visibly. "What is that?"

"I don't know. I can't get it off."

"It's how we stay connected, Theia. I'll always know where you are."

Donny exploded. "You put a supernatural tracking device on Theia? Are you crazy? What are you, a stalker now?"

"I love her," Mike answered. "We're supposed to be together."

Haden's face turned to stone. While his anger was usually white-hot, it seemed even more dangerous when it was ice-cold.

Mike inched in his seat, sensing his doom and ready to make a break for it. "Don't side with the devil. Haden is the one with all the tricks. He's got you all under his spell. Mara is the one who will save us."

"You're delusional," Haden said, his voice firm with resolve. "And whatever plans you have for Theia are hereby canceled."

Mike looked wild, hunted. He pulled a small vial from his pocket. "Mara warned me that I might not be able to save you all. I didn't want to believe her, but she's right. We planned for this."

He threw the vial to the floor and a fog filled the room, murky and sulfuric. As the smoke of brimstone filled my nose, covering the rest of my senses, I began a long descent into a bleak, desolate place. My body stretched like rubber and ached with intense pressure.

And then I knew no more.

CHAPTER FOURTEEN

ᘒ

Sunlight streamed through my curtains and I rolled away instinctively. *Just a few more minutes.* I slipped back into a shallow slumber, but something nagged at me. Was I late? I couldn't even remember if it was a school day or not.

The nagging thoughts persisted, poking at my peace until I gave in and sat up. Fine. Obviously I was forgetting something very important. My thoughts felt wrapped in cotton, incoherent.

It was a school day—that much seemed to sink in. I checked the time and had plenty. I hadn't overslept, so I went about my daily routine. As I scraped my curls back into some semblance of a ponytail, I gritted my teeth. As usual, I thought about a haircut, knowing it would please Father and probably make my life easier, with fewer headaches. Both from making him happy and not having to pull it back all the time.

The pestering feeling of unease returned. What was wrong with me? I tried to shake it off as I descended the stairs. Did I not finish my homework? Was there a test?

The sunshine had been replaced with fog outside—much like the inside of my head. I hated to think I was getting sick and hoped this wasn't the precursor.

When I noticed an envelope with my name on it sitting on the polished table, it seemed as if time stopped. The sound of my heartbeat filled my ears. For some reason that card scared me. I swallowed hard. I was being ridiculous, of course. What could an envelope do to me? I scraped my bone-dry well of courage for enough to open it.

I touched the corner of the envelope and then waited to see if lightning would strike or the bottom of my world would fall out. Using one finger, I dragged it closer to me. The writing was my father's. Why on earth would he leave me a card?

I pulled the envelope apart with shaky hands. Whatever was inside portended disaster, at least according to the state of my stomach. I opened the card.

Happy 17th Birthday, Theia.

Love, Father.

Surely it had to be a mistake. My birthday had come and gone months ago, hadn't it? I was so puzzled. I couldn't grasp the memory, yet I knew it was there. I dropped the card and stepped away from the table, hugging my arms to my chest.

What in the world was going on? Why would my father put out a birthday card when I'd already turned seventeen?

It didn't matter. I needed to get to school.

"Earth to Thei."

I blinked at Donny across the cafeteria table. "Sorry. What were you saying?"

Donny rolled her eyes and stole another Tater Tot from my lunch tray. "I asked if you had figured out your prison-break plans for this weekend."

There.

Again.

All morning long I'd been experiencing the strangest déjà vu. We'd had this conversation before. I knew everyone's lines as if we were in a play.

"Ame, help me convince Theia that she needs to cut loose with us this weekend." Donny bit the tip of her pizza, the cheese stretching a mile before breaking. Only Donny could make that sexy. When I ate pizza, I cut it into bite-size pieces.

Ame unpacked her lunch from the reusable tie-dyed sack she brought every day—she was very conscious of her carbon footprint. "Theia, if you don't cut loose with us this weekend, I will have to listen to Donny bitch about you all night and it won't be any fun at all. *And* I won't have anyone to talk to when she ditches me for the first pretty boy that comes along. You have to come."

On top of the strange sensation that this had happened before, another awareness of an intangible wrongness coated my brain, dulling my reactions. I blinked and saw the inside of a nightclub, the one Donny was always trying to get me to go to. I felt the music, its hard beat reverberating in my chest. My skirt was too short and I felt exposed. And his eyes . . . whose eyes were those that were so dark and saw right through me?

I stood up quickly, knocking over my milk.

"Theia? You okay?" Ame asked.

I shook my head. Something was wrong. Very, very wrong. "I have to go."

They were both wide-eyed at my unusual reaction. I always tried too hard not to be noticed or make a scene. Donny offered me a ride, but I was already running for the door. I left campus without a look behind me.

The house was empty, but it felt full of something that shouldn't be there. Some kind of static, and it overwhelmed the inside of my head too. I tried to figure what was out of place, but it seemed that it was only me that didn't belong.

I couldn't shake the misplaced feelings. Nothing fit. My life was exactly the same as it should have been, yet it wasn't.

I needed music.

An overwhelming urge to play assailed me. It seemed an age since I'd picked up my violin, though I'm sure if I could remember correctly, it had likely only been since yesterday. I ran upstairs, pulling out the tight hair band. I didn't bother with any of my usual preplaying rituals—no tuning, no scales. I needed to play, to immerse myself, to lose myself. With shaky hands I fumbled with my bow until it finally reached the note I was looking for.

I began playing a song that I'd never heard before, yet knew like my own heartbeat. As the music swelled, flashes of a handsome boy filtered through my mind's eye. I didn't know him, but I wanted to.

Wait. That wasn't right. I *did* know him. It was like trying to remember a dream. I saw things in senseless pictures that wrought feelings from the bottom of my heart to the surface. Feelings of love, deep and true. And passion that I knew I'd never experienced yet inexplicably understood to belong to me.

Then, as I got closer to the kernel of truth that would answer it all, I woke up to the sunlight streaming through my curtains.

I couldn't recall what had happened after I played the violin. I just awoke to the sunlight and a new day. I patrolled the house for signs of my father, but he'd already gone to work. We must have had dinner the night before—I would have asked about the card. Why couldn't I remember?

I looked at my phone. The date read the day after my birthday . . . so I was wrong. I must have dreamt that I'd turned seventeen months ago. Why didn't I check the date yesterday? My brain was fuzzy and clouded. Almost like I was dreaming that I was awake.

Not knowing what else to do, I went to school. I leaned against the lockers waiting for Amelia to fetch her binder. I was so tired they needed to make a new word for tired. Every time I blinked, I swore the backs of my eyelids were made of sandpaper.

"I have play practice after school tomorrow if you want to come over after." Ame stopped. "You're really pale. Are you sure you're okay?"

Nodding, I pushed off the bank of lockers. "I just haven't slept well the last two nights."

She dug in her pocket and handed me a crystal. "This one restores energy. If you can keep it on your skin, it will work better."

I nodded, pretending I believed her. Pretending that every word we traded didn't feel like a program I'd already seen.

As we walked down the hall, I pulled the band out of my hair to ease my growing headache and finger-combed my curls. As we passed the windows of the admin office, time blurred into slow motion. I shivered and a rush of cold seeped into the marrow of my bones, as if someone had just stepped on my grave. And danced on it as well.

I looked up, expecting to see him.

Who? A memory was almost in my reach, but then it was gone again, like the spent flame on a candle with no wax. He should have been there. *Where was he?*

My heart began to crack, missing someone I had no memory of.

Ame grabbed my arm. "Are you all right? You look like you've seen a ghost."

"Please keep walking," I squeaked.

She slung a protective arm around me and ushered me into the nearest bathroom. I slumped against the wall, trying to catch my breath, but my lungs didn't want to work correctly and I exhaled when I should have inhaled.

"What is wrong with you? Do you need the nurse? Should I call your dad?"

I shook my head, which did nothing for my already poor balance. "No. I just need a minute."

The door burst open and the surge of energy that always followed Donny came in with her. "Hey . . . what's wrong?"

Amelia answered, "She just freaked out. It was the weirdest thing. We were walking down the hall and everything was fine. Then she—"

"Oh, God," I cried. "There is something really wrong with me. I think I have a brain tumor or something."

The conversation was still one I remembered, but different. A name flashed through my mind, crystal clear. *Madame Varnie.*

A small piece of the puzzle finally fit. Sort of. The name was familiar—like a memory that I couldn't exactly remember. "Amelia, do you have an appointment with someone named Madame Varnie this week?"

She knit her eyebrows together in concern. "How did you know that?"

"It doesn't matter." I crossed to a sink and wet some paper towels to hold to my forehead. "But we all have to go."

"Who is Madame Varnie?" Donny wanted to know.

Ame studied me while I answered. "He's a psychic."

"He?" Ame asked.

"Just trust me," I said. "There is something going on. And somehow I know he's the one who can help. We need to go today. I think . . . I think it's a matter of life or death."

I convinced them to leave right then. Donny was always up for skipping class, so it was Ame we had to drag out by her sleeves.

I tried to explain my déjà vu lapses on the way there, but I knew I wasn't making any sense. I rambled on and on, knowing that only Amelia was taking any stock in my story.

When we reached the bungalow belonging to Madame Varnie, I couldn't get out of the car fast enough. I bounded up the steps and punched the doorbell, knowing this wasn't how it was supposed to go. Amelia was the one who should have been racing for the door, not me.

I gestured for the girls to hurry up. Somehow I knew that the person who opened the door would know how to help me. I'd never believed in psychic readings before—that was Amelia's hobby, not mine. While we waited for someone to open the door, I tried to picture what Madame Varnie might look like. Why was I so certain that someone who went by "Madame" was a male?

Since I had no expectations of what Madame Varnie looked like, I have no idea why I was so very surprised at his appearance. To say that he stunned the three of us into silence when he opened the door would be an understatement.

I suppose the first thing that stood out was his lilac turban, which matched the shapeless shift he wore. The shiny fabric formed a large beehive on his head, and in the middle of it was a glass eye the color of peacock feathers and surrounded by fake jeweled beads. It was about twenty-four inches of nonsense, but unfortunately it was not the oddest thing about him.

Madame Varnie's face was overly made up. Too much powder, too much shadow, and too much lipstick were spackled onto a face that was distinctly neither middle-aged nor female, as the costume seemed to suggest. Instead, Madame Varnie was very clearly a younger man in drag.

And I had somehow known it.

"Well, hello," he said, in a breathy, effeminate voice. Then his mouth formed a surprised O. He didn't want to let me in. I could tell. He smelled like fear.

Wait a minute . . . he smelled like fear? How would I know what fear smelled like? Did fear even smell? *It must be a tumor.* That would explain the way my brain was misfiring and that I was imagining scents for things like emotions.

We held a wordless gaze for a few moments, Madame Varnie and I. "You have to help me," I whispered.

His face somehow paled even more under the makeup, but he stepped aside and let us in. He gestured to the living room area but went into the kitchen and came back with a handful of soft drinks and a bottle of beer for himself. And no turban.

He told us to sit on the couch and he flopped onto a chair and took a swig. A pretty big one, actually.

We made hasty introductions while Donny and I sat down, but Ame stood in front of his chair, studying him. "Are you old enough to be drinking beer?"

All three of us snapped our heads to look at her.

"What?" she asked defensively.

Varnie wiped his mouth with the back of his hand, smearing his lipstick. "Sugar, we've got a few more important things to discuss than California liquor laws."

Ame crossed her arms over her chest. "That means no, you're not. How old are you anyway? It's hard to tell with all the . . ."

"Maybelline?" Donny finished for her. "Ame, focus."

"I'm nineteen," Varnie answered.

Ame leaned over and peered into his eyes like she was looking into the windows of an empty house. "There's something strange about you," she murmured.

"There's something strange about everyone, Miss Amelia," Varnie said quietly. "Look, girls . . ." When Varnie had our attention, he looked uncomfortable, like he didn't know what to do with it now that he had it.

I rubbed my temples, but it did nothing to soothe my headache. "Let me guess," I began. "*This town is changing. There's a bad juju and it's getting worse.* That's what you were going to say, weren't you?"

"How did you know that?" he asked me.

I laughed one of those derisive grown-up laughs. The ones you hear right before they say, *Who said life is fair?* or *You'll wish you hadn't been in such a hurry to grow up someday.* I finally understood why people became cynical. "For the last two days, everything has been a replay. The problem is, I don't remember my lines right—it's all off-kilter and disjointed. I need you to help me get back on track, Varnie."

"I don't think that's wise," he said.

"Please."

He shook his head.

"I know you're a part of this, Varnie. You can see through it. I think . . . I know this is going to sound crazy, but it feels like this is all fake somehow . . . manufactured." Despite Varnie's unkempt appearance, I trusted him. "Please."

"I don't know why you think I can help you. I'm just a guy who sees too much of what nobody else can see. The best thing I can do for you is to warn you to go while you still can." He tipped his beer. "That's what I'm going to do."

"Please," I pleaded.

"I'm just a coward—what do you want me for?"

I shook my head. "You're not a coward. I have a feeling you're probably the most heroic person I know."

He laughed. "Right. Look, when I first got to this town, I thought it had the most wicked cool energy of any place I'd ever been. It was the purest high for a guy like me. But it's getting murky and I'm scared. I wish I could help you, but I can't."

Amelia joined me. "It would really mean a lot to me if you could try to help my friend."

They locked eyes and I felt like I'd just intruded on a very personal moment. Something passed between them and it was palpable to both Donny and me as well. Varnie nodded and Amelia smiled.

He stood up and I joined him in the middle of the room. He exhaled loudly, as if to voice his doubts, but his eyes were kind. He took my hand, turning it over to inspect the lines of my palm.

His touch was like a cattle prod directed at my brain. We both jerked back, surprised.

"What happened?" Amelia asked, concerned.

I looked to Varnie for an answer, but he appeared shaken, like he'd seen a ghost. "I don't know. It's never been like that before. Are you sure you want to do this, Miss Theia?"

Of course I didn't want to, but I nodded my assent and held my palm up again.

He stared at it for a long moment, his emotions crossing his face in waves of anxiety. "There is something powerful protecting something it doesn't want you to see."

"Which is why I need you to help me see it, Varnie. I just *know* you have the ability to shine the light on the dark. I can't explain it, but I know you somehow."

"That happens a lot in my line of work." His lips flattened into a thin grimace and he picked up my hand again. Like flashes of lightning, grotesque and morbid images strobed in front of me until all I could see was the montage.

Goblins dancing, skeletons, mangled women sewn with dark-laced seams . . . a writhing beast on a platter, a pink-tinged smoke, a man too old to be a boy but too young to be a man, a red dress . . . my father collapsing, shadows disappearing on a wall . . . a black rose, a red dress, a top hat, a first kiss . . . people glowing, a promise, hell, heaven, falling . . . a perfect heart, an imperfect desire, a woman with black eyes . . . a machine torturing my father, an aching hunger . . . I jerked away from Varnie, the sensations still thrumming through my blood like electric jolts. None of the visions made sense, but Varnie looked shaken too.

"I'm not sure what just happened there. Usually I just pick up glimpses, but your energy packs a wallop." He ran a trembling hand through his blond hair. "Who is Haden Black, Theia?" he asked.

Haden Black. The sound of his name opened up a vein. Haden Black.

He was everything.

"I need to find him."

"I'm not sure that is a good idea," Varnie said.

I squeezed my eyes closed and bunched my fists. *Remember, Theia.*

All of this, my current situation, felt manufactured. A spell maybe? When had I started believing in spells? I just had a sense that I was dreaming awake, that reality had blurred edges and blind corners. I glimpsed a shadow moving in the corner, but when I turned it stopped moving. "I don't know how to make you all understand this—but we aren't here. Or maybe we are, but it's an alternate version of us."

I looked into their faces and knew they didn't understand. I didn't understand either. What should I do? Amelia and Donny had been uncharacteristically quiet during the whole episode. They looked spooked.

Donny cleared her throat. "I had a dream about some guy dueling with a skeleton last night. He told me his name was Haden Black."

Amelia clutched at Donny's arm. "I had the same dream! Only there were more boys there too. Gabe from your English class and some guy named Archibald."

Varnie whipped his head around. "What did you say?"

Ame wrinkled her nose cutely. "I said, I had the same dream, only there—"

"You said Archibald." He was practically accusing her.

"Yeah, and . . . ?"

He moved into her personal space warily. "I'm Archibald."

"I thought you said you were Varnie."

"Wouldn't you go by your last name if your first name was Archibald? My middle name is worse. Life seems to go much smoother if I just sign everything 'A. E. Varnie.'"

"Okay, this is all very intriguing," Donny began, but then changed her mind. "No, this is all very creepy." She pressed her lips together firmly and her jaw squared with tension. "Your name and your dress code are very interesting, but not what we need to be focused on. What should we do?"

"I think we wait," I said. I began to feel a chilling darkness deep in my bones, in my soul. Whatever was coming would find me. I had a feeling it wouldn't be long.

A note on the fridge from Muriel let me know that my father would be staying in the city that night. How convenient. I hadn't seen him since the disjointed episodes had started. Was that another indication that this reality wasn't true? My arsenal for fighting whatever was happening was pretty slim: I could play the violin and recite by heart every line said by Mr. Darcy in *Pride and Prejudice*. I was likely the most ineffectual girl to save anyone, and yet somehow I felt as if I was the one who had to save us all.

I pulled out some snacks while I concentrated on the name Haden Black. He was the key to it all. He was what was missing. My charm bracelet clinked on the plate. I held my wrist up to examine it. It seemed like I'd always worn it, but for the life of me I couldn't remember how I'd gotten it. Another strange trick my mind was playing on me.

"Hello, Pussycat."

A cold shot of fear spiked my blood. I dropped the plate and whirled to face a woman in my kitchen. I dimly heard the clatter of the plate hitting the floor under the roar of my heartbeat. The mad pounding of my pulse made me light-headed. I wanted to run, but all I could manage was a silent scream.

"Whoopsie. I didn't mean to startle you."

She traced the fingers of one hand over the countertop as she walked towards me. Her fingernails were bloodred talons. Her slinky gown was black and looked like what some women would call a slip and wear *under* their dresses. Silver serpentine cuffs in the shape of snakes coiled from both wrists to her elbows. As if they knew I'd noticed them, their forked tongues wiggled.

Her other hand held a pink gift bag with curly ribbons and tissue paper peeking out the top. The whole thing had been bathed in glitter and sparkles. She held it out to me, but I shook my head, the only part of me that wasn't paralyzed in fear. Whoever she was, she was my nightmare.

The smile that stretched across her lips filled me with more dread than a sneer would have. I had a feeling she was always most gleeful when she was at her most wretched. "My sweet little poppet, don't be rude. I've brought this a very long way just for you."

My hands shook as I reached for the sack, but I could not will myself to open it.

"Relax. It won't bite. I'm too subtle for the obvious. The suspense is just killing me. Open it."

My lower lip trembled. I had to bite the inside to keep from bursting into tears. I removed the tissue carefully. It looked like a snow globe inside the bag. Why would she give me a snow globe? I pulled it out slowly, not trusting that it wouldn't snap at me.

"Shake it."

Reluctantly, I did as she asked and held it up so I could see the scene inside. The "snow" was actually red and black hearts.

"They're rose petals. Aren't they precious?" the scary woman said.

As I peered into the heart-shaped confetti, little figurines replayed my misplaced memories in the glass with startling clarity. All of them. And now that they were there, I longed for the perfect state of ignorance once again. I remembered all the thoughts and feelings she'd stolen . . . and also the ones I didn't want. The fears and doubts came back like a runaway car on a roller coaster in my mind.

As the hearts began to settle on the bottom, a new scene played out in the globe. Tiny people representing my friends were being swarmed by some kind of hairy beasts and skeletons. The fight wasn't fair—they didn't all have weapons.

"They're in danger."

"Are they? Maybe they aren't. Maybe this is a trick, my darling. Or maybe this is a choice."

"A choice?"

She placed the globe on the countertop. "You get to choose their fate. This"—she gestured to the kitchen—"or that." She pointed to the globe.

Her words took their time sinking into my brain. "So, if I choose this, this unreality you have concocted, then they are all safe? What about Haden?"

"Ah, there's the real question. *What about Haden?* Well, you see, in this reality, you never met Haden. None of that abysmal falling in love ever happened—you're both safe."

"And my father?"

"He never fell ill." Mara pursed her lips. "I'm disappointed that he did to begin with. I really thought he'd have lasted longer. I must have been greedier than I realized."

There was a catch, of course. I just needed to figure out what it was. "Why are you offering me a do-over? I know it's not out of the goodness of your heart."

"Don't be impudent, child. I've extended an olive branch. I'd suggest you take it."

I began moving slowly away from her, trying to put the kitchen island between us. "Where is Haden really?"

"He's still home, where he belongs. Where he's always be-longed." She shrugged and we began circling the island. "He's as mopey as ever. That boy tries my patience. But he hasn't met you, you haven't met him, and the world is safe from your evil, demon ways. Why aren't you happy? It's what you wanted, after all. You haven't been able to control yourself as a demon. Everyone is in danger because of you. Here's your chance to fix everything."

All the action in the snow globe had stopped. If I could save them . . . and my father, I should. And yet I knew there was more to it, more that she wasn't revealing to me. "Does he remember me?"

"No. You never happened. This should be an easy choice. You give up Haden and you and your friends—and your father—get to live. It will all go away as if it never happened."

I closed my eyes and remembered what it felt like to fall in love. All of that would be gone. Mara would be more careful with Haden now. He would never get to live as a human. He'd either spend his life longing to be human or he'd embrace his demon heritage and hate himself for it. I'd seen firsthand how important his human relationships were to him, how much he enjoyed belonging. And did I honestly believe that he would be better off never having loved me, even though we couldn't be together?

"You're asking me to choose between loving Haden or saving my friends and my father?"

"Heavens, you're as sharp as a marble." Mara reached across the counter and grabbed my wrists roughly, her talons drawing blood, but her voice was syrupy smooth. "Yes, that is exactly what I am asking you to do. Haden is squandering all his gifts to be a worthless human like you, like his father. I want him back. He is to inherit my kingdom and if you're very lucky, he won't decide to take over your realm someday as well." Her voice became reedy with a venomous edge, no longer even resembling a human woman's voice. And, oh God, her eyes. They were windows into hell. "I will stamp out every trace of humanity in him. It will be a glorious time for Under—he's going to be the king of nightmares, Theia. I'll make sure of it."

She was the master of illusion, evil incarnate, and I knew in my heart she would never give me what she offered—absolution from what she perceived as an attack. "I don't trust you, Mara. I'm not making this choice, because it isn't a choice at all. It's not real."

She let go of me and crossed her arms. "I don't understand what he sees in you. You're worse than boring . . . you're milquetoast."

I blinked and we were no longer in my kitchen. It had been a fake reality after all. The room had one chair and nothing else but stone walls and floor and a door guarded by two of her skeleton henchmen. "Why did you put me through all of that? Why bother with all the drama and the mind games?"

"I had to see if you were ready." Shrugging, she pointed to the snow globe. "Enjoy the show."

"What show? Ready for what?"

"It's going to be very amusing. I can hardly wait."

Amusing? "You didn't answer me. Why would you go through the trouble of tricking me or making me think that I could save anyone?"

"I like games. Surely even you have figured that out by now." She cupped my jaw in her hand, a hand I knew could break my bones like twigs if she so desired. "Your human minds delight me. I enjoy poking into the crevices and unearthing your deepest, darkest fears . . . and desires. They're all the same to me." My heart stuttered as she went on. "And I know your deepest fears, my little poppet. You're afraid you'll be just like me . . . and that is one nightmare I relish fulfilling for you. You'll learn to love your work, Theia, just as I love mine. You think my blood is a curse, but you'll soon realize it's a blessing. I'm going to get you started with a front-row seat. You think you know your friends, but now you will see what they are really made of. Shake the globe, dear. Donnatella is ready for her close-up."

She left me alone, taking her henchmen with her, though I suspected they would stay on the other side of the door. I picked up the glass globe from its perch on the chair. It was my only window in the stone cell. I remembered how Haden used to watch the human world from a mirror that served as a portal, how it was his torment and pleasure at the same time. I had no doubts that what I would see in the snow globe that acted as a crystal ball would only add to my anguish, but it was the only link I had. Haden had told me at the bowling alley that the *not-knowing* was scarier than knowing. I didn't believe him then and I certainly didn't now.

I sat in the chair and took a breath to steel my nerves. I shook the globe and peered into the glass and watched all of my friends live out their personal nightmares.

up is still down

CHAPTER FIFTEEN

Donny

I've awoken surprised in other people's beds before. Not a lot, but it has happened. It's a horrible feeling.

I sat up and looked around, not comprehending anything.

Think, girl.

The last thing I remembered was . . . crap, the cabin. Mike was spewing all sorts of weird stuff about Mara, Amelia had been in some sort of stupor, and then there was a gray fog and a lot of nothing.

So where the hell was I? And where was everyone else?

Okay, start with the obvious. I was on a bed. A nice one too. Big carved pillars of dark wood were posts. I was lying on a velvety duvet in a deep red color, and I could roll over four or five times before I found the other edge of the bed. There were candles lit everywhere—on tables, in sconces—but no electric lights. I looked down at the floor; it was pretty far down there. A really plush fur, hopefully fake, served as a rug. A staircase would have been nice. Why would someone make a bed this high off the ground?

The rest of the room was as opulent as the bedding—lots of velvet- and satin-upholstered furniture by a fireplace. Hundreds of candles did a good job for lighting, but there were some really long shadows. I didn't care for the shadows. If I was in Under, which I suspected I was, since this room was similar to the one Theia had told me about, then I needed to be very wary of the shaded areas in the room. How did I get here?

I slid off the bed carefully, losing my balance as my feet hit the floor. Something was very wrong. I felt . . . changed, uncoordinated. I looked down and couldn't see my feet.

Ohmyeffinggod.

My stomach was huge. I cried out. Had I swallowed a beach ball? My shirt rode up over the roundness. I had no belly button—my innie was totally an outie now. I stared at my belly for a long time, too long. I just . . . couldn't believe it. I didn't wear the kind of clothes that could accommodate that kind of weight gain.

And then it moved. It felt like a small animal, only I felt it from inside my skin.

Ohmyeffinggod.

There was a baby.

Inside of me.

Oh crap oh crap oh crap. Just how long had I been unconscious?

I was pregnant. The thought paralyzed me. I'm a careful girl. I've had sex for the wrong reasons and I've made terrible choices, but never, never, never have I had unprotected sex. A baby is the very thing I never wanted. I never wanted to babysit them or hold them. I'd tolerated my little brother, but never actually liked him until he could play without smelling like diaper.

I'd never thought babies were cute and I pretty much believed every teen mom I saw had been hit with the stupid stick for not only getting herself in that position but keeping it besides. I'd been on the pill since I was thirteen, and nobody got near me without a condom *and* spermicide, which I carried in my purse at all times.

And now one of them lived inside of me?

Had I been in Under for so long that I slept through eight months of gestating? And then, as the thing rolled around like it was doing a somersault, my blood ran cold. What if . . . what if it wasn't a *baby* baby? Like not made the normal way, with assistance from Gabe, who so help me was going to pay for this. Unless it was some kind of demon-possession thing.

I was so not cool with birthing demon spawn.

I needed to find my friends. Hopefully, Ame had snapped out of her trance—I needed her advice in a huge way. She would know what to do, I told myself as I padded across the floor. My center of gravity was all off and I felt wobbly. And a little hungry.

I shuddered. What if it wanted me to eat raw meat or something?

I wanted to cry and scream. This was not fair. My body was

mine. I didn't want to share it and I didn't want to contemplate how I might have been violated. I never thought I'd be in a position to pray that Gabe had knocked me up, but oh, my God, if it wasn't Gabe . . .

The huge wooden door was locked and immovable. That didn't surprise me. I paced, awkwardly, trying to get used to my new shape and figure out how to get free.

There were no windows in my room, but there was a huge fireplace blazing, flanked by tall bookshelves on either side. I pulled a few books off the shelves, but none of the words made any sense, so I put them back. What had I been hoping for? *The Secret Way Out of Your Room*? Maybe a copy of *What to Expect When You're Expecting Satan's Offspring*?

Tears tried to force their way out of my eyes, but I held them back. I would not cry. I hated crying. Just because I felt helpless didn't mean I was. I just needed to find Amelia. She would know what to do.

There was a little statue of a pregnant-looking woman on the shelf. I picked it up, thinking that, if nothing else, I could use it to hit someone in the head if they came in.

As soon as I held it up for further inspection, the bookshelf began to swivel. I jumped back as the shelves disappeared and a skeleton sitting against a stone wall took their place.

I screamed.

It screamed back.

I screamed some more, holding my weapon threateningly. Because I could totally kill something already dead, right?

It wasn't made completely of bones like the skeleton hanging out in the biology lab. That would have been better. Way less creepy. Instead, it had a beefy, normal body, but a skeleton head. No eyes, no skin, no hair . . . just white bone.

Still, even with no tongue or throat or lips, it was able to scream like *I* was the abomination. It got up, and I whimpered and backed away. It didn't come at me, just stared at my belly. I put one hand over the baby protectively.

Seriously? I was protecting it?

Yes, yes, I guess I was. "Don't come near me!" I shouted. *Please wake up, Donny. This is a horrible dream.* "Wherever you just came from, go back."

It shook its head, rattling its jaw, and pointed at my huge middle. "Donny, what the fuck?" the thing asked.

It felt like someone slammed an icicle into my heart. The *thing* had Gabe's voice. My Gabe's voice.

"Where is he?" I screamed, completely losing it. "What have you done with my boyfriend?" Did it eat him?

It tightened its fists the way Gabe sometimes does when he wants to throttle me. And then it ran its normal human hand over its bony head the way Gabe does when he ruffles his hair. "Shit," he said.

I dropped the statue and stumbled backwards a few steps. I wanted to curl into a ball on the floor but there was no floor. The bottom of my world had fallen out.

That thing had Gabe's voice, it wore his clothes, it mimicked his mannerisms to perfection, and it was clearly upset about my surprise pregnancy and its own lack of sandy brown, perfectly tousled locks of hair.

"No," I said, deciding that this was just too much. Maybe it was a trick.

"Donny, I . . . You . . . What the hell?"

"Are you really him?" I asked softly, looking at the thing. He was terrifying. This couldn't be happening. Please let this be a dream. Was he a demon too? All three of us fell for monsters? Maybe all men were. That would explain a lot.

"It's me. I swear," he said.

"How can I be sure? Tell me something only you would know."

There went his hands to his hair again. And when that frustrated him, he did the fist thing. So far, he was very convincing. "You want trivia right now?"

"Yes!" Why did he always make things so difficult? Add another check to the "He's probably Gabe" list.

"Like what?"

I had to stop looking at his head. "I don't know. What tattoo do I have on my left boob?"

"I thought you said to tell you something only I would know."

I glared at him, right at his empty eye sockets.

"Fine. You have a secret picture of us in your compact thing."

I tried to put my hand on my hip, but it was all . . . not my usual hip. I had the graceful lines of a rhinoceros; there was no way to pull off my usual haughty stance. "I so do not keep your picture in my makeup compact. It's a mirror, genius."

"Yes, you do. I saw it. It's not the one you use all the time;

it's the brown one in the bottom of your purse. The picture is from the night we had a picnic at the beach, but it rained so we ate in the car. I teased you about the S Club 7 CD you still had in your glove box, and you sang one of the songs to me really badly. Then we took pictures with your cell phone. One of them is in that mirror thing."

All I could do was blink at him.

"Remember the time you told me I had lettuce in my teeth and to grab a mirror from your purse? I grabbed the wrong mirror first."

My heart seized a little. He'd never said a word.

Clearly, the thing to do here would be to pass out, but it was a luxury I couldn't afford. I had to deal.

The fight had gone out of me, though. It was a lot easier to be tough when Ame and Theia had my back. My aching back. I lowered myself onto the couch, holding the small of my back like I'd been practicing being pregnant for a long time.

"Are you okay?" His hollow eyes were trained on my stomach.

"No," I said. "Are you?"

"How bad do I look?" he asked.

I so didn't want to tell him. "What happened to you?"

He shrugged his human shoulders. "I dunno. I woke up like this. I don't remember anything. You?"

"I woke up like this too."

He sat in a chair across from me. I stared at his feet. The rest of him was too much to contemplate.

"We need to get out of here," he said finally. Neither one of us wanted to discuss my pregnancy or his . . . condition.

"I couldn't find a way out," I said. "Are you a demon like Haden or something?"

"What? No. I'm just me."

"Gabe, you don't have a face."

"Right. I'm pretty sure I'm not a demon, though." He paused. "What about . . . ?"

He'd gestured at my large tummy. The baby was settling down, not rolling around so much. I wondered if it was sleeping or got more active when I was walking around. I purposely didn't know much about being pregnant. Did babies sleep in there? What else was there to do?

Gabe was still waiting for an answer. I shrugged. "I just don't know. Honestly. I'm trying not to think about it too much because I will probably go insane if I do."

"Were you late? When we were at the cabin and stuff, before we came here, were you late?"

It was tempting to answer with a joke. I knew what he meant, though. I shook my head. "Not that I know of."

"Would you have told me if you were?"

His words hung on the air like the accusation had nowhere to go except be stuck between us.

I shook my head again. "Probably not."

"Damn it, Donny. Why can't you share stuff with me? Am I so awful?" Gabe held up one hand. "Obviously, right now I am. But before I turned into Skeletor."

"What's a skeletor?"

"He was He-Man's archnemesis . . . but that's not the point. I'm your boyfriend and I've tried to be a really great one. Why can't you ever rely on me? If you were pregnant, you should feel like you can come to me."

"This conversation is stupid," I said. Damn those tears trying to make a break for it. "If I was pregnant before we got here, I didn't know it, so there is no point to be made. Maybe I would have told you—I don't know. But *what if* and *maybe* aren't helping us get out of here."

"Do you think it's mine?" My eyes must have widened because he quickly covered. "I know you didn't cheat on me. I'm not asking if it's another guy's kid . . . you know what I mean. Do you think . . . ?"

"Do I think this baby is human? I don't know that either." I touched my stomach with one finger. I still had a hard time believing what I was seeing was true. "I'm very conflicted. On one hand, I don't want to be pregnant. On the other, I feel . . . I don't know . . . responsible? To keep it safe, ya know? It seems pretty innocent."

"It sounds like you mean you're feeling maternal."

I scrunched my nose up. "God, I guess you're right. I feel kind of maternal."

I tried the word on and risked a look at his face. God, I missed his eyes. They were always so warm. "Do you feel . . . fathery?"

"I'm not sure. I feel . . . worried about you. Like I need to take care of you more than usual. But I'm not sure I feel anything about the . . ."

"Baby. It's called a baby." Oh, fabulous, now I was defending its honor. "Look, it doesn't matter anyway. It's not like I expect you to go to childbirth classes or anything."

"You're awfully snappy," he said. I couldn't disagree with

him, but I certainly wasn't about to *agree* either. "And why can't you expect me to go to childbirth classes with you? Maybe part of the problem is that you never expect anything from me."

"Part of what problem? The problems I'm looking at right now have nothing to do with what I count on you or don't count on you for. We're trapped in a hell dimension. I'm near the end of gestating a baby of unknown origins, and you have turned into a feature creature of some kind. Childbirth classes are a zillion miles from where we are."

"Maybe, but like you said. Here we are . . . trapped. We're in hell, together, and the worst things that can happen to us . . . have." He held out his arms. "I'm still here, though, Donny." He pointed to my stomach. "Whether that is my responsibility or not, I'm still here."

"Where else are you going to go?" Okay, yes, I was being churlish.

But what if this was my life now? What if we were stuck in hell forever and I had to raise this baby with Gabe the skeleton man? What if it came out like some kind of monster too? I didn't know if I could love a normal baby, but somehow I might have to love some kind of demon? It could come out with scales or vampire fangs. Would Gabe still be around then? Could I stand to look at him every day for eternity the way he was now?

I'm not as shallow as the sneetches, but this was extreme. I like boys a lot. I like the good-looking ones best of all. Gabe was the hottest guy I'd ever been with. I was extremely attracted to him, which is why I put up with all the things I'd never wanted before to be with him.

I heard a little voice inside me. *Liar.*

Okay, maybe there was more than physical attraction, but whatever was left would have to be really strong to overcome the fact that he had no face.

"Donny." His voice lowered to that warm, rich tone that always curled my toes. "Please, this one time. Can you need me just a little this one time?"

I looked at him. Hard. It was possible that we were going to die. Why couldn't I let my guard down? Okay, so he was really hideous-looking, but he never let me down. No matter how hard I'd pushed him, Gabe stayed.

He'd been a looker, but it was probably past time that I realized he was even better-looking on the inside than he had been on the outside.

"I do need you," I whispered. And then I added, "Bone-head."

Gabe took a deep breath. "If I come over there, are you going to let me be nice to you?"

I nodded. Quickly. "That would be appreciated."

He moved to the couch and sat next to me, so I rested my head against his chest. It was easier this way, to not look at where his face used to be. God, I missed his face like, whoa. We stayed quiet for a long time. But then I decided I needed to know what had happened to him.

Gabe tensed when I asked. "I woke up in a dungeon. I was surrounded by skeletons and corpses and even though my cell was unlocked, there was no way out of it until you activated that secret passageway into your room.

"I don't know what happened to me before I woke up. I'm kind of glad about that, I think."

He stopped talking but the way he breathed suggested he was working up to continuing, so I didn't butt in. Finally, after several long seconds, he asked me how ugly he was.

"You look like . . . an X-ray of you. That's all." I tried to say it brightly. I'm pretty sure I failed. "This is your worst nightmare, isn't it? Waking up without your perfect hair?"

He chuffed out a laugh. "I'm less concerned with my hair than most people think. But yeah, waking up hideous is horrible. Does that make me shallow?"

"No. I think waking up a skeleton would freak anybody out."

"Donny, I don't know who I am if I'm not good-looking. That's probably stupid, but that's how I feel. If we get out of here alive, I can't go back like this, Donny, I just can't."

His heartbeat sped up beneath my ear. "We'll burn that bridge when we get there. Rest assured, I'm not going back pregnant either. God, Gabe. I swore this would never happen to me. Like ever. I know everyone at that damn school is going to think it's no big surprise. So the class slut got knocked up—"

Gabe covered my mouth gently. "Don't talk about my girlfriend like that. You're not a slut. That's not what I see when I look at you."

I had to shift because not only was the conversation making me uncomfortable, but the baby was doing something to my internal organs. "What do you see?"

"Okay, but if I get mushy, you can't get mad because you're the one who asked."

I poked him in the ribs. "Why do you stick by me when I know all your friends tell you I'm easy?"

"First of all, anyone who makes the mistake of calling you names is not a *friend* of mine. Second, you are the opposite of easy. You're the most challenging person I know. I'm a guy, and not a very complicated one, but even I can see that you use your hotness like a suit of armor. You let very few people see what you look like under the front you paste on for the world. I want to be one of those people more than I can remember wanting anything."

Little earthquakes shook the walls around my heart. There was nothing to hold on to while I rode out the aftershocks, one after the other as each moment of my time with Gabe replayed all the ways he'd become indispensable. As the wall crumbled, I realized that it hadn't been keeping my heart safe from Gabe after all. He was already on the other side of it.

"So is waking up pregnant your worst nightmare?" Gabe asked, politely ignoring that I hadn't responded to his eloquent laying of his heart at my feet.

"God, yes," I answered. Knowing I needed to grow up and be honest, I squeezed my eyes closed and continued. "Also, I don't know why I'm such a bitch. I know you have been nothing but nice to me. I realize that you have been cutting yourself off from the sneetches at an alarming rate in order to stay with me. I know it bugs you that I don't let you say mushy things to me like a normal girl would. I just— Why do you put up with me?"

"I'm not gonna lie. There are times that I wished I'd chosen a different girlfriend. Somebody sweeter, less complicated. A nice girl who enjoys the same things I do, doesn't mind my friends, and is maybe even proud that I'm her boyfriend." He stroked his hands through my hair.

"Dream on, dude."

He chuckled. "This fantasy girlfriend also wouldn't be friends with demons, or half-demons, and our dates would not end with me not knowing where the hell she was when I woke up lying on a curiously damp dungeon floor surrounded by cadavers in various states of decomposition.

"But no. I had to choose you, a girl who can't even have a normal girl name, a girl who would prefer it if we only met up when it was time to have sex and then I left her alone the rest of the time, a girl who tries to drive me into jealous rages whenever I *can* convince her to go out in public with me. It's like you choose your clothes with the express goal of effing with my head every single day."

"I really do. I love it when you think I'm dressed totally inappropriately and you want to be mad but can't because all you think about is getting me back into that janitor's closet. So, again, I ask . . . why are you still even here?"

"You're the best thing that ever happened to me." He said it so simply, so matter-of-factly, that for the first time ever, I believed that maybe I really was.

I never knew what I had to offer Gabe, other than the obvious. All the times I got mad at Amelia or Theia for their low-self-esteem issues, and I'd been packing around the same ones wrapped in different paper.

"I don't want to be pregnant and I don't want you to be Skeletinator or whatever."

"Skeletor," Gabe said, correcting me.

"Whatevs. But I do want you to always think I'm the best thing that ever happened to you. And I hope you never give up on me. I will try really hard to be less difficult and maybe occasionally I will surprise you with being nice."

"That's all a guy can ask for."

A noise outside the door sent every hair on my body straight up. By the time I got my ungainly ass out of the chair, Gabe was already across the room. He had a fire poker in his hand. Why hadn't I thought of grabbing a fire poker earlier? I was so not cut out for scary castle living.

"Stand back from the door!" It was Varnie's voice.

Gabe and I exchanged relieved glances. Varnie was hitting the door from the other side, probably trying to smash the lock. As the wood splintered and he made progress, I lost my marbles again.

Gabe noticed the look on my face right away. "What?" he asked.

"I don't want him to see me like this." I panicked.

"Hey." His voice was smooth. Gabe had a way of laying on the butter that always chilled me down when I got worked up. "It's going to be okay. Varnie will help us figure out what to do, right?"

I nodded, but tried to tug my top down over my huge belly. Gabe pulled off his hoodie, his T-shirt below riding up with the action. His abs were still perfect, his skin still that healthy shade of bronze. While his face was covered with the shirt, I could imagine him the same. But once it was off, the sight of his skeleton head cut me all over again.

He handed me his shirt and I sank into it, pulling it over my plus-one gratefully. "I'm going to stretch out your shirt."

Even a skeleton head can portray an eye roll. "I don't care about the shirt."

I didn't care either if he cared, actually. He wasn't getting it back. The familiar scent of him soothed me—his soap, his cologne, and something that didn't come in a bottle or bar, something that was unique to Gabe. I used to chalk it up to pheromones, but I suspect it was more than that.

And then the door burst open. Varnie rushed in and stopped in horror at Gabe. "Duck me!"

"It's okay," I said, stepping in front of Gabe. "The bonehead is my boyfriend."

Varnie swung his head to look at me and his jaw dropped at the sight of my rounded stomach.

"I'd rather not talk about it," I said. "But I suppose that is way too much to ask for right now. Let's get out of here first and then we can figure out the whole Renesmee thing I've got going on."

Varnie whistled. "How long have we been down here?" He shook his head. "Wow."

"Where's Ame?" I asked him.

"Follow me," he replied, and we tried to keep up with him.

He was moving pretty fast through the corridor. I tried not to take in too much of the scenery. It was damp and chilly, like cold sweat. Varnie was a man on a mission, though, and I didn't blame him. Nobody wanted to think of Amelia all by herself in a place like this. Especially if she was still being all lights-are-on-but-no-one-is-home.

It was hard to keep up with my new body, and Gabe hung back with me, not willing to chance a separation. Thank God.

"Is it too much to ask that we look for a kitchen? I'm starving."

The boys halted and stared at my baby bump.

"You guys need to stop. Am I the first pregnant woman you've ever seen or something?" I rubbed my belly. "I would sell my soul for a grilled cheese sandwich right now."

Gabe clapped a hand over my mouth. "Are you crazy? Don't even joke like that around here."

Varnie looked sad for a moment and then shook his head. "We need to keep moving."

We followed him around a corner, but it was like he poofed.

"Varn?" I whispered. "Varnie?"

"Where could he have gone?" Gabe asked.

I didn't like the prickles his sudden absence left behind. "Let's just hang out here until he doubles back when he realizes he's lost us."

Gabe nodded but we both wondered if and when that was going to happen.

CHAPTER SIXTEEN

◈

Amelia

I know everyone assumed that just because I couldn't respond from my catatonic state I was also unaware of what had been going on around me.

Man, that would have been way better. Trust me.

It's really claustrophobic to be trapped in your own head, unable to talk or control your body. Unable to help or explain to your friends what you know is happening and ways to stop it.

I know Theia totally blamed herself for all this. She believed that we should have left her in Under to begin with. That all of our problems would have been gone and we would have been safe from Mara.

Theia was very, very wrong.

I was still trapped, though now I was sitting in a hard wooden chair in a room that I didn't recognize. I wasn't in the cabin and I was alone. The wall in front of me was stone. Not brick but cold, gray stone, and it bled. The wall pulsed like wounded skin under the rivulets of red.

That's all I could see because it was all that was directly in front of me and I had no control over my eyes. They stared straight ahead and I blinked occasionally, though not when I tried. I couldn't even control my own eyelids. This was totally a mega-suck.

I'd never been in a castle before, but I guessed that's where I was now—Mara's castle in Under. I'd have shivered if I could. She was bad enough when she was on our home field; I hated the thought that I was on hers now.

And then I felt Varnie. He wasn't in the room with me, but he was near. Maybe not physically, but awareness of him blew around me like a breeze. His name, his face, his heart—the things I counted on every day swished through my head and around my senses. But something was off.

I wanted to push through, find that bond, hold on to it. I thought that I probably could. But I hesitated.

Which I'm not good at, by the way, hesitating.

If I had learned that skill—that one that makes you think before you leap—it's possible that none of us would have been in this situation to begin with. No one but me knew that *I* was the reason Mara was in our lives. Me. Not Theia. I realized that the moment I saw who Mara was at the bowling alley—the moment I recognized her.

Somehow I had to find a way to make it right again.

So before I reached through the veil to find Varnie, I hesitated to think. Was that what I really wanted? Was it for the best? If he was in trouble, would I distract him? Would he then be too worried about me to take care of himself? He made a big show of being a coward, but he wasn't. Not really. Varnie was there every time I turned. If he had been my partner in the trust-building exercises we had in contemporary issues class last week, I wouldn't have fallen on my butt during the fall-back-and-your-classmate-will-catch-you segment.

Varnie would always catch me.

Mike Matheny wouldn't even realize I was falling. I knew that. I'd always known that.

I'd heard Theia in the cabin when she said she saw something ugly connecting the two of us and I knew exactly what that was now, even if Mike didn't. Part of me really wanted to strengthen that connection, but that would have been a mistake. No matter how much I wanted him to love me, he didn't. And now I knew why I couldn't let go.

The thing that connected me to Mike wouldn't let me. The vile magic that hugged my heart like a noose pulsed and throbbed and tied me to him forever.

Amelia.

Varnie was looking for me. I sensed him stronger than ever.

I stilled the freak-out parts of my brain that were going nuts because I was essentially trapped in a box of my own body and reached out to his voice through the bond we'd made metaphysically the past few months.

Varnie?

When I heard nothing, I shouted his name in my head

again, but I realized I was not the only one shouting. Disembodied voices were screaming and moaning all around us. There was whimpering too, but I think that was me.

The anguish the voices projected was awful. What had happened to them all? I was frightened, but I was also angry. They were evidence of Mara's appetite for destruction. They were lost, angry, sad, humiliated—and they were all trapped here. Just like me. Just like Varnie.

I centered myself, like Varnie had taught me to do, and let the sounds wash over me, trying to figure out where they were coming from and what was going on.

Through the din, I heard his voice, strong and true. *"The beach, Miss Amelia."*

Our favorite visualization place.

I had to open all my senses, which wasn't easy because I was totally freaking out. I visualized myself sitting cross-legged on a sandy beach, focusing on the briny smells, the sound of the surf and the gulls, the texture of the sand. And then I concentrated on Varnie. His shaggy blond hair, his sun-kissed nose, the way he made me laugh. For a brief second he was there, in front of me, and then he was gone again.

The picture in my mind kept shorting out, the way the television loses the satellite signal at my house whenever someone uses the microwave. I focused harder. I felt him hovering, then disappearing. The next time he reappeared in front of me, I grabbed him, pulling him towards me with all my strength. I wouldn't let go.

I. Would. Not. Let. Go.

Varnie began dissipating again, so I grappled at him more, harder.

Stay with me, damn it!

We tumbled backwards on the sand, Varnie landing on top of me. He tried to ease up a bit, since I was carrying all his weight, but I was terrified he would disappear, so I clutched him tighter.

"Miss Amelia," he said, his face less than an inch from mine. "Did you just swear?"

Without thought, I scrunched my hands into his sunbleached hair and removed that last inch between us with a kiss I didn't know I had in me.

Varnie responded instantly. In a distant part of my thought process, I'm sure I understood that this wasn't real. We weren't really on a beach. We weren't even really together.

I poured everything I had ever felt, *ever*, into that kiss. My fears, my joy, my excitement, my dread—he would know what to do with them all. And he did. He took them like they were the first drink of water after crossing a desert.

And then suddenly we stopped kissing and stared at each other.

Hello, awkward moment.

I felt guilty because I knew my heart didn't belong to me. It belonged to Mike, and even though I finally understood that it was a lie, I couldn't stop the wrongness from creeping in. As for Varnie, he probably wondered why the hell he was kissing some high school kid.

"Are you okay?" he asked finally, after years and years of uncomfortable silence.

I nodded, aware of all the distance that was so not between our bodies at that very moment.

"Am I hurting you?"

I shook my head.

"Good," he said. But he didn't move. His eyes were so intense. He didn't seem like his usual humble, shy dude. He seemed like a guy who ate his Wheaties, saw the finish line, and wasn't going to let anything get in his way.

That was so hot.

I blinked hard, trying to clear the jumble of thoughts I wasn't used to having. This wasn't right. Varnie wasn't Mike. And then I tried to rethink that as well, because I knew one of those thoughts didn't matter. I just didn't know which one. Finally I gave up. I couldn't do this on my own anymore.

"I have to tell you something." My voice sounded very grave. I didn't like feeling all serious and stuff. It wasn't me.

"Okay," he said amiably, and then he began kissing me again.

I never thought about kissing anyone who wasn't Mike before. I think I'd just become accustomed to the fact that I might never have my first kiss because, well, Mike didn't know I was alive and I would never give my heart, or my lips, to someone who wasn't him. I wished I'd thought to wonder why I didn't think it was strange that I'd let that happen—that I'd let myself be dismissed and write off love.

I know my friends thought it was weird. After the first year of my "harmless crush" they'd tried getting me interested in other guys. It was like most of my brain agreed with them but there was this voice inside my brain that said, "Under no circumstances." My heart was available only to Mike Matheny and that's all there was to it.

And the only person I could blame for my stupidity was myself.

So as I kissed Varnie on the beach like in a scene from some cheesy movie (without the surf splashing over us), I felt equal parts amazement and guilt. The voice was screaming at me to stop. The rest of me felt like I'd been waiting for this moment my whole life.

Maybe we could stay like this forever. Maybe whatever happened to our bodies in Under didn't matter now.

He stopped kissing me, his eyes dimming in intensity and changing to concern. "Miss Amelia, you're crying."

"I am?"

Varnie wiped a tear with a careful swipe. "I have to admit it's a first. I've never made a girl cry by kissing her before."

"It's not you, it's—"

Something about his eyes made me shut up. He pushed off of me and I missed him so much I thought I would break into a million pieces.

I sat up and ran my fingers through my sandy, clumped hair. "Varnie, you don't understand—"

"I'd rather we not have the 'It's not you, it's me' conversation right now. We can save the demoralizing for a different day maybe. What are you doing Thursday?"

He joked, but he was wounded. I'd probably been hurting him for months. That was a shame. I'd spent my life being the girl who looked out for people, who took care of their feelings, and all the while I'd been stomping his heart into the ground without even thinking about it.

"You need to listen." I scooted closer to him, but he returned his gaze to the water, shutting me out, ignoring my tentative touch on his arm. "It really is *me*. You're a great guy—"

"Amelia." He growled.

"Just listen. When I was a freshman, Mike Matheny . . . Don't you start tuning me out, Archibald Egnatius Varnie— you need to listen."

He stared at me now, with wide-open eyes. "How did you figure out my whole name?"

I groaned. "I looked through your wallet one day when you went to the bathroom."

"You looked through my wallet?"

"Can we focus for a minute?" I rubbed the sand from my palms onto my pants. "So, I thought Mike was cute. I had a little crush and I was just starting to get into the metaphysical. And I was thirteen. It was kind of a bad combination. Sort of the perfect storm of uncontrolled feelings meeting uncontrollable forces."

His brow furrowed. "What . . . you did a spell?"

"Sort of." I couldn't look at him. I was so ashamed.

"Miss Amelia, lots of girls do love spells who know nothing about magic. It's a layperson's playground. They're simple charms but they don't carry real weight. It's like playing a harmless game. Don't be too hard on yourself."

"It's not such a harmless game when you live in Serendipity Falls and accidentally summon someone." I snuck a peek at him through my hair. "I didn't know who she was until I saw her again the night at the bowling alley."

A slow wave of understanding passed over his face. "You summoned Mara?" He exploded from a sitting position into full-on angry pacing, kicking up sand as he went. "I can't believe this. How could you not tell anyone?"

I covered my face with my hands. "I didn't know. Everything happened so fast at the bowling alley and then when I realized where I knew her from—well, then it was too late. I've been trying to figure it out, but it wasn't until Theia saw the . . . intestinal thing between me and Mike that I put it all together."

"Enlighten me."

"Could you sit, please? You're making me nervous." He glared at me again, but took a seat. "Okay, so I was thirteen and crushing on the new guy. I Googled some love spells and put out some serious mojo but nothing seemed to happen. Then one night I woke up and Mara—who I didn't know was an evil demon at the time, thank you very much—was in my room. She was wearing a pretty dress and was all glowy and she told me she could bind me to Mike forever."

Varnie jumped up again. "And you let her?"

"I thought she was some kind of angel," I protested. "I didn't understand what she was offering. I was *thirteen*. Forever is a different concept when you're thirteen." I kicked at the sand. "I thought I was being offered the fairy tale, so she did a spell, took a hank of my hair, and was gone." God, if I could take the night back. "Obviously, Mike didn't wake up in love with me. I chalked it up to a very strange dream."

"But you never got over him?"

I shook my head. "I'm still not, Varnie. That's what I'm trying to say. Logically, I know that what I feel for Mike isn't real. It's manufactured. She bound me to him, but not him to me. But my heart . . . my heart doesn't understand the difference." I got brave and looked at Varnie, really looked at him. "My heart isn't free."

He reached for my hand and gripped it firmly, possessively. "It certainly doesn't belong to Mike Matheny, I can promise you that." He forced me to look at him, not letting my gaze retreat.

Even knowing that I was bespelled to love Mike didn't change the fact that I *did* love him. "You understand, don't you? I brought Mara here. It's my fault she's obsessed with us. I summoned her, unintentionally, but I did it."

"You can't blame yourself for Mara's appearance four years ago or now. Like you said, you didn't know what she was. She's evil. You can't be held accountable for her actions." He pulled me up, and we stood facing each other. Holding both my hands, he closed his eyes. "It's time to unbespell you."

"You can do that?"

"I'm certainly going to try."

I should want this. I should want Varnie to help me bludgeon the ball and chain that had kept me from moving on for four years. But I didn't. I wanted to clutch the endless longing I had for Mike like a security blanket. I began to tremble. "I can't do this." I didn't want to stop loving Mike. It was all I knew.

"Amelia, that is fear talking."

"I don't care." I wrenched my hands out of Varnie's grip.

"You don't know him like I do. You don't understand." Even as I said the words, I was shouting from within, *Don't listen to me, Varnie.*

I was irrationally angry. It was the spell talking, I'm sure. It was ripping me to shreds inside. God, when I had seen Mike on the ground, unconscious, my whole psyche shut down. The spell was strong. Stronger than me.

"You can still love him."

I met him with a startled gaze. "What?"

"You can still love Mike." Varnie circled me slowly, like he was afraid I was going to bolt. Then I realized he was actually toeing a circle in the sand. Our circles have power. "I'm not asking you to change what you feel in your heart."

My eyes narrowed into suspicious slits. "I don't believe you." I followed his movements from inside the circle. "You want me for yourself." I slapped my forehead. "Oh God, Varnie. I'm sorry. I don't even know why I said that. It's like there are two people fighting for control of who I am right now."

Varnie stepped into the circle and palmed my shoulders. "There now, hush. It's the magic. It's trying to protect itself. That's probably what's got you catatonic too. Just relax and look at me."

I inhaled shallow breaths that did the opposite of relaxing me.

"I swear, Amelia. You don't have to give him up. You can love Mike Matheny." He paused, his lips thinning as he tightened his jaw and said the words he didn't want to say. "You can love him until the day you die, if you want. We just need to get the dark magic out, okay?"

I nodded. Justifying it. He was right. I could still love Mike. "Okay, I'm ready." And then the panic set in again.

Varnie held my arms firmly, his eyes closed. He would use a different sense to look inside of me. "Let me see it. Let me see the spell."

I twisted in his grasp, but he didn't loosen or relax his hold. I could feel something burn inside. Varnie was using his psychic light to find the darkness coiled deep in my heart like a cancer. It burned hotter, like a hot knife in slick butter. He was strong but I was stronger. I could push him out. I could . . .

I closed my eyes, and I saw it too. It was so ugly, the dark magic. God, that had been inside me all this time? It looked like putrid flesh decomposing into . . . jelly. I gagged. That thing had been living in me for years. "Get it out, get it out, get it out!"

"Easy, Miss Amelia. I can't get it if you don't relax."

Breathing had never been so difficult.

"Open your eyes for a second," he told me.

I focused on him. Waiting.

"You have to trust me," he said finally, when he was sure I was paying attention.

"I do."

"No . . . I mean really, really trust me."

"I do," I repeated. "Wait, why?"

"Do you understand that I care about you?"

"Yes. Varnie, what is going on?"

"Do you know that I would never do anything to hurt you?"

"You're freaking me out here," I answered. Panic began

churning in my stomach like a shaken can of Coke freshly opened.

Varnie rested his forehead on mine. "The thing, Mara's spell, has entwined with your own energy. I think that's part of the reason you've become so strong in magic so quickly, why you're so intuitive. It's going to hurt you a lot to separate the two, and you might not have the same . . . strength." He took a deep breath. "I have to tear you apart to put you back together again."

I could feel the darkness slithering inside me. I'd enjoyed the magical intuition it had given me. I liked being special, seeing things nobody else could see, controlling elements, being strong. But it was wrong, evil. "Get it out. I trust you."

I think it would have hurt less if he had been ripping out my actual organs instead of the foul binding Mara had implanted in me. I felt things being tugged loose that I didn't want to lose—faith, hope, dreams. They were all seamed together with ugly lies and manipulation and it was as if he reached into me with a hot poker and singed the good with the bad. I was losing more than Mike. I was losing me.

"Don't give up, sweetheart," Varnie said as I jerked in pain and cried out. "Remember, I promised to put you back together too, as soon as the hard part is over."

I whimpered and lost control of my legs, falling into Varnie. I was a rag doll. No substance, no nothing . . . but then the pain ebbed and something else replaced the gaps inside me. Something pure and white. I clung to Varnie, letting him do all the work.

I began to feel better . . . but less. Less open, less aware, less me.

Varnie let me down easily to the sand again. He kept murmuring. Nonsense words. They comforted me, though. He sat behind me, pulling my back to his chest. The esoteric Amelia began putting herself back together inside me wearily. I think the only reason I was centered enough to stay in the visualization was because of Varnie.

We stayed like that for a long time.

Then I opened my eyes, and I was back.

"I've become the girl who had to be rescued by the boy," I lamented, a little disgusted with myself. Some savvy divinator I was, right? Haunted by evil for four years while I ran around yammering about the healing power of crystals.

"I got to be the white knight. I'm pretty stoked about it actually. How do you feel?"

"Shaky, sick, embarrassed." I looked deep inside myself. "Free."

"I love you, Amelia. I'm sorry I waited to tell you until it was too late."

His declaration surprised me. Too late? "Varnie . . . I—"

"It wouldn't have mattered if I had told you before now, when you were still in that thrall with Mike, but it just seems a colossal shame that all that time is wasted." He rested his chin on my shoulder. "I'm really, really sorry."

"Varnie, what are you talking about?"

Varnie didn't answer my question, but continued talking as if I hadn't asked. "Running away has always been what I do best. But I didn't run this time, did I?" His voice seemed sad . . . or maybe resigned. "Staying on the go, that's what kept me alive those years when I had no one to count on."

"Why did you have to run?"

He took a deep breath, coming back to the conversation and not whatever was going on inside his head. "Sometimes the things I see in my visions can see me back. And they don't appreciate being noticed. And then there are the medical professionals with their pills and syringes and fancy jackets with the arms in the back. They poked and prodded and overmedicated me and *still* my visions came. It's a hell of a lot easier to outrun a pissed-off creature of the night when you're not doped up on clozapine, so I've learned to keep moving and keep away from white coats."

He never talked about his life before we met him. I couldn't imagine what it would be like to have his visions and no support system. "You didn't run this time," I said, encouraging him the best I could. "What changed? What made you stay in Serendipity Falls?"

He cleared his throat. "My biggest fear used to be that my psychic talent would get me killed. But the first time I was the recipient of one of your world-famous smoosh hugs, my biggest fear was that I would let you down. That when you needed me, I would abandon you or not be able to help you."

I turned so I could see him. I'd never noticed that his nose was crooked before. Just a little, like maybe he'd broken it once. It made me want to kiss it. "You've never let me down."

"When you were in my arms, in the cabin, you felt so small. You were so gone . . . vacant. I swore I would do anything to bring you back. And it's time to go back now, sweetheart." He stared at me like he was memorizing my face. He picked up one lock of my hair and smiled. "Pink."

I didn't want to leave the beach, but he was right. It was time to go find our friends and get out of Under. "I'm ready whenever you are."

Something passed through Varnie's eyes, and even though he was smiling there was an unbearable sadness. My palms turned icy cold. Something was terribly, terribly wrong. I brought my hands to his cheeks, felt the scruffiness there. I needed the physical connection because something between us was fading even as we sat in the sand. "What?" I asked on a shaky breath.

He wrapped his warm hands around my wrists. "You need to know what you'll be seeing when you wake up."

My eyes began to burn with forming tears. "Whatever you're about to say, I don't want to hear."

"Gabe and Donny are just about to your cell. You won't be alone for long." His Adam's apple bobbed. "There is blood."

"The wall? I saw it in front of my chair."

Varnie closed his eyes. "Not the wall. Amelia, there was a struggle behind your chair. You weren't awake, not even in your catatonic state, when we first got to Under. There was a creature, a . . . troll, for lack of a better word. He was going to hurt you. I had to fight with him."

My brain raced to catch up with what I somehow already knew in my heart. I let myself live in denial a little longer. "You killed him?"

"Yes," he whispered. "Amelia . . ."

"No!" No. If he didn't say it, whatever came next wouldn't be true.

"I couldn't let him get you. He wanted to hurt you. I

couldn't let him . . . but . . . he had a weapon, a sword. He stabbed me. Amelia, I killed him, but he killed me—"

I sobbed. "No! No, you're just wounded maybe. We need to go back in there and stop the bleeding. I can maybe heal you—"

"It didn't hurt for very long. I was so full of adrenaline that I barely registered that I was stabbed until he was dead and then things got hazy. There really is a light, sweetheart, and it's beautiful. But I couldn't leave you, not until you woke up."

Waves of cold washed over me. Over and over, drowning me in disbelief and denial. "Then we'll stay here."

"Amelia."

"I can't go back there knowing you're gone. I just want to stay with you. Please, Varnie. Let's just stay here at our beach."

"We can't stay here. You need to go back and live a big, full life. You're free of that spell now, and our friends need you." He kissed my hands, tears spiked on his lashes. "I need you to keep going, keep living. I need to be able to take the next step and know that I didn't let you down when you needed me most, Amelia." He kissed my lips. A sound, hard kiss that tasted like good-bye. "You have to go back now."

"I can't leave you."

"I'll always be with you."

We both watched the tracks of each other's tears as they rolled down our cheeks. "We didn't get to be together. We didn't get our chance. I'm too selfish to let you go."

It wasn't fair. He sacrificed everything for me and he didn't get a shot at happiness? I believed in karma and a universe that provided and could be trusted. This was all wrong. It just couldn't happen.

"I wouldn't change a second of it. I would fall on a thousand swords to keep you safe, but, sweetheart, you have to be strong for both of us now. You're still in danger and I can't protect you out there. I barely had enough energy to show Gabe and Donny how to find you."

If I died, his act of bravery would be in vain. That's what he was saying. He needed me to honor his life by living mine.

"I understand."

Most people don't get a long good-bye. Maybe it was better that way. There was so much pressure to say the things that had never been said. To hold on to every second. I would miss his friendship, his mentoring. He'd taught me so much. And he'd saved me—not just from a monster but by plucking out the darkness from inside me. I owed him everything.

I traced my finger around his lips. "Thank you."

"You don't have to thank—"

I pressed my mouth to his to stop the words. In the kiss, I gave him a piece of my heart that would always belong to him. I knew that wherever he went next, he would take care of it.

"It's time," he said, and then he was gone. It was so abrupt, but at the same time it felt like a clean cut.

I heard Donny calling my name. I closed my eyes and clutched a handful of sand. When I opened them again I was sitting in a chair. I opened my fist and the sand fell through my fingers.

CHAPTER SEVENTEEN

Theia

Every time I tipped the snow globe, another terrible scene depicting my miserable friends brought me low. The scenes in the red and black petals would last only until the last heart-shaped confetti settled on the bottom, so I had to keep turning the glass ball. I wanted to send it crashing to the wall, but it was my only link to the people I loved and I desperately needed to stay connected somehow.

It was frustrating not to hear what they were saying, but I could see enough to know none of us would be the same. I'd watched in horror as Varnie gave his life to save Amelia from the sickening creature who was going to hurt her. My heart seized as Varnie's blood poured from his wound, as he took his last breath. I shook the ball again, hoping, praying that I was wrong. That Varnie would get up. I just couldn't accept that he could be gone. His absence would be a hole in our hearts forever. I cried until my heart felt like a wrung-out rag.

Like a hero, even death hadn't stopped him. His aura changed in front of my eyes as it rose out of his body in a ghostly form. It solidified and roamed the castle in search of someone to save Amelia.

It had taken a lot of energy to break down the door. I was surprised that Donny and Gabe didn't seem to notice that Varnie was becoming more and more transparent as they neared Amelia's cell.

I shook the beautiful globe and it showed me ugly things once more. Gabe and Donny, such as they were, had found Amelia and they mourned Varnie, though not for long. They seemed to know it would be best to honor him by finding a way safely home. I cried as they pulled Ame away from his body, and rage built like an inferno inside my soul.

I hated Mara.

I'd yet to see Haden, though whether that was a blessing or a curse, I didn't know. My three friends got lost in the twisty corridors of the castle. I couldn't warn them that the halls changed on a whim. They held hands as they searched for a way out of the concrete nightmare and I knew they would never find one.

They came upon an atrium with a high arched glass dome for a ceiling. Above the glass roof, huge winged creatures soared, occasionally diving at one another in aggressive combat. It was daylight outside, but they looked like bats. Huge bats with red eyes and wingspans about six feet across. One landed on the glass. It wasn't a bat but more like a twisted black goblin, and it was staring at them, licking its lips.

My perspective of the scene changed. No longer could I see the atrium roof inside the glass, but the globe I held became the roof. It was then that I noticed my friends could see me back, as they pointed at what must have seemed like the eye of a giant staring at them as if they were a live-action diorama.

Then the flying horde, hairy and slimy, found a way into the atrium through an opening in the glass. My friends huddled together in the middle as the beasts swooped over their heads like dive-bombing birds. I realized I was going to watch them die. I wanted to look away, but could not. The monsters were maniacal as they terrorized their prey with grins of huge teeth, sharp and yellow. One swooped low and slashed a talon across Amelia's cheek. I choked on my sobs as the red blood welled up on the cut.

The goblins began landing and circled my friends. There were dozens of them and more yet in the air.

Then came Haden.

He was magnificent. He entered the atrium, an army of creatures behind him, each ghoulish and unsettling, but obviously on his side. Dressed in black from head to toe, Haden wielded his sword with grace and cunning, slicing his way through the horde of creatures.

Those who fought with him represented the myriad nightmares Mara brought to humanity. A spider the size of a Volkswagen skittered alongside a hellhound with large ruby eyes. A man with no facial features, just taut skin, carried a club of iron spikes. A woman with hair made of asps floated above the ground making horrible clicking noises. A horned demon with oozing skin lesions lumbered in behind a row of skeletons.

Haden moved with a preternatural grace. Though I was frightened for him, a part of me was in awe of his skill, his strength. He was single-minded in his purpose. I marveled that he was the same boy who looked at me with love, for this man was someone I'd not yet met. The pride I felt was a bittersweet pill, for he was there to save me but he wasn't mine anymore, and this man, the one who battled so valiantly, had kept himself a dark secret when we were together.

I think my heart stopped beating altogether as I tried to keep track of the chaos. There was blood. A lot of it. I tried to keep watch on Donny and Amelia—the skeletons that had come in with Haden gave my friends weapons and were protecting them, but things were changing fast.

Haden looked up once, into the eyes of the giant, and I knew he recognized me. In the seconds that he'd been distracted, an enemy got too close. I cried his name and gasped as I saw him go down—but the last heart-shaped petal fell and I had to shake the globe once more.

Instead of taking me back to the atrium, the scene displayed was one of the many hallways in the castle. I shook it again, frustrated. What had happened to Haden? Again, all I could see was the hallway. I peered closer, wondering what Mara wanted me to see when all my friends were in another part of the castle. I looked deeper into the ball, holding it so close that it touched my skin.

An almost imperceptible change in the shadows caught my interest. I sensed the movement before I saw it. The shadows seemed to gather into themselves and take substance. As the lines became more defined, an icy sensation grew inside me. There were no features, no hands or feet. Just a cloak of darkness that continued to grow. And then it moved.

Chills raced up and down my spine. I felt like I was watching the embodiment of fear. It was even worse than Mara, and every instinct I possessed warned me of impending doom. The creature created from the shadows would have no match. I knew it was death. It was unforgiving and obscenely graceful as it slithered through the corridor. It seemed as though it wasn't moving so much as the distance was stirring to accommodate where it wished to be.

It left a trail of frost in its wake.

I didn't want to see it anymore. The stark dread pooled inside my limbs so that I felt I couldn't move. I was paralyzed when the moment came that the scene changed once again. Death's cloak slipped through a wall and descended upon a girl sitting in a chair.

Holding a snow globe.

CHAPTER EIGHTEEN

Haden

Even their blood was putrid. I pulled the sword out of the freshly slain goblin and heaved when the aroma reached my nose. Jesus. Even if a person could survive the talons and the feral temperament of the damn things, the smell might be enough to kill you.

I looked up and Theia was gone. I shook my head. I couldn't give in to wondering how she'd become a giant or what was going on outside of this damn atrium. I had to trust that she would do what she needed to do to survive.

From the corner of my eye I saw yet another creature descending on me. How many had my mother sent? Even if I couldn't see it, I'd have smelled it coming. I pivoted and thrust just as it tried to take a swipe at me. As I gutted the beast, I hoped my soldiers were able to get through the carnage with the extra weapons for my friends. Each of my skeletal guard knew who they were assigned to protect, but in the thick of battle, especially a battle against goblins, things often went awry.

As if to punctuate the thought, I found my feet stuck to the floor. A quick glance showed me that all of us—the skeletons, the creatures, and the humans—were stopped and stuck in midmovement. A shift in the atmosphere echoed in my bones. Something was not right—even for Under. The floor began tilting, even though we were stuck to it. As the laws of nature were breached, up became down quite literally.

There was nothing to hold on to, but I wasn't falling anyway. The goblins screeched in fear, a sound no one should ever have to hear, and I heard my friends shouting. I looked down at the glass roof now below me. Everything quaked, shaking loose a dusting of flower petals. Heart shaped. And then we pitched and rolled once again. A carnival ride of terror.

I focused on not losing the contents of my stomach. The smell combined with the constant jostling made that task difficult at best.

Theia. Something was wrong. I felt it in the change of my heartbeat. An unwelcome sensation overtook me. What if she was gone?

I don't think she ever understood that she'd already saved me just by breathing. It was her quiet presence that stopped me from following the path Mara had laid out for me. It was her heart that showed me a new way. If I died today, it would be worth it. I didn't fear death as much as I feared becoming the monster.

As long as she was alive, I had reason to live. I would earn back the trust I had sacrificed in order to save her.

And then the dome cracked. Shards of glass began falling like raindrops, each one hitting the floor with a ping and then a crunch and they began falling faster, a downpour.

Suddenly freed from the floor, I resumed the battle against the goblins. It was much later when I realized the girls were gone.

down is up again

CHAPTER NINETEEN

❧

Theia

I blinked awake, tied to some kind of table. Above me, a single lightbulb hanging by a cord swayed back and forth. The ceiling was stark white and the coppery smell of blood tinged the air.

I couldn't sit up; the straps were as strong as they were snug. Panic lodged itself in my throat. *Breathe, Theia. And think.*

What had happened?

The shadow had entered my room. I'd been too frightened to turn around, my body literally paralyzed, so I'd watched in the globe as if it were happening to someone else. It approached the girl in the chair from behind and as it melded into her, my blood froze, all sensation stopped, and I dropped the globe.

I couldn't remember anything else. I had no idea how I'd gotten to this room and all I could feel was surprise that I was even still alive and the ever-present fear that hadn't gone away since I'd first met Mara.

What had been in that shadow and what had it done to me?

I didn't feel as if I'd been physically harmed, other than the fact that I was tied down. In fact, I felt less . . . helpless than I had. What had changed? Did the shadow do something to me?

The straps holding me down chafed my skin. If I could access demon speed and blow up glass . . . maybe I had other, unknown powers. Strength would be ideal. I accessed the others when I was upset and agitated—that's when I saw auras too—so I focused on my feelings of fear and anger to see if I could get untied. If I was going to be cursed with demon blood, I might as well use it to my advantage.

My whole life I'd been trained to choke emotions, hold things inside, but now my source of power was intricately woven into the volatile core of my heart. Tapping that power, really focusing on my rage, I flexed beneath the straps and they snapped off as if I were the Hulk instead of, well, me.

I swung my legs over the table and tried to get my bearings. I wore a hospital gown, but the room was too dingy to be a hospital room. Ancient medical equipment flanked the table next to me. Rust coated the surface of the metal in patches of varying shades of oxidation, as if some indefinable liquid had pooled time after time but had never been wiped down.

Unlike my father's hospital room, no disinfectant odor concealed the fusty, malodorous air. In one corner, an industrial-size hose hung on a hook, and in the middle of the floor, a drain cover clogged with bits of hair and . . . something . . . sat there menacingly.

I remembered a field trip to a grocery store once, when they took us to the butcher room in the back with a similar setup. I remembered what they did to the meat in that room.

I needed to get out of there.

I gasped and choked on my breath when I saw the lines on my arm. Someone had drawn on me with a black marker. I hopped off the table. I didn't want to know why that had been done. I just wanted out of that place.

Halfway across the room, I stopped short when the door flew open and Donny and Amelia were brought in by skeleton guards. They too wore hospital gowns. They too were marked up.

Donny struggled more than Amelia. "Don't you hurt my baby!" she yelled. Ame saw me then. "Thei!"

It all happened so quickly. More guards came in and rushed me. Behind them, several more came with two additional gurneys and a rolling tray with instruments. Even with all my fear and rage, I couldn't shake the skeletons on either side of me. They herded my friends and me to the middle of the room and watched the door, so that is what we watched too.

I glanced down at the marks on my arm and then back at Amelia's and Donny's arms, and then I knew.

Oh God.

Thoughts gave form to fears I'd never let myself dwell on before. The handmaids. Had they been hacked apart and re-stitched like foul jigsaw puzzles in this very room? Were we next?

At the door, Mara appeared, still wearing the same slinky outfit from my kitchen. On her arm a small old man shuffled in alongside her. She escorted him gently into the room, patting him endearingly and smiling as if she were on the arm of Brad Pitt on Oscar night.

The old man was shrunken and white. Every step wavered him precariously closer. Time had carved deep grooves into his translucent skin. He had no teeth left and his jaw worked uselessly as he made nonsense sounds in a frail, old voice. Spittle collected in the corners of his mouth.

His tattered lab coat had been stained to the color of bisque, with blotches of brown and red.

They stopped in front of us. Mara spoke a little louder than normal, enunciating her words carefully with a gleeful enthusiasm. "Here are your patients, Doctor. They are all ready for you."

Amelia whimpered while Donny struggled. The "doctor" made a few sounds like "mah, mah, mah" and he raised his shaky hand towards my cheek. I flinched. His eyes were clouded completely over. He couldn't see a thing.

"We're all very much looking forward to seeing your work again, Doctor. You've always had such a way with the scalpel."

The maids came in then, each bringing a different-colored dress of the same style. They hung them on a bar and cooed at each other happily. Their heads wobbled unsteadily on their necks at the point where there was heavy black stitching. Their mouths had been seamed closed with black Xs.

The dresses they brought in were identical to the ones they wore.

Oh, God. This could not be happening.

Mara's eyes cut like black diamonds when she looked at us. "I've been impressed by the strength of your friendship, ladies. It occurs to me that you should have a more permanent bond to celebrate that substantial link you share. The good doctor has agreed to help us transform your relationship to the next level."

At that, the guards hauled us to the gurneys. We didn't make it easy for them—I'm sure after seeing the maids, Donny and Ame realized we were going to be an encore production for the invalid doctor.

We all struggled, but the skeletons were too strong. It was impossible to hurt them, for they had no soft flesh to punch or kick, no organs to protect. Just bones and a viselike grip.

There was a tray of sharp objects next to my bed, all of them dirty and rusty. I managed to kick it over before they forced me to lie down. It didn't matter. The skeletons just picked up the instruments from the dirty floor and put them back on the tray. It took six of them to hold me down.

We all continued screaming and thrashing, trying to get away. Donny's fever pitch broke my heart. She was so concerned for the unborn child in her belly. I didn't understand how it came to be there, but it didn't seem to matter to its mother.

"I think you should sew their mouths closed first, Doctor." Mara loomed over me so I could witness her cool smile. "That might quiet them down."

The doctor had a scalpel in one shaky hand. "Mah, mah, mah," he said, gumming his lips and coming closer to me. The knife shook terribly as he got closer and closer to my eyes. He wasn't even seeing me, just coming towards where he thought he should make the first cut.

The seconds lasted too long. They were stretched and drawn tight so that every excruciating detail could be remembered in perpetuity. The last things I would ever see with my own eyes would be the crags on his face, the strange wiry whiskers that grew like tufts of white tumbleweed on his chin, the vacant milky eyes. I'd remember the sour smell of age and death and senility bearing down on me to ransack my youth and sanity. Slower and slower, the shaking instrument that would take me away from myself for good continued to inch towards me at a godforsaken crawl. A maggot crawled out from his nose before oozing back into it.

That high keening sound had to be coming from me. It was the sound of desperation. I bet Mara loved it.

The doctor trembled so hard and his hand was so weak that he dropped the knife just as it was about to make contact with my skin.

I whimpered with relief and a certain letdown. The reprieve was temporary. I would only have to go through it again.

The scalpel landed on the gurney next to my head and Mara picked it up and put it back in his hand, folding his fingers over the instrument. "There, there, love," she told him. "Do try again."

There would be no anesthesia, no drugs to block the pain or dull the senses. And it would take hours and hours for him to finish this job. He was too weak to make effectual cuts; they would be dull and painful and ugly.

Death would have been kinder, but people don't die in Under unless Mara wants them to.

Like Varnie.

My heart filled my throat. How would we ever be the same without Varnie?

Remembering his bravery and his sacrifice sharpened my desire to live. I wouldn't let what he did be in vain. Not while I had breath in my body. Shoving past the fear, I found that place in the center of my soul and pushed with everything I had. A sharp crack filled the air as if I had summoned a lightning bolt. More cracking and popping followed and I was free from the oppression that had been holding down my limbs. The power inside me grew and grew, filling me with a confidence and strength I'd never felt before.

And then I remembered. The shadow creature hadn't hurt me or tied me down. It had found me because it was *my* shadow—it had been looking for me because it belonged to me. It was the darkness I shared my soul with. The darkness I tried to deny.

I accepted that now—that I was made up of more than human flesh and bone. And that darkness would not be caged. The beast within had simply been biding its time, waiting for me to accept it as Haden had needed to reunite with his demon side to save me.

I might damn my soul forever, but maybe I deserved no less.

One thing was certain: my demon cried for vengeance.

I sat up and watched as each of the skeletons in the room snapped and splintered, collapsing as their bones became brittle and ground to dust. As *I* ground them to dust. It felt incredible.

Donny and Amelia were still tied to their tables, so I

pushed the ancient doctor away and we tumbled to the floor. I grabbed a scalpel from the floor and rose to cut their straps, but Mara stood in front of me, blocking me.

"Get out of my way." An unusual bravado filled me to overflowing. I was so done with all of this.

Her eyes narrowed. "You forget yourself."

"I know my place and it's not here. Your reign of terror is over, Mara. You keep coming at me with everything you have and I keep thwarting you because I will not give up."

I thought of every strong woman I knew about—my mother, Muriel, my best friends . . . Buffy the Vampire Slayer . . . I would not back down. I would not surrender.

Everything boiled down to its most basic form in my head. A certainty, almost an epiphany, solidified there. Like a spotlight shining on a single thought, I realized I wasn't afraid. I was free. Perhaps also insane, but free from fear.

I kept moving towards Donny and Ame, scalpel in my hand, and Mara actually backed up. I felt like maybe the insanity was taking over a little, but I also felt empowered. I had something she didn't have.

I wagged the knife at her. "Your evil is strong, but I shouldn't have to tell you that my love is stronger. And that is what makes you so angry, isn't it? Of all the things your kind can do . . . all the damage you wreak and all the power you hold, you still can't defeat humanity. You never will. You keep searching for a way to steal our strength because you're jealous."

She hissed. "I'll kill you. I'll kill all of them. We'll see how strong you are when I eat your precious little heart."

"You're nothing but a big bully. You've made a career of scaring people, but it's all tricks. Smoke and mirrors. What are you going to do to me, Mara? Send more skeletons? I'll kill them. Send the doctor after me?" We looked at him, unconscious on the ground at our feet.

"You unworthy little tart! You don't think I can cut you without the doctor? You will be just like those handmaidens you dread—mark my words. I will dismember you one piece at a time."

I chuckled. I actually chuckled. "You really don't understand humans at all."

She let her face register surprise.

"I won't stop fighting you. You've thrown everything you had at me. You tried to erase who I was by kidnapping me the first time, and you tried to make me forget who I love by playing with my memory and taking away the people I care for—but I'm still here and I'm still fighting."

"You would do well not to give me more ammunition, child. You forget that I'm still standing too."

"Not for long, Mara." Okay, some of my bravado was bluffing. "You're so jealous of me."

The snake bracelets on her arms began hissing and coiling as her anger built. "I'll destroy you."

"You hate that Haden loves me—that he can love but you don't know how. More than that, you hate that humans have souls and you never will. It doesn't matter how many you steal or destroy in your quest to possess one, you will never have a soul of your own."

She smirked. "Have you seen your father lately, Pussycat? Do you know how he suffers? It's all your fault. You brought this on him. All of them."

"Don't listen to her, Theia." Amelia's voice rang out, clear and true like a bell in the din of my doubts. "Mara brought this on us all, not you. She's been playing with us like toys for a long time."

Mara laughed. "Oh, Amelia, you pathetic child. You owe me so much and yet this is how you repay me. You were nothing—you still are nothing. Without my gift, what do you have?"

"That wasn't a gift. You cursed me!"

Mara shrugged. "Without my curse, how will you fight me? My spell gave you power, Amelia. Now you have nothing."

I remembered the day on the beach that Mara sent something dark after the three of us. We stood together and buffeted her magic then. We could do it now.

I began reciting the spell Ame had taught us the day on the beach. "Though in the shadow, darkness hides."

Mara snapped her soulless gaze to me.

"This spell protects and thrice provides."

She hissed.

Amelia's voice joined mine. "For whom I trust the dark divides."

"Crap," Donny yelled. "I totally don't remember the words."

Ame and I continued, "But whom I love my *will* decides."

Mara grew several feet taller and her skin began pulling back from her face, exposing a chilling horror beneath her flesh.

I whimpered a little. Ame yelled, "Again, Theia!"

"Though in the shadow, darkness hides."

"Hides," repeated Donny.

"This spell protects and thrice provides."

"Provides!" What she lacked in memory, Donny made up for with gusto as she repeated the last word of every sentence.

"For whom I trust the dark divides." The straps that had been holding the girls to the gurneys snapped and flew across the room. Mara's talons grew longer, sharper. Donny's voice joined ours for the last line. "But whom I love my will decides."

The words made little sense, but the meaning went beyond the words. I'm pretty sure Amelia got it out of a new age spell book that probably had no business trying to fight real evil. Still, it was the three of us claiming our power, our bond. Mara leaped at me, claws out. I barely had my hands in front of me when she was repelled away as if she'd hit a wall. Amelia's smirk let me know she wasn't as powerless as Mara thought.

Amelia and I ran to Donny, who was having trouble rolling off her gurney in her state of advanced pregnancy. She must have been so scared. Mara rose up and grew at least another foot taller and began shedding her human form altogether. Under her skin, she was made of slimy scales.

The smell of brimstone filled the room.

Mara bared her teeth in an inhuman snarl. In a voice that grated on my eardrums, she told us in detail how she was going to dismember us. "I'll roll in your blood, Theia. I'll gnaw on your bones and sate myself on your souls before I swallow your brains."

She grabbed Donny by her throat, raising her easily above her head while Donny thrashed helplessly. Without thinking, Amelia and I plowed into Mara. Her slime stung my skin through my hospital gown.

We all toppled over, a mass of arms and legs and feminine shrieks. Mara swung one arm out and Amelia flew across the room. She yanked Donny off her by the hair. She wasn't so lucky with me.

My strength was no match for her, especially now that she was in this form, but I held on, trying to reach her throat. I kept sliding and the burn continued singeing my skin. She couldn't get me off her, though, and in my tenacity I realized I was growling like an animal.

Mara continued growing larger. With one giant heave of her now beefy arm, I found myself flying, landing on top of the doctor.

Mara half crawled and half slithered across the room towards Amelia. "I need a little pick-me-up, my sweet," she said to her in a chunky, phlegmy voice. "You don't mind, do you?"

Mara laid her hands on Ame's shoulders and began draining Ame of her essence. I found a reserve of strength and leaped across the room as if I had wings. I pummeled Mara's slippery flesh with my fists. I couldn't stop her. She just kept draining Amelia. I saw Ame's light getting dimmer and I ceased thinking; I just reacted.

I used my feet to roll Ame away from Mara and pushed my friend as far as I could, and then I used the last weapon I had. The weapon Mara herself gave to me.

I began to feed on Mara.

The world fell away as I consumed all the evil that resided where the mare demon's soul should have been. I wished I could say that it was horrible or unappetizing, that it repelled me or sickened me. Instead, it lit me up inside, filling the emptiness and the gnawing ache of hunger she herself had put there months ago.

The darkness tasted like a rich chocolate—lush and decadent. Power rushed through me, swirling in waves and waves of electric energy. I must have surprised her—it took her too long to fight back, and by the time she tried to buck me off, I had already absorbed enough of her essence to weaken her.

After only a few moments, Mara stopped struggling beneath me, reducing in size and returning to her human form as I continued to take and take. Everywhere my skin touched hers, the energy seeped in. There came a moment at a crossroads. I didn't have time to rationalize or think it through, but I knew one instant of crystal clarity where the option was to cross the line or back away.

I didn't back away.

From someplace far away, I heard Amelia begging me to stop, but I was too entrenched in feeding to answer. The choice had been made. Maybe it had never been mine; maybe this was what I'd been hurtling towards this whole time. The first time Varnie had ever read my tarot cards, the death card appeared three times in a row in a deck that contained only one. We'd all thought that something was trying to kill me—that I was in danger. Maybe I had *been* the danger all along.

I saw no way to stop Mara other than to become her. With each passing second, I felt my old life slipping further away from me. With Mara gone, someone else would have to take her place. Would it be me?

Something pulled me away from the currents of energy zinging through me. I wasn't ready to let go and I fought the strong arms that yanked at me. Dim voices pleaded with me and then one poked through the mist that fogged my mind.

"Stop it or I will tell everyone about that time you had a crush on Jake Martin in ninth grade." Donny tugged harder.

Her voice found its mark and the haze began clearing. *Donny. Amelia.* I was still human enough to care. I found an ounce of will and pulled my hands off Mara, dizzy from the potency of her.

I stared at her lifeless body while mine thrummed with something new, something grave and old and undoubtedly dangerous.

Moving away quickly, as if distance could undo the last two minutes of my life, I heard a strange gasping sound and realized it was coming from me. I stared at my bloodless hands. What had I done?

Donny and Amelia eyed Mara's prone body carefully as they scooted closer to me. We huddled together in our matching hospital gowns. Everything had changed. I shook, not with cold but with the chill of unholy magic coursing through me, changing me. Rearranging all that was. It felt like my DNA strands were tangled, looping and knotting in a pattern that might look right but wasn't quite.

"You never told me you liked Jake Martin," Amelia said accusingly.

Donny let out a shaky laugh.

"Jake is very smart," I whispered with mock defensiveness. "And he has nice teeth."

Donny snorted. "He has a mullet and he drinks vodka Red Bulls in first period every morning."

"Well, he didn't in ninth grade. Except for the mullet part." I shrugged and then began to cry. I let Donny and Ame pull me into an embrace.

"That was really stupid, Theia," Donny said into my hair. "What did you just do?"

"I'm not sure."

I began shivering and the three of us huddled on the floor not knowing what would happen next. We had each other, but for how long? Would more horrors come marching through the walls? Would I turn on them myself? Would Mara wake up? Was she dead? Was I her now?

"Donny," Amelia gasped. "You're not pregnant anymore."

Donny's hand went to her flat tummy, her eyes wide with panic. "Good," she said after her brief reaction. "It was all like a bad dream." But tears spilled down her cheeks and Ame and I hugged her closer.

The door flew open and we shrieked. Haden raced in with a sword, behind him some of the castle inhabitants I remembered as being loyal to him. His army. He stopped suddenly and surveyed the wrecked room. The wound Mike had given him had reopened and his face bloomed with bruises. Lowering his sword, he said dryly, "Well, I see I'm just in time to save the day."

His eyes found his mother on the floor and he looked at me, the question raised in his arched brow.

What had I done?

Haden and I traded speaking glances in a wordless conversation while in the background Donny freaked out until she saw Gabe come in. Gabe, whose hair was somehow perfect, despite the fact that his clothing was tattered and full of blood and who knew what else. Despite the fact that when last I'd seen him, he was a skeleton with no hair.

Haden's chest rose and fell in shallow pants and he swallowed hard. His eyes grew glassy as he looked away from me to his mother and back.

"Is she . . . ?" He didn't finish his sentence. He didn't have to.

"I don't know." My heart lurched in my chest. I wanted to touch him but I was afraid. What if he hated me for what I'd done to his mother? "Haden?"

Another wordless conversation passed between us. Seconds ticked by as a series of emotions crossed his face, each more devastating than the last. He stepped towards me and I jumped back, my nerves skittering around blindly, not knowing what to expect. His eyes traveled to my marked-up arms, to the most likely dead doctor slumped against one wall, and then to his most likely dead mother slumped against another. "You've been busy."

I bit my lip. "I'm sorry."

This time when he took a step, I ran to him and his arms locked me in a tight embrace, one that I wished would last forever and transport us out of the hell that we'd trapped ourselves in.

"What have you done, lamb?" he murmured as he patted me gently to make sure I was really all there.

"I don't know. I had to stop her. I didn't think, I just—"

"Shhhh. It will be all right." He pulled off his black coat and wrapped it around my shoulders.

"I don't think so, Haden. I think I've done a very bad thing."

More of Haden's guards filed into the room. Some were beasts, all of them different but chilling. The skeletons were there, as always, but also men with no faces or faces so deformed that it hurt to look at them.

One was completely blue and about seven feet tall. He had no hair—not even eyebrows. He stooped to Mara's prone form. "She's gone."

It was as if the entire castle exhaled a surprised gasp. His voice echoed off the four walls, getting louder and louder. *She's gone . . . she's gone . . . she's gone.*

A rounder creature with four arms joined him. "She killed the queen," he said, and turned to me with an accusing stare.

An eerie stillness precipitated the creaking of the skeletons' bones as every one of Haden's guards turned towards me. Fear bubbled in my chest. I had to get to the door, but they were blocking it. Haden pulled me behind him, but they encircled us.

Their macabre masks, terrifying and unsettling, were all

looking right at me. Creatures I had no name for, all with unforgiving scars and misplaced facial features, stared at me with lurid intensity.

"You killed the queen," one said, and then dropped to his knee. "Long live the queen!" The rest followed, bowing their heads and murmuring words I didn't know or understand.

Haden's arm snaked around my waist, pulling me against him even though the imminent danger had passed. We realized, at that moment, that a new danger had just begun.

I was their new queen.

CHAPTER TWENTY

As the creatures pledged their loyalty to me, I felt the foundation of my existence shift once again. I couldn't be their queen. I didn't know the first thing about being a queen. They bowed their heads, the skeletons' joints creaking in horrible cacophony as they swore fealty to me. Haden must have read the panic in my eyes because he got them mobilized and back out the door while I sank to my knees next to Mara.

She looked peaceful, like she was sleeping. How did she fit so much evil into that body? How had I managed to eradicate it all? She was supposed to be immortal. Why had she given me the very key to her demise?

Haden knelt beside me and reached for my hand. I searched his face for a trace of anger. I'd killed his mother. How could he hold my hand? "Are you okay, Haden?"

He rubbed his temple absently. "A part of me is glad she's dead. What kind of bastard does that make me?"

I traced the shadow of a beard forming on his cheek. "I'm actually more worried about the other part—the one that's upset that she's dead and blames me."

"I can't blame you for defending—"

He cut off his words as his face tightened into a grimace.

"What's wrong?" I asked.

"She's not dead."

I looked down at her body, startled when her chest rose. I rolled onto my haunches, ready to bolt, but she remained prone and quiet. Her breath was shallow and she showed no other signs of life. I hadn't killed her after all. Part of me was relieved, yet I couldn't shake the wariness.

"She's still gone. I can't feel her at all," Haden said, watching her breathe.

"What does this mean?"

"Everyone under her tyranny can feel that her presence has lifted, but she's still alive, technically."

"Like my father?"

"I'm afraid so, love. She's drained beyond hope of recovery."

"Which means my father is too."

"I really don't know, Theia."

He helped me up and began ordering the soldiers and servants to different tasks. They were to secure Mara, find my father and make him comfortable, get our friends to guest rooms so they could rest and refresh themselves. He took his time describing the food trays he wanted delivered. He was very specific. Food could be frightening in Under. Some of the inhabitants preferred their meals still squirming.

Then he ordered a search of the castle to find Varnie. All of us stopped and stared.

Varnie.

He didn't know. Ame crumpled into Donny and Gabe and they took her out while I tried to find the words.

"Haden, I'm so sorry."

He paled. "Why?"

But he knew. I could see the realization spread as his color returned.

I took his hand and held it close to my heart. Every bone ached with weariness and loss. I was so tired I didn't think I could stand much longer and yet so much needed to happen. I licked my lips and tasted the salt of tears I hadn't realized were falling. "Varnie was killed while saving Amelia."

Haden's entire body tensed and the blacks of his eyes overtook the white. Varnie was his best friend and he was gone because we brought him into our lives. I could see the guilt and the pain coming off him in waves. He raised his chin to the ceiling and bellowed a harsh curse and the walls around us began to bleed in streams of dark red.

The guards that had remained took a step towards him, but I held up my hand to halt them. "Leave us," I ordered as if it was the most natural thing in the world to command skeletons to do my bidding.

Haden thrummed with a wild energy. I lowered myself to the floor and pulled him down until his head was in my lap. I stroked his hair, which felt like cool silk rushing against my fingers, and murmured words in a language I didn't know I knew. He shuddered with silent tears and I comforted him, though it felt that so much had happened we would never feel whole again.

My father had been unleashed from the torturing machines, but he only stared blankly and unseeing, unable to respond. I stood at his bedside, knowing he was in two places at once, but I could do nothing for his broken spirit or body. I pleaded with him to just wake up until I grew hysterical.

Haden pulled me away from my father's bed and guided me into the hall. "You need to rest, love."

"Rest?" Was he joking? I couldn't rest until my friends were safe. Until my father woke up. I wanted to throw myself on the floor and scream like a child who had suddenly realized that life was unfair. "I have too much to do to rest right now."

When Mara collapsed, some of her leftover magic spells sparked brightly and chaotically and some of them faded or disappeared instantly. As a result, Under became even more disordered than usual. There were thousands of souls that had been freed from the forest trees, but they were disoriented and still trapped in the realm, angry and confused. Some of Mara's *experiments* were having strange reactions: people were spontaneously combusting or going mad—well, more mad than they already had been. The entire dungeon had disappeared, causing the castle to shift precariously as it settled into its new shape.

And until some of the magic stabilized, my friends were trapped in Under as well.

Haden kept guiding me away from my father's room. "If nothing else, you need to at least sit down. When was your last meal?"

"About an hour ago," I answered, reminding him that I'd fed recently and that was why we were in this mess.

He turned me to look at him so I could get the full effect of his stern demeanor. "Mara can't get out of her cell even if a miracle happens and she wakes up. Your father is as comfortable as we can make him, and I have sent for the finest witches in Under to discover a way to restore his essence to his body and reinstate the portal back to Serendipity Falls. Donny, Gabe, and Amelia are sleeping safely under guard." He tapped my nose. "You need to rest."

I nodded grimly. I had very little energy left to argue. Haden whisked me away to a quiet parlor removed from all the revelry that was happening throughout the castle as the inhabitants of Under celebrated their freedom from the tyranny of Mara.

I'd never been in that room. Everything in it felt old and delicate. The spindly furniture would have made a lot of money at an antiques sale, and there were lace doilies on every surface. I think Haden chose the parlor because it was the least influenced by Mara. There was nothing of her decorating taste in it—no statues carved from human bones, no paintings of people dying terrible deaths.

He built a fire in the hearth while I stared out the window

at an impromptu party that had begun on the grounds outside. I pulled the dark velvet curtain closed. I didn't want them to see me. I felt exposed and raw.

"This was my father's parlor." My quizzical look prompted him to carry on. "My mother tried to make him more comfortable, so she had it decorated to match the room she'd abducted him from. She was . . . a complicated woman." He ran his hand over the back of a chair, going back in time in his mind. "I would sit on his lap in front of the fire. He stopped talking when I was about six. He would just stare at the fire and I would sit with him every evening."

"I'm sorry, Haden."

"I'm sorry that she managed to do the same thing to both our fathers."

The lines on my arm still mapped a course of Mara's evil and they itched beneath Haden's coat, which I wore over the hospital gown. "I need to clean up." I wanted them scrubbed off me. I'd cut them off if I had to. And the hospital gown made me feel weak and naked. Haden pulled a golden tasseled cord and directed the skeletal servant who entered to "make ready a bath."

"You sound even more old-fashioned when we're in Under," I remarked.

He looked older too. The worry lines on his forehead weren't usually as pronounced. His aura flared and I noticed he still had a gap where he'd been stabbed by the silver knife. He'd been moving a little slower, now that he wasn't in battle any longer—it worried me that he wasn't healing as fast as he should.

He noticed me staring at him. "What are we going to do,

Theia? You can't possibly stay here. I don't care if they think you're their queen. You can't take her place."

"I have to. Varnie said humanity needed nightmares and the mare to survive. I'm *her* now."

"You are nothing like her." He raked a hand through his hair. "Under is no place for you. You'll wither slowly as it takes everything you've ever known from you. It's no place for a beautiful young woman with her whole life ahead of her."

I shrugged. "I'm not exactly excited about being the queen of the underworld, Haden . . . but I'm not going to wither away." I hoped. I thought of my willow tree and the heart-shaped petals . . . of the song that haunted me. "Sometimes I even kind of like it here."

He rolled his eyes to the ceiling. "You'll grow to hate it and hate me for it. You can't stay here. You'll miss your friends and your family. There is a whole life you won't get to lead." Haden pushed aside the curtain and watched the merrymaking outside. "There is nothing in Under but fear and heartache."

"And you." I hadn't meant to say it out loud.

He turned sharply to look at me, dropping the curtain. "As I recall, you decided we can't be together, remember? You threw me over." He grinned. "Not that I ever took that seriously. You can't break up with me. Not when I feel your heartbeat in my chest."

He stared at me darkly, waiting for a response. Haden had always advertised that getting near him was risky, but at the same time, I could never resist the heart that lived beneath the danger.

I recalled our first meeting, when he was nothing but polite,

but warned me of the peril of being near him while simultane-
ously daring me to take him on. And then almost begging me
to stay while pushing me away.

"Haden, we are broken up. Now is not the time to discuss
our love life."

"Or lack of love life."

Feeling like a wrung-out dishrag, I had nothing left to argue, so when the servant let us know that my bath was ready, I
followed the skeleton without reservation and without respond-
ing to Haden.

I don't know how long I'd been in the tub, but the water was
still magically hot despite my pruning fingertips. I considered
never getting out. Every inch of my body held so much tension
I was surprised I hadn't burst.

The candlelight glinted off the frothy bubbles like millions
of diamonds. Every time I moved, a whisper of jasmine scented
the air. My skin softened from the moisturizing treatment of
the soap, and the plate of chocolates on the little table next to
my oasis were caramel bites of bliss.

But could I really stay here?

Could I give up my human life? Under was strangely fascinating, but would I ever be completely at home here? There was never
a place to get your footing, not really. It changed and rearranged
itself constantly. Its beauty was matched only by its viciousness.

A long sigh escaped me. I should get out of the bath. There
was so much to work out—I was being selfish by hiding in the

stolen moment of luxury. I reached behind my head to massage away a knot in my neck muscles.

"If you have stiff muscles, I am more than happy to offer my services."

Haden's voice surprised me and I sank lower into the bubbles, sloshing water over the sides of the tub. "What are you doing in here?" I shrieked.

He chuckled. "We were worried that you'd fallen asleep."

His voice got closer and I panicked, sinking farther below the water and arranging the bubbles to make sure he couldn't see me. "I'm fine. I'll be out in a minute."

He crouched at my head and blew a breath playfully at the bubbles, laughing at my squeal. "Relax. You're wearing more bubbles than even your long nightgowns cover."

I inclined my head just enough to look at him from the corner of my eye. "This is completely inappropriate," I said.

"Yes, I'm aware of that. Can I scrub your back for you?"

I gasped. "Haden! No. Get out."

He stood up, but instead of leaving, he grabbed a short stool and brought it back to the tub.

"I'm very uncomfortable."

He leered at me over his too perfectly sculpted nose. "Maybe you should sit up a little, then."

I splashed him.

"We need to talk about us." He stole one of my chocolates. "I figured since you'd be a captive audience, now would be the best time."

"This is the most ridiculous time ever to discuss our relationship." Since he wasn't going anywhere, I decided to distract him from discussing our relationship by bringing up Mara. "Haden, what did I absorb from Mara? I thought she didn't have a soul, that only humans have them."

"Honestly, love, I didn't know you could do what you did. Demons don't have souls, at least not the ones who don't have a human parent like I do. Apparently, her power had a tangible form, like the human soul has an essence, one that you had access to since she cursed you with her blood."

"So I'm more of a demon now. Like you. Not just poisoned by one, I *am* one?"

I caught Haden's gaze. If I was a demon, then I was no longer off-limits. We were no longer bound by the demon-taking-an-innocent-therefore-we-can-never-have-sex rule. The bathwater was suddenly much too warm.

He smiled wryly. "I suppose that is a very interesting development we'll need to explore in depth at a later time, love." He leaned over and wiggled his fingers in the water. "The girls and Gabe have awoken and are waiting for us in the parlor."

"They know you're in here with me?" I covered my face with my hands. "Oh God," I whimpered.

He chuckled. "A true queen doesn't care what other people think of her actions."

"She does if she has to put up with Donny's teasing afterwards."

"Theia." His voice grew serious. "We really do need to talk. This breakup is a horrible idea. You need to stop pushing me away. It isn't fair."

"Can we discuss this after I'm dressed?"

"We can discuss it some more after you're dressed, certainly. But right now I need you to listen. Are you sure I can't scrub your back for you?"

I groaned with frustration. "I just wanted . . . I didn't want to drag everyone down with me. I thought if I could separate from you and everyone that I could keep you all safe. I wanted you to have a real life." Instead, nobody was safe. Not my father, not my friends, not Varnie.

"I thought you understood. After I came for you in Under the last time, I thought you must know . . . but I guess I was wrong."

"Know what?"

"You *are* my life."

"Haden—"

"This stops now, Theia. You can't continue to push me away. I don't want you making grand sacrifices for me that pull you out of my life and make me more miserable than ever. Stop thinking you have to do this on your own. You're not alone. You have me. You have Amelia and Donny. Surely you can see that every time you don't count on us, you hurt us."

I'd never thought of that before. I'd been so wrapped up in trying to undo my mistakes that it didn't occur to me that my lack of faith was hurtful to the people I wanted to protect the most.

"What about you? It's not like you were planning a surprise party behind my back, Haden. You were strategizing an entire war. And you weren't going to tell me about it before you left. I think we've both decimated each other's trust."

He frowned. "You're right. Absolutely right. We both need to stop pushing each other away to prove our love. From now on, complete honesty. We're young and reasonably smart. I'm sure we can learn from our mistakes. . . . Please?"

His face in the candlelight, the way he looked at me as if I were the only thing in the world that mattered—any girl would swoon. But it wasn't his looks, and it wasn't his demon speed or the way he carried a sword or wore a cravat that made me love him. It was the weaknesses he showed only to me. The moments when he was unguarded, unsure of himself—when he needed me. Why was it so hard for me to grasp that I didn't have to be perfect for him any more than he needed to be perfect for me?

I would do anything for him. I loved him the minute I laid eyes on him. Perhaps the least I could do was trust him.

And my friends . . . what a disservice I'd done them by not leaning on their strength. If I'd told them what was going on instead of keeping everything locked inside, they could have helped me. Maybe if I'd told them about the hunger and the dreams, they could have prevented me from my nocturnal essence stealing.

While it was true that I didn't want to drag them into my hell, they came anyway. And they were strong and smart and it was our bond that gave me the power to overcome Mara's evil. Now that her evil lived inside of me, I needed them more than ever. They made me better and stronger.

"Okay," I said.

"Okay?"

"You're right. I won't push you away anymore and I'll stop keeping things bottled up inside and let you all help me."

"What's the catch?" he asked.

"I can't just leave. Mara is gone—but her legacy is mine now."

"And me, Theia. I am her son, after all. The demon legacy is *my* inheritance. I'm sending you back. I'll deal with Under."

I rolled my eyes. So much for not pushing each other away to prove our love. "You're sending me back?" As if he could if I didn't want to go. He wasn't getting rid of me that easily. "You mean to take over, don't you? Become what you hated? Haden, after everything we've been through, it's not fair."

He grabbed my hand. "But you think it's fair that I let you become what I didn't want to?"

We once had to write an essay in history about Lord Acton's famous quote "Power tends to corrupt, and absolute power corrupts absolutely." Mara had too much power and nothing to temper it. She twisted the souls of humanity for fun, just because she could. Would anyone taking her place fare any better? Would Haden eventually become just like her . . . his greatest fear?

Would I?

I shifted beneath the water and Haden's breath hitched. I wasn't sure if I revealed anything or if it was just the thought of me revealing something, but his cheeks grew pink.

"Maybe we can continue this conversation later?" I suggested.

Haden smiled the shy-teenage-boy smile and not the

demon-who's-seen-everything smile. I admit, they both did the same thing to my tummy.

He leaned in very carefully to kiss me. It was a sweet kiss, his lips soft as they feathered gently over mine. I gathered suds on my hands and reached for his cheeks, soaping his face. Not one to bow out of a fight, he grinned against my mouth as he splashed the top of my head with water and bubbles.

"Minx," he whispered before he left me to get dressed so that we could plan our new destiny.

CHAPTER TWENTY-ONE

The first thing I noticed when I entered the parlor was Amelia pretending she was fine. She smiled at me, but it was a fragile thing that only showed her sorrow. Amelia was everything that was good and true and sweet in the world and I hated that her heart had been broken.

"Ame," I began, but stopped because what else could I say?

The three of us moved towards her until we were huddled together. Varnie's absence was an ache.

"I'm so sorry, Amelia." I squeezed her tighter. "I wish there was something I could say or do."

"I miss him so much," Amelia cried. "He saved me, you know."

I nodded. "I watched it in a crystal ball. He was so brave. A real hero—that's how I'll always remember him."

She used the back of her hand to wipe her tears. "Not just

that. When I was out of it? He found me inside my head and helped me get centered. That thing you saw connecting me and Mike Matheny was a spell Mara put on me when I was thirteen." We all gasped, so she kept talking. "I didn't know it was her—I did a stupid love spell. She showed up that night but I thought she was a dream. She tied me to Mike all these years, but that magic she put in me was why I was so strong. It's gone now. Varnie helped me get it out. That was his ghost, wasn't it?"

"I think so, sweetie." I rubbed her back.

"His ghost led us to Amelia's cell," Gabe said. "It was so weird. He looked so real, and then we lost him. . . . He was just gone."

Haden wrapped his arms around my waist and rested his chin on my shoulder. It was so hard to talk about Varnie and know he wasn't coming back.

Donny hadn't said anything. She absently rubbed her flat stomach, and then looked up quickly to make sure nobody had seen her do it. I pretended not to notice. "I keep thinking maybe it's not real. Like my bun in the oven or Gabe's skeleton head."

"What?" Haden asked. "You're pregnant?"

"I was . . . for a little while. Mara did some weird stuff to us . . . like our worst-nightmare stuff. So did Varnie really die? Maybe that was just another scary thing we had to face?"

Ame shook her head. "He's really gone. I felt him leave."

Gabe cleared his throat. "I think it's because the stuff she did to us was like a magic spell or something, you know? And when Theia beat the crap out of her, it was like all the spells got broken. But Varnie's dying wasn't a magic spell. Mara didn't turn him into a ghost like she turned me into Skeletor. It really happened, so it couldn't *un*happen."

We were quiet then, remembering our friend. And then we began to discuss what we'd each been through on this trip to Under. I told them all about the flowers, how I was afraid that I had been draining souls from our school. And the little girl that I'd frightened.

I kept my eyes closed the whole time I talked. It was possible that they would hate me, but it was important that I be honest. Their lives were still in danger and they were still stuck in Under. The very least I could give them was the whole truth.

"How are you going to control that now that you are even stronger?" Donny asked. There wasn't judgment in her voice.

"I don't feel any different. I thought, when I started taking her essence, that the real me would get lost or taken over. I still just feel . . . like me. Actually, I almost feel like I have more control now."

Ame took my hand and led me to the couch. "I wouldn't have you change for anything, Theia. I'm glad you feel the same—but you're not. You need to understand that. You're still mostly human . . . probably . . . well, maybe . . . but your feet are planted in two very different worlds now. You're powerful; the rest of us can see the change even if you can't."

Everyone took seats and stared at one another for uncomfortable, awkward moments. Finally, Gabe said, "So, Theia is the new mare queen, so she has to stay here and rule the underworld?"

"She is not staying," Haden said.

"Of course I am. I can't just return to high school. That part of my life is over. I belong here now."

"No. Absolutely not." Haden stood, his aura flashing and sparking around him except for the place where he'd been stabbed. "This is my fate. I was raised to take over one day."

"Uh, dude? What about all those people that live here that are partying down and calling her the queen?" Donny asked.

Haden shook his head. "We'll figure it out."

He moved too sharply and winced, holding his hand to his side. I concentrated on his aura and the gap seemed larger than it had been earlier in the evening. It was getting worse, not better. Instinctively, I knew I could fix it. "I need to do something and you're probably not going to like it." I stood in front of Haden and hovered my hand over his wound. "You have an opening in your aura where the silver knife wounded you. I think, if you . . . um . . . feed from me the way I did Mara—"

"Absolutely not," Haden argued.

I had powers now. Powers I didn't understand, exactly, but I felt a certainty in my bones that I could heal him. "I think if you take some of my energy through the gap, it will close."

"No."

Amelia rested her hand on Haden's shoulder. "There is an energy transference that happens in healing. Varnie and I were studying a spiritual healing process called Reiki. It's about life force energy—it's ancient and safe. Just a laying on of hands and transfer of light."

He wanted to please her, I could tell. He warred with himself about giving in because she'd had such a horrible blow, but as quickly as the indecision flashed over his features, the stubbornness set in again. "She's asking me to actively feed from her and I won't do it."

Ame sent me a look that said the ball was back in my field . . . or whatever that American saying is.

"I know it will work, Haden," I said. "It's like this primal voice that I feel compelled to listen to."

The dark and forbidding expression on his face was likely supposed to make me back down. He narrowed his eyes to slits when he realized it wasn't working and then exhaled a frustrated breath. "I doubt I could stop myself from draining you completely if I started. You know better than to test my control like that."

"We're all here to stop you if you can't stop yourself, Haden." Ame joined my side.

Haden shook his head. "No, Theia."

"I trust you." I used my eyelashes the way Donny taught me when I wanted something from a boy. "Do you trust me?"

He scoffed at my blatant attempt at flirting, but it still worked a little. His resolve weakened, even if he wouldn't admit it. "It is a terrible idea."

"Please." I felt the energy growing warmer between my hand and his body, so I concentrated on it, pushing what felt like light into the gap of his aura. My arm began tingling as the luminosity stopped going just the one way and I felt a return of power coming from Haden. It wasn't like taking Mara's essence. It didn't feel like *taking* at all. Instead, I felt like a conduit. The energy channeled from me into Haden and back until it became circular. We shared it until instead of two different glimmers of essence, it fused into one shaft of light. The pattern became something other than the two of us; it morphed into its own entity, swirling through us, around us, between us.

I had no idea what kind of power had transcended us, but I felt connected to him on a new level. Something bound me to Haden. Not in the creepy way that Ame had been attached to Mike. This felt strong, good. Almost pure.

"That was beautiful," Ame said, her voice full of awe.

It felt a bit disconcerting to realize we weren't alone. The healing had felt intimate. I think they all felt the same way because they quickly made excuses to go back to their room, leaving Haden and me alone.

As soon as they were gone, Haden began pacing, a scowl etched into his face. Finally he stopped right in front of me. "Theia, I want you to have your life back. You deserve to go to college and have a career, have babies . . . Whatever you want, I want you to have it."

"I want to do all those things too, Haden. But I want you to do them with me. We can't have that life, so let's have this one. Together." Haden and I got lost for a second in each other's eyes. We could make it a good life. I knew we could. "You know I can't just go back. Too much has happened."

I felt it like a tug on my heart when he realized I was right, but still he wanted to be certain this was my choice. "You're not really the queen. You don't have to be anyway. I want you to be sure you really want this before you step into her role."

"What are you saying?"

"There are no magical rules of the realm that automatically dictate that you take Mara's place if you kill her, any more than there are rules that her reign passes on to her firstborn son. Mara made up all kinds of conventions while she lived here, but there isn't one of them that can't be broken. The people of Under respect you for killing their tyrant and bewitching their prince, but that doesn't automatically make you the next mare demon ruler."

I let his words sink in. "Who else can do it, then? Besides you?"

"Another demon would likely make a power play in the absence of a ruler. They still might try, but you've got Mara's power and the loyalty of the realm, so unless you abdicated the throne . . ."

"So what you're saying is that whoever is the most powerful is in charge. When it was Mara, she made the rules for this realm."

He bobbed his head slightly in agreement. "Basically, yes. There are rules of nature that don't get broken easily—demons will naturally do what they do best, or worst. Under is and will always remain the birthplace of nightmares. Mara was the most powerful mare demon, so she made the kingdom of Under what she wanted it to be."

"What are they like, the other mare demons?"

"Unpredictable. They're demons, love. You met my demon form once, when it was without my human soul, and you've met Mara. They're not as powerful as she was, but they're not cute puppies either. They also take perverse pleasure in giving humans nightmares, something Mara encouraged."

I shuddered, remembering how cold Haden had been when he'd been separated from his human side. "So, if we let one of them rule, instead of me, Under would end up with another Mara."

"It's possible. I doubt any of them would be a benevolent leader—but it doesn't have to be your problem. You can still walk away."

I set my jaw. "I don't want to walk away. Not anymore." I was surprised that I felt so strongly about it, but leaving Under to someone else made me feel the same jealousy I had for Haden when it came to other girls. It was my realm. I was needed and part of me needed Under just as much.

"I can't deny you have a lot of power, more than me now. But you don't know how to use it or rein it in. I can help you with that." He took my hands. "I would love to help you with that."

"You'll rule with me?" I asked, hopeful and already reading the answer in his eyes.

"It won't be easy for you. Or me. The hardest part will be the children."

I bit my lip. Primal fears were passed through nightmares, and it was going to be my duty to continue that. "Maybe there's a better way? Or maybe we can, I don't know, supervise the other demons better and not give as many nightmares as Mara did?"

"We'll need to rule over them very watchfully, but I think, as powerful as you are, they'll have no choice but to be reined in. At least a little." He lost his scowl and began to look hopeful. "Also, I think we can, and should, live in both worlds."

I thought about what that would be like. Maybe I could still go to college. I could still play my violin under the willow in Under and eat Muriel's scones in Serendipity Falls. And most of all, I could still be with Haden. "I'd like that very much."

"You say that now. I'm not sure what this job will entail, love. We have a lot of work to do getting rid of Mara's legacy and forging our own. And there are going to be times when you hate yourself for what you have to do."

"But we'll do it together."

"Aye. And I hope you don't grow to hate me for it."

A few days later, after we'd seen our friends home safely, I found myself restless and unable to sleep. I crept down the hall and slid silently into my father's room.

His spirit had been so traumatized that it remained in Under even though we'd set it free. Without rejoining my father's body, the wounded spirit kept them both trapped in this limbo state.

"Hullo, Daddy."

I took my chair next to his bed. He didn't sleep. Not ever. He just stared.

Folding his cold hand into mine, I began telling him about the upcoming ball preparations. I talked to him about everything now—well, almost everything. If he'd heard me on some level over the past few days, he knew that I was now the queen that presided over Under. I'd told him how we defeated Mara, how we were changing the kingdom.

How I missed him and regretted that we'd wasted so much time being distant.

I wondered if my father would have shared this life with me if he had been himself again. Would he understand what I was trying to do for both our worlds? I hoped he would be proud. I suspected he'd have fought me every step of the way.

I reached down for my violin. "Tonight, I realized it's been far too long since you've heard music. You used to listen to me play all the time when I was a little girl. Do you remember, Father?"

The memories assailing me were bittersweet as I raised my instrument and began to play one of his favorites. Near the end of the song, I fell into the familiar zone I found only with my music. Instead of finishing the tune, I soared into another, one I was making up as I went along. The song was cool and sweet, like the first taste of strawberry ice cream on a hot August afternoon. It spoke to me of childhood—pigtails and shiny patent leather shoes, scraped knees and the zoo. Through the melody, I told my father that I used to long for his closeness. I wanted to call him Daddy and for him to tuck me in at night and read me stories. The song wailed about all the things I never had allowed myself the luxury to cry for.

And then, somehow, the song carried into my father's ears and woke him up from his sleep. He began to blink. I didn't falter, instead coaxing out more emotion, hoping to stimulate him further. At some point he looked at me. Right at me. And his eyes focused and he came back.

I stopped, lowering my violin slowly. "Hi." I exhaled more than spoke.

"You're really here?" he said, his voice gravelly from lack of use.

"I really am."

"I'm not sure . . ." His face screwed up into confusion. "I don't recall . . ."

"It's okay. It will come back to you. Don't try to force it."

"I tried to die. Why didn't I die?"

I shrugged. "I don't know. I guess it wasn't your time yet."

My father closed his eyes, the pain of remembering clenching his jaw. "I heard you . . . like you were at one end of a tunnel telling me all these things I didn't understand. Didn't want to understand. And then, the song. The music made me remember your childhood. How I wished I could have been warmer, all the mistakes I made. I ran back to find that little girl again, to tell her I was sorry. And then I woke up."

"Well, you have to stay now. The girl still needs you."

He blinked at me, absorbing what I said and perhaps all the other things I'd told him during the week. "Yes, I suppose she still does. I'm very tired now."

I stood up and smoothed his blankets. On an impulse, I leaned down and kissed his cheek. "Rest, Father. We need to get your spirits up so you can rejoin your body."

He closed his eyes. "I'm going to pretend that makes sense. We'll talk later about all this boy nonsense." He smiled slightly when he said it and my heart lifted.

"Yes, later. Good night."

I left my violin in his room. I was done playing for the night. As I closed my father's door behind me, a huge weight lifted free from my chest. He was awake. There was hope.

CHAPTER TWENTY-TWO

D onny pulled back the curtain. "They're still partying out there? Have they even slowed down since we left and came back? It's been a week. This castle is like one big frat house of the living dead." She turned back to me. "Are you sure I can't do your makeup for you?"

"It's under control," I said and then promptly stabbed myself in the eye with the mascara wand. Donny had a heavy hand with cosmetics, though, and I wanted a fresher look. It was important that everything was perfect tonight.

Amelia sat next to me on the bench in front of the vanity. "Are you absolutely sure you want to go through with this?" she asked, wringing her hands while her foot tapped nervously.

I stared at my reflection. The girl who stared back was nearly a stranger compared with who she had been only a few months ago. "I'm sure." I scooted around and stood, a little wobbly on my high heels. "How do I look?"

Ame clapped and Donny gave me a thumbs-up. I was decorated in one hundred yards of white tulle and taffeta. A floral sash of black roses tied around my waist and my hair was a confection of curls bejeweled with black and white diamonds.

A girl gets coroneted only once.

"So there's no backing out after this, right?" Donny asked.

"I'm already considered the queen. This is just a formality. I'm glad you could come. It means a lot to me."

It was a very special occasion. We'd decided that while Haden and I would travel between the realms often, our friends should come to Under only on rare occasions. This night, however, was too important to keep them away. They each had a stake in Under, having lost so much, and while they wouldn't rule, their guidance would always be a part of our management. I was counting on Donny and Amelia to keep me grounded. And human.

And we all wanted to honor Varnie by never letting Under become what it once was.

This night was all about celebration, however. And although the kingdom had been celebrating quite well on its own, we wanted to have some type of organized party and formal coronation.

"What's it like to be a queen?" Amelia asked.

"It's not as glamorous as you would think. We've been spending most of our time going room by room and eradicating traces of Mara." I shuddered. "It's going to take a long time. She had a fascination with blood that I really don't want to discuss right now."

I also had to get used to seeing ghouls and beasts and skeletons everywhere I looked. All the things that scared me most were constantly popping out of the shadows. And my three handmaids were a handful. They were completely insane, but astonishingly earnest in their desire to please me. Unfortunately, they tried to please me the same way they took care of Mara, by bringing me "delicacies" that turned my stomach. Every day they laid out a dress for me, and every day I repeated my desire that they burn every item of clothing in Mara's wardrobe. I would not wear anything of hers. They cooed and gurgled, but kept trying to interest me in their former mistress's gowns.

And looking at them made me realize how close I'd come to becoming one of them.

I traveled back and forth more frequently between Under and home than Haden did. Now that we were in charge, Under was more his home than it had been while he was growing up in it. He enjoyed the challenges of reshaping the world. I did too, but I also wanted that elusive high school diploma and summer classes had already begun. Luckily, I didn't need as much sleep as I did when I was "pre-mared" as Ame called it, and when I did sleep, I could visit Under in my dreams.

I also spent a lot of time talking to my father—both to his body in his hospital bed at home, where he was still comatose, and his bed in the castle, where his spirit lived and was getting stronger every day. We'd been cautious with each other, but it was starting to feel like we were making progress. I had no doubt that once he was strong enough to return to his body we would begin a battle of wills regarding my future. I almost looked forward to it.

A knock on the door signaled it was time.

My best friends looked beautiful, if a little nervous, in their ball gowns. We were quite striking as we checked ourselves one last time in the mirror.

"This is so much better than prom," said Ame.

"It had better be," Donny added.

We linked arms as we ventured down the long hall. The castle still moved however it saw fit, but somehow I always knew how to get to whatever room I wanted—even if it was in a different place from the last time I'd been there. There would come a time, I thought, when I would stop trying to figure out how all of it worked. That time wasn't now.

As we neared a sideboard against the corridor wall, it jiggled. I didn't like the look of it and slowed. It jiggled again and we stopped. The chair next to it wobbled and then the four legs began walking away from the wall like an animal. The furniture started coming at us, and we turned and ran the other way.

"Somebody watched *Beauty and the Beast*, I take it," Donny huffed.

"Her magic is still alive in pockets around here," I answered as we ducked back into my room and slammed the door. "Sorry, guys, this will just take a minute." I tugged the tassel that signaled the servants.

Since I wasn't very good at letting people wait on me, they knew that when the bell rang I was serious.

"You're not even scared, are you?" Amelia asked.

I thought about it. "No, I guess not. Not really. You have to take the good with the bad around here."

"The good better be extraordinary," Donny said, fluffing her hair in the mirror. She was doing a good job of pretending not to be scared, but I could smell the fear.

That was another reason why I spent a lot of time going back and forth. I was constantly aware of human essence around people now. I could tell when people were lying, when they were ill, when they were happy or afraid—and I needed the frequent times in Under just to take breaks from being overwhelmed by all the human souls. It was easier to control my hunger in Under, and I hadn't fed on an essence since Haden stopped me with the flowers.

A servant knocked, and apologized when he entered. "The unfortunate furnishings have been removed, Your Majesty."

"Mr. Pickerling, what have I told you about that?"

He bowed deeply. "Miss Theia," he corrected himself.

I hated all the "Your Highness" this and "Your Majesty" that. We settled on "Miss Theia" because it reminded me of the way Varnie used to call me that.

"Shall we try again, girls? I'd really like to show you what I meant by the good. You've only seen the worst of Under."

Ame looked a little green. "Um, Theia? How many eyes did that guy have?"

"Seven." I pulled them back into the hall, where we were escorted by two skeletons to the coronation ball. I feared I would never get used to the sound of their rasping joints.

The doors to the ballroom stretched in a high arch of solid

oak. As the doormen pulled them open, I wanted to see my friends' expressions. We'd prepared them for the macabre dancers they would see—but I hadn't tried to explain the dazzling ball itself.

On a dais of red carpet, an orchestra of skeletons dressed in black tuxedos played a song that, like Under, was beautiful and endearingly creepy. The tones produced by their strings were not heard in our realm; it was like being bitten in your heart while at the same time receiving a breathtaking kiss. Dancers had already begun swirling in intricate patterns across the shiny floor, their gore matched only by their charm as they swayed past in lavish clothing of rich satins and silks. The women wore makeup, whether they had faces or not, and the men wore suits in every color imaginable.

The girls stepped farther into the room, their eyes drawn to a chandelier so immense and bright it was like looking at the sun. The crystals broke the light into patterns on the wall and then dipped those shapes into a rainbow prism.

Amelia gasped when she saw the chocolate buffet that Haden had come up with on his own to please me. Chocolate renditions of famous sculptures lined the middle of a long table, each surrounded by a bounty of chocolate in varied sizes and colors. At one end, a chocolate fountain the size of a wading pool gurgled plentifully.

"Oh, man, am I having naughty thoughts," Donny said.

Gabe reached for her. "That is exactly what I hoped you would say."

"Theia, you look pretty," Mike Matheny said with a little bow, though not enough to dislodge the food from his plate.

"Thank you, Mike," I said after a curtsy.

318 · GWEN HAYES

We hadn't known what to do with Mike. We found him in the castle, locked in a replica of his room from home. We tried to explain to him what Mara was, what she'd done to all of us, including brainwashing him. It took him longer to recover from the shock than the rest of us. Probably because he'd been blindsided by Mara when the rest of us had at least known she was coming.

He'd refused to leave his room in the castle for days—and he still hadn't returned to Serendipity Falls. We tried to coax him back to his old life, but he simply wasn't ready to go back. I was surprised he'd agreed to come to the party. Usually he spent most of his time in his room.

"I shouldn't be here," he said, looking at his plate as if it had answers. "It's a celebration and I don't belong."

"What happened to you wasn't your fault. Mara used you. She used all of us."

"I feel so dumb. Those things I said to you at the cabin . . ." His coloring changed from pink to red. "I'm really embarrassed." It was the first time he'd talked to me about that night.

"We were all pieces on her chessboard, Mike. She made you think that you needed to save me—and I didn't help matters by unknowingly using the Lure around you. Tonight is about new beginnings, though."

He huffed out an imitation of a laugh. "I stabbed Haden with a knife. I don't know that I will ever be able to forget that. I'm pretty sure he won't." Mike lifted his right hand from his plate. "I didn't know I was capable of stabbing someone."

"I've done things I wish I could take back too. We still don't know whether I'm the one who drained our classmates.

We may never know. It's how we go on from here that counts. You thought you were doing the right thing . . . saving me from a demon. You didn't know."

He seemed to shrink into himself. "You're trying to make me feel better. I get that . . . but it's going to be a while before that happens, okay? She really messed with me. And because of that, your friend died and Amelia hates me too."

"She doesn't hate you. Amelia couldn't hate anyone. She's hurting and she's as embarrassed about what Mara did to her as you are. Try to have a little fun tonight, okay?"

He nodded and took his plate to a table.

Ame was standing alone, watching the dancers, so I joined her next.

"You miss him," I said. Varnie's absence was painful for us all, but I knew Amelia and Haden paid a bigger price.

She nodded. "Who's to say if we would even have worked out, you know? I just wish we'd gotten our chance. He was a good, good guy, wasn't he?"

I squeezed her hand. "He was the best."

"I suppose I'm going to be stuck dancing with Mike all night since he's the only other human here."

"Be nice, Ame."

"You're right. I know it's not his fault that Mara did that magic, but I still feel like he cheated me out of a love life for four years."

"Don't say her name too loud. I don't want a riot tonight." We watched the dancers for a few minutes more. "Mike blames himself for Varnie's death. Because he sent us here."

Amelia closed her eyes. "It's not his fault. It's no one's fault but Mara's."

"I tried to tell him that."

"I'll talk to him." She had to steel herself to go to him, but she would do it. Amelia was the strongest person I knew. She would help Mike even at a cost to her own pride.

I felt a prickle of awareness and turned towards the source—Haden. From across the room, I met his gaze and the world just stopped. He moved towards me with a pantherlike grace and a predatory gleam in his dark eyes, weaving through the dancers and setting my heart drumming a primal rhythm.

The sounds of the party dimmed under the rush of my heartbeat—and Haden's. I felt it keenly as they matched beat for beat. He moved with agonizing slowness as I ached to be near him—it was always like this. This elemental longing, this dangerous desire. Still, I held my position and let him come for me.

As he got closer, his eyes told a story. Our story. A tale of hunger and desire, of love and sacrifice, of the beauty and the beast that lived in each of us. Ours was a dark fairy tale where the princess sometimes saved herself but didn't need the prince any less.

We hadn't yet tested the theory that we could make love without peril. There had been no discussion, just an unspoken agreement that for now we preferred to stoke the fire between us. We would know when the time was right, and wasn't it just delicious to anticipate when that would be?

The smoldering expression on his face suggested that maybe my dress that night would be the tipping point.

He stopped directly in front of me. His nostrils flared

slightly as his eyes roamed over me, searing me with the possession in his hot gaze. "I'm not going to tell you that you look beautiful," he said finally.

I sent him a quirky grin. "You're not?"

He shook his head, but the look he sent me from his heavily hooded eyes made the air around me shiver.

"Then I won't tell you either." But he did look beautiful. Oh, how he did.

"'Beautiful' isn't strong enough to describe how delectable you are. It would be a throwaway word. Meaningless."

The butterflies in my tummy went wild. "I don't need the word, Haden. I can see how you feel just by looking into your eyes."

He swallowed hard. "Dance with me?"

He bowed splendidly in his starched tuxedo. I curtsied, transported into another time when courting was so much more graceful. He led me to the floor and we waltzed as if we had no cares but to spin the world.

It was later, as we stood on the dais and accepted our crowns, that I realized Mara had gotten exactly what she wanted all along.

In the predawn hours after the ball, restlessness hummed through my body, strumming impatient chords of an impetuous song. Something had changed tonight. I felt content and yet suffused with a feeling that I was in transit. That I was about to embark upon something unfamiliar.

I wandered the halls barefoot in my ball gown, hoping to

cure my restlessness by discovering something new or at least burning off some of the energy that seemed to be lighting me up from the inside. I began to take stock of my current situation, surprised, really, at how it all seemed to be just as it should be.

So, sure, I was mostly a demon now and queen of an underworld and, yes, my father was still *technically* in a coma in another realm. My life was different from what it should have been, maybe, but it was a good life.

Donny and Amelia would never let me down and they accepted me even when I changed so much. I had music again—it no longer seemed to be rote and boring, but a place that I could go to explore my own spirit. And I had Haden, the boy who woke me up when I was sleepwalking through my own life. He always saw what I tried to deny about myself, and he always accepted that those were my greatest strengths.

I found myself standing outside his door instead of my own.

Perhaps I would knock and tell him I couldn't sleep. If he wasn't tired, maybe we could watch a movie or just listen to music.

Or perhaps not. Maybe my restlessness brought me to his room for a reason. Was I ready for more?

Inhaling deeply, I lifted my hand and prepared to knock just as the door opened. Haden stood, sleep-rumpled and smiling wickedly, as if he'd known all along I would end up at his door.

Perhaps tonight would be the night we fell all the way under.

Perhaps.

Gwen Hayes lives in the Pacific Northwest with her real-life hero and a pack of wild beasts (two of whom she gave birth to). She is a reader, writer, and lover of pop culture (which, other than yogurt, is the only culture she gets). Visit her on the Web at www.gwenhayes.com.